REDBALL

REDBALL

A Sarah Pribek novel

JODI COMPTON

Dear Reader,

If you're disinclined to read author's notes, here are the very basics that you need to know:

This book is a period piece; it's set in 2005. However, the days of the week don't line up with actual calendar dates from that year. For reasons essential to the plot, this book involves Devil's Night and Halloween; in addition, certain things needed to happen on weekdays and others on weekend days. Moving the storyline back to 2003 would have made the days and dates line up, but raised the prospect of introducing other continuity errors which, at a late stage in the revision process, I was unlikely to catch. Besides, there's such a thing as going too far in search of unimpeachable authenticity.

This book is a work of fiction. While I drew from several real-life crimes in inventing the plot, ultimately I work from my imagination. All the characters in this story are fictional. Resemblance to actual persons, living or dead, is coincidental.

Finally, if you read the first two Sarah Pribek novels when they were published in 2004 and 2005, or not long thereafter, and have been waiting ever since for the end to the trilogy... I am more grateful than I can say for your loyalty, and I hope this book will be everything you've anticipated.

Best,
Jodi

TABLE OF CONTENTS

PROLOGUE

A hard rain fell over central Wisconsin as I drove up to the prison. It wasn't in a populous area, and only darkness showed beyond the fence line. In the upper Midwest, by the middle of autumn, full dark comes in late afternoon. Now it was early evening, but could as easily have been midnight, particularly under an opaque rainy sky. The automated chain-link gate, operated by some unseen person, rolled back to let me drive through.

In the prison yard, I left the Nova's headlights on, shining into colorless drill bits of rain as I got out and ran to the shelter of the nearest building. There wasn't another person in sight, and for a moment I stood awkwardly under the overhang of an outer walkway. Ahead of me was a door painted an industrial shade of olive green. Flush against the wall, with no markings and no handle on the outside, it was clearly used only for exits, not entrances.

The door opened and a tall, almost thin figure emerged. Shiloh. It was the first time in nearly two years that I'd seen him in street clothes. He wore faded jeans, running shoes, and a flannel shirt loose over a black T-shirt. He carried a brown paper bag of his effects.

His hair had grown long, too. I'd always liked it on the long side, the way he'd worn it during his narcotics-work days.

"Hey," he said, when we were standing close together.

"Hey," I said.

For a moment we were like two strangers on a blind date. I said, "You look ... older." I winced and amended my words. "I mean, thinner. You've lost weight."

"It's okay," he said, gently. "You look the same. You look great." Then he looked out at the yard. "This weather is strange. It's winter, we should be well into snow, shouldn't we?"

"It's okay," I said. "Shiloh, I missed you. I really did." I touched the end of one curling strand of russet hair. "I can't believe they let you grow your hair this long in prison."

Shiloh said nothing, but in the dimness his eyes were full of regret.

"They wouldn't, would they?" I said.

Logic, like external water pressure, breached the fragile walls of the dream and it fell apart.

ONE

November 2, 2005

"Detective Pribek, good morning." Lieutenant Prewitt, to whom I reported at the detective division of the Hennepin County Sheriff's Department, nodded toward his guest chair, and I sat. It was 9 a.m., three hours after the vivid dream woke me not to rain, but to the brightness of snow reflecting sunlight onto the walls and ceiling of my bedroom. It was the second of November; we'd woken to the first snow of the year on Halloween morning.

Prewitt had a letter on his desk. The short quadrangle of text was visible but not readable from where I sat, but I knew what it said. I'd written it. Prewitt had undoubtedly read the letter before this meeting, but now his face inclined downward as if taking it in afresh. I waited.

There was a photo on Prewitt's credenza I hadn't seen before. In it, a very new and pink-skinned face looked out at the world with the bemused blue-gray eyes of early infancy.

"So," my lieutenant said. "You're leaving us."

"Not right away," I said. "I'm taking an EMT-Basic course in night school. I won't be certified and ready to ride for another three months."

"Ultimately, you want to be a paramedic?"

"Yes, sir."

1

"There are a few questions I have to ask you about this. It's just standard."

"I understand."

He tapped a pen against the letter. "I'm not making judgments here, but you must know most people would consider going from detective to paramedic a retrograde career move."

"I know."

"So what's motivating this?"

"I just…I know it's an honor to be entrusted by the community with this public trust that — "

Prewitt cut me off. "In your own words, Sarah. Like you'd explain it to your next-door neighbor."

"I want to stop the bleeding. I never get a chance to do that as an investigator."

"But good investigators," Prewitt said, "prevent blood from being spilled at all, by putting away those who would hurt others again and again if uncaught."

"I know that," I said. "But I've always felt most at ease in a first-responder's role. My strengths are in aid at the scene. If what we do out there is a war, I feel like I was meant to play a different role in it. Call it a combat medic's role."

"Mmmm," Prewitt said, noncommittally. "Let me put something out for your consideration," he said. "There's such a thing as burnout. Sometimes detectives find that transfer into a different position helps." He scanned a page in my file, again feigning absorption of facts he'd reacquainted himself with before this meeting. "You were one of the best shooters in your Academy class," he said. "You never did anything with that, never tried out an assignment with a crisis-response unit."

"I didn't get into this line of work to shoot people."

"Sometimes that has to done."

"I know," I said. "Police work has its harsh realities. It's just that I'd feel better about those realities if I knew I were helping in the best way I'm suited for."

2

"You sound like you've been giving this a lot of thought," he said. "You understand that you're going to take a hit in pay?"

"Yes," I said.

"You've discussed it with your husband?"

It was rare for my colleagues, all of whom had known Shiloh, to mention him. "Yes," I said. "He wants me to do what I feel is right for me."

Prewitt moved my letter to the side, as if taking the topic off the table. "I have a request of you, then, before you move on." He tapped the folded *Star Tribune* on his desk. "You've been hearing about Jessie Ryan, I trust?"

"The student who disappeared," I said.

"The student who was murdered," Prewitt corrected. "Her body was found late yesterday afternoon in a dumpster outside a print shop in South St. Paul. We've been able to keep it off the news while her mother made the ID and gave the news to the immediate family."

"Who found her?" I asked.

"One of the shop's employees. The St. Paul detective who took the call recognized Jessie and called us. It's looking like cause of death might have been head trauma. The autopsy's scheduled for today."

His next words didn't seem to come as easily. "This is quickly becoming a difficult case for several reasons. It wasn't initially treated as a potential abduction, so it wasn't worked very aggressively. It's obvious now that it should have been." He paused. "Jessie Ryan's grandfather was something big in the State Patrol. That shouldn't make a difference in an investigation, but of course, it does."

He rubbed the side of his nose with his index finger, then said, "In other words, this case is what on the East Coast they call a 'redball.' To catch up with the situation, we're getting a small task force together. I want you and John Vang to represent the Sheriff's Department. Are you up for it?"

"Why me?"

"Why not you?" Prewitt responded. "I'm familiar with your record. While you've made some unconventional choices on the job, there's nothing wrong with the work you've done for us."

Nothing wrong wasn't a compliment, but after the difficult past year, I'd take it and be grateful.

Prewitt leaned forward, picked up a paper clip off his blotter, and straightened it. Then he said, "Nobody holds it against you that your husband is in prison, Pribek."

There was a world of unspoken implication behind that simple statement, and I admired his discretion. "Thank you, sir," I said.

Prewitt leaned forward and wrote on a notepad, then tore off the top sheet. "Joe Santarella, with the BCA, is heading the task force," he said. The BCA was Minnesota's Bureau of Criminal Apprehension. "This is his cell number. Call him and let him know you're in. He'll have a copy of the Ryan file made for you."

"There's one other thing," I told him. "A 'redball' investigation like this runs virtually around the clock for the first couple of days, but I have school three nights a week, including tonight. I can miss one or two classes, but there are attendance requirements. I miss too many, and it's an automatic incomplete."

"Let Santarella know," Prewitt said. "He'll work something out with you."

"Thank you, sir," I said. I hadn't really wanted to bring it up, but I had a healthy respect for my class's instructor, Nate Shigawa. He was a paramedic that I'd known since before enrolling in his class; we'd crossed paths on the job, the way cops and emergency medics often do. Tall and quiet, he'd struck me as courteous and preternaturally capable for his age of 26. But as a teacher, Shigawa intimidated me a little bit. He had no problem calling out the late, the lazy, and the unprepared.

More than that, he'd started our first EMT lecture with a pointed diatribe about how compulsive risk-takers and adrenaline junkies do not last in the emergency trades, and his eyes had landed on me for somewhat longer than other students. I didn't think Shigawa had forgotten that the night he'd first met me, I'd jumped into a rainstorm-swollen canal after a drowning child, with no plan for how I'd get back out.

Prewitt glanced out the window, where fresh snow brightened the city streets. "I don't know where this year went. Before you know it, it'll be the holidays." Then he returned his attention to me. "Well. Carry on."

"Thank you, sir," I said again.

My husband, Mike Shiloh, was in prison for auto theft. How he came to commit that crime is part of the story of the murder of Royce Stewart, a small-time criminal turned unpunished murderer, in Blue Earth. Shiloh didn't kill Stewart, and I didn't either, though I suppose neither of us were entirely guiltless in his death. The whole story was one I was never free to tell anyone, and neither could I speak up to exonerate myself when, for a time, I had been the main suspect. There were probably some in the department who were less willing to discredit the old rumor, but I'd learned that was beyond my control. It was that to which Prewitt had so gracefully alluded in his office.

He'd also discreetly touched on the fact that when Shiloh was released, his employment prospects were not good. Police work would forever be closed to him, and even in the civilian world, Shiloh would face the more general employer mistrust of ex-cons. Shiloh's bleak job prospects made it all the more extraordinary that he'd encouraged me, without reservation, to enroll in the EMT class. To head off money troubles, I'd already taken in a roommate, another decision to which Shiloh had given his blessing.

We'd have a crowded house, and our finances would be at low ebb, but if the parole hearing in January went well, Shiloh would be home, and that was the main thing. Even with five frigid months of winter looming ahead, and all the uncertainty that Shiloh's life after prison would bring, I couldn't repress a small itch of pleasure, a healing itch after the difficulties of the past year.

TWO

The Ryan file was ready when I arrived to pick it up, and I took it up to the law library atop the Government Center. It had been Shiloh's favored place for reviewing files, back in his days of working cold cases.

Finding an unoccupied table, I got to work immediately, wanting to be well-prepared at the first task-force meeting. Prewitt recommending me for this kind of a case still surprised me. I'd never thought of myself as a cerebral investigator of Shiloh's caliber, making up for it by putting my shoulder to the wheel. Well, I'd have plenty to pit myself against now.

I spread out a one-page summation, eight witness statements, several maps, and some color photos, and the flyer I'd been seeing around town. Prewitt was right: It didn't add up to a lot of investigative effort for a missing persons case, even without the hindsight of knowing that this one would become a homicide.

Help Find Jessica Ryan, the flyer read, with stats underneath. Height, 5'2; weight, 104; hair, reddish-blonde; eyes, blue; no scars or tattoos. At the bottom was the tipline number, and underneath that, Help Us Find Our Friend Jessie!

Usually, there was more information than that. I clicked my pen into life and wrote in the margin, *Where's the last-seen information? Incl. clothes last seen in?*

I turned to the narrative summary and began to read.

Jessica April Ryan had been a 21-year-old junior at the University of Minnesota. Her parents had split up when Jessie was young. Her mother, Katharine, had taken her two daughters and moved back into the home of her own father, Roy Nedegaard. Katharine Ryan found work as an administrative assistant in the Democrat Farmer-Labor Party of Minnesota, but had never moved her two daughters from the Nedegaard home in an affluent residential enclave in Washington County, an area near the Wisconsin border but still part of the what was called the 'seven-county metro area' around the Cities.

As a teenager, Jessie had been a figure skater with hopes of competing at the national level, but a knee injury had wrecked those plans. She'd recovered fully, but only after the girls she'd once practiced with and competed against had hopelessly passed her up in skills. At the University, Jessie studied theater arts with a concentration in dance, hoping to work as a skater's choreographer later.

Despite the fact that her family lived less than a half-hour from the University, Jessie was never a commuter student. She'd lived in the residence halls her first two years, then moved into a Como neighborhood house with two other girls. During her student years, Jessie had worked several part-time jobs, mostly in retail. She was described as bright, sociable, and vivacious. Her friends laughed at the idea that someone could have wanted to hurt her.

On October 30, a Thursday, Jessie and her roommates hosted a "Devil's Night," or night-before-Halloween party. The party was a great success, partly in thanks to Jessie, who was lauded by her friends as an excellent planner and organizer. The next day was a school day, and Jessie's roommates didn't see her at all. This wasn't unusual in their hectic household. That afternoon, though, Jessie's roommate Angela Eastman had complained that Jessie seemed to have "ditched" them with the cleanup from the party, which all of them had been too tired to deal with the night before. It wasn't until Jessie failed to come home in time to dress and get made up for a fraternity masquerade that her other roommate, Kori Lindegard, began to feel stirrings of concern.

Jessie wasn't answering her cell phone. A few phone calls to mutual friends confirmed that no one had seen her all day. Kori went into Jessie's room and found both her school backpack and a handbag there, along with Jessie's wallet and cell phone, the phone out of juice. At nine o'clock, Kori called Jessie's mother and told her what she knew. Katharine Ryan, shortly thereafter, called the police.

I was halfway through the summation when my cell phone chirped discreetly. I picked it up. "Pribek."

The smooth voice on the other end didn't identify itself. "I'm standing outside a courtroom during a fifteen-minute recess that I had to ask for because my witness in the Jones case wasn't outside the courtroom like she said she'd be at — "

"Oh, *shit,*" I said, the word sibilant as a whisper but loud enough to make a family-court judge nearby straighten up and scowl at me. "Chris, I'll be right there, I'm just upstairs."

The elevator took only a minute, but when I arrived, county prosecutor Christian Kilander was at his leisure in the hallway, all six feet five inches of him leaning against a post, looking as though he were about to light up a cigarette.

"I'm ready to go," I said. "Really."

Kilander shook his head, immensely pleased at my discomfort. "Too late now, girl," he said. "I got a recess, and now the judge is going to take his full fifteen minutes to check sports scores or whatever it is he does in chambers. You can sit down and cool your heels."

I'd known Kilander since my early days on patrol; we'd both been frequent competitors in pickup basketball games at the government-employees' gym. Shiloh, too, had played in those games and knew Chris, but there was bad blood between them. That was professional, something about points of procedure in a old vice case and Shiloh being an uncooperative witness. It was before my time, and I'd always refused to let it influence me, because personally, I liked Kilander; he'd always been decent to me.

I sank onto a bench, rummaging in my shoulder bag. "Okay, do you want to review — "

"No, I most certainly do not wish to discuss anything related to my very tedious textbook prosecution of Ed Jones."

Jones was a would-be stalker who'd broken into a never-gonna-be girlfriend's house to steal panties, feed her tropical fish to death, and make about ten spelling errors in the handwritten complaint of a rejected lover. What Jones lacked in gravitas as a romantic antihero he also lacked as a legal mind, but he'd insisted on representing himself. Kilander considered the trial a sort of vacation.

"He's defending himself, for God's sake. On cross, all you have to do is get out of his way and let him screw himself up." He looked through the plate glass at the far windows and City Hall beyond it. "Let's talk about your ascension to the Ryan task force and working with the F,B, pause to genuflect, I."

Kilander soaked up gossip like a cactus, so I didn't ask how he knew I'd been tapped to work the Ryan disappearance, now a murder. Instead, I said, "The FBI? I didn't hear that part."

"Hadley and I shot some hoops last night," he said. Skyler Hadley, a mutual friend, worked major cases for the MPD. "He mentioned that some kind of Quantico hotshot was coming out to lend a hand on the Ryan case. Sky was bitching about having to go get him at the airport, because his flight landed at 8 a.m., right in the middle of morning drive time. I told him, they also serve who only idle in traffic on 494." He inspected a clean thumbnail and added, "Sky also mentioned you'd taken in a roommate. A rookie cop, I think?"

"Yeah. Temple Lockhart." It didn't surprise me that Hadley had heard that; he and Temple were both MPD, though Hadley was a detective and she was patrol.

I wondered, though, why Kilander had asked. He seemed too discreet to pry into my financial affairs, but on the other hand, he'd never gotten along with Shiloh. If he could trace back my money worries to the fact that Shiloh, who'd once earned more than me as a cold-case homicide detective, would be unlikely to earn much after his release from prison — well, that'd certainly give him a reason to look down on my husband. Not that he'd ever needed one.

To forestall that, I said, "It's good to have the company. I mope when I'm by myself too long."

Kilander seemed about to respond to that when his long, mobile face shifted slightly, an inward-focused look of distraction. He shifted his weight off the post, took out his phone, and checked the screen.

"Ready?" he said. "The judge is about to bring the jury back in."

Kilander was speedy and efficient in his direct examination of me. After that, things slowed to a crawl. I had no problem, as Kilander had advised, saying the minimum and letting Jones flounder in his cross-examination, but I wasn't prepared for how very slowly he'd do it. He questioned me on points of fact that weren't being contested by either side. He referred to "the alleged fish," as if it were in question not whether he'd dumped food into the aquarium until the fish bloated and died, but whether the pets had existed at all. At the defense table, Kilander steepled his hands so that they covered the lower half of his face, and I knew he was hiding his amusement.

Then the time came when I started wondering if I was even going to make the beginning of the task force meeting on time. I realized that I should have mentioned it to Kilander outside, but hadn't, because it was my fault we were late getting started. *Come on,* I told the judge, mentally. *Start getting annoyed at the waste of your time. Tell this clown to wrap it up.*

But Jones apparently felt he'd reached a high note, because he said, "No further questions."

Kilander must have read the combination of irritation and desperation in my eyes, because he didn't wait to be asked before telling the judge, "I have no re-direct here, your honor."

"I'm glad to hear that, counsel," Judge Stern said, putting a subtle dry emphasis on *glad.* Then, to me: "You may step down, Detective."

Kilander winked at me as I crossed the well.

THREE

The powers that be had made room for the Ryan task force on the top floor of City Hall. The stairs leading up were smooth marble, a risk to life and limb in smooth-soled indoor shoes, but I took them at a run anyway, clutching my Ryan case file to my chest, the smaller spiral notebook I'd consulted on the stand riding on top of it. Outside a closed door with a frosted glass window, I took a few seconds to catch my breath from the run, then shifted my papers into my left arm and opened the door. As I did, the notebook slid off my tilted manila file and landed with a flat slap on the floor. I sat on my heels to pick it up. "Sorry," I said, straightening. "I got hung up in court."

It wasn't a big room, dominated by a rectangular table in the center, four men seated around it. There was a white dry-erase board at the front of the room, a few research materials — photos and maps — clipped to its top railing. The case was still young; that collection would grow.

"You must be Detective Pribek," said the man at the head of the table. "You're hardly late. We were just making introductions. I'm Joe Santarella."

He was fortyish, with a wrestler's powerful barrel chest and black curls trimmed to within a half-inch of his skull. As if to compensate for this stevedore masculinity, Agent Santarella's clothes were crisply pressed, and a gleaming platinum watch mostly overpowered the curling black hairs that escaped the French cuffs of his shirt. The man next to him, in contrast, looked like a Ph.D. student who'd made a wrong turn on the way to the University's west bank campus. Short and slight — I thought he'd probably come to about five-six or five-seven, standing — he wore a simple brown cardigan over a white T-shirt and jeans. He had a deep olive complexion and thick black hair cropped artlessly short, and broad, hawk's-wing eyebrows.

"I'm told you know Skyler Hadley," Santarella continued, "and of course John Vang."

Vang, a Hmong with an incisive mind and a dry sense of humor, was my now-and-again partner in Sheriff's Department investigations. Hadley, an African-American MPD detective and Kilander's source of departmental intel, was also a familiar face.

"And this is Syed Hasan," Santarella continued, coming to the man seated next to him, "with the FBI. Syed, this is Sarah Pribek, a detective with Hennepin County."

"Sarah," Hasan said. I saw now that his eyes, not the brows, were his dominating feature; large, dark, and lambent.

"Pleased to meet you," I said.

"Syed's background is in psychology," Santarella said, "and he's been working in behavioral sciences at Quantico, so he's going to help us with the victimology on Jessie and to assess suspects as they come in. He's not going to be in the field much, he'll be working off the information you bring him." Santarella looked to the profiler for confirmation, and Hasan nodded.

"And, as I was just about to tell everyone," Santarella went on, "since he's new here, don't hold out on your secret downtown parking spaces and best spots for takeout. Syed, anything else you'd like to say, in an introductory vein?"

"Just that my wife's flying into town in a day or two, and might like to meet you all when things get settled," Hasan said. "Natalie doesn't usually travel with me, but we're expecting our first child in about five months."

There was a general, congratulatory murmur around the room. I moved around the table to take the empty seat next to Vang. Santarella

14

straightened his sheaf of papers against the conference table, a coming-to-order sound. "I was called into this case late yesterday. We're all starting from about the same level on this case. The original detective on this case is on medical leave, but we've got his notes."

Hadley was rubbing the bridge of his nose, and I wondered what he knew that he wasn't saying.

"I don't know how much time all of you have been able to dedicate to reading those notes, so I'm going to briefly go over what we know so far."

I put my pen down and listened as Santarella ran through the biographical material I already knew, then into how the investigation had proceeded — or, at first, failed to proceed.

Halloween is not an ideal day to go missing. Something about the holiday breeds irresponsibility, as the normally straitlaced put on masks and costumes and slip out from under the harness of conventionality. The police field higher-than-usual calls about children who do not return as expected from trick-or-treating and normally responsible adults who stay out partying. A 21-year-old college student not being locatable by her roommates on Halloween eve had not been cause for alarm. Even so, a Detective Nelson of the MPD had gone to Jessie's house and taken a report and a few statements. It had been a perfunctory response, if Nelson's brief and undetailed report was any indication.

It wasn't until late the following day, after some irate calls from Jessie's grandfather, former Captain Roy Nedegaard of the Minnesota State Patrol, that Santarella had been called at home on a Saturday and asked if he could take on a special case.

The shift into overdrive came too late; yesterday afternoon, the grim discovery had been made: Jessie's body in the dumpster, naked but wrapped in several bolts of brown velveteen fabric.

If Jessie's last day of life had, in fact, been Halloween, it was proving terribly difficult to reconstruct. She'd been at the Devil's Night party she and her roommates had thrown the night before, and according to one guest, had been asleep in her room at eleven-thirty, when that guest ducked into her bedroom to make a quiet phone call. Supporting that witness assertion was the fact that the clothes Jessie had worn to the party were found in her room, draped over her chair. The next day, her bedroom door had been closed all day. Neither roommate, upon getting up, had been certain whether Jessie was sleeping in or had gone out early, and soon they'd left for school without giving it further thought.

Jessie's one class on Halloween had been a survey course on astronomy, held in a large auditorium with over a hundred students attending. No roll was taken, and 45 minutes of the 50-minute session had been on a slide show that accompanied a professor's Halloween-day presentation on the role of the stars in occult traditions. In other words, they'd been in the dark.

About a half-hour after that, a student named Mark Nilson reported, he'd seen Jessie Ryan ascending the steps to Walter Library but hadn't spoken to her.

But the very idea that Jessie had gone to school was suspect in itself: Why would she leave without her backpack, wallet, or cell phone? The one item that was missing were her keys; everything else seemed accounted for.

When Santarella reached that point, he stopped and straightened his papers by tapping their bottom edges against the table. "So," he said, in a tone of summation, although no conclusions had been reached, "this is probably a good time for a break. Let's take ten minutes, go get some water or some coffee if you want it, and then we'll talk about where we're going from here."

Vang and Hadley, rising, fell into what was obviously the continuation of a conversation they'd been having, about the Green Bay Packers; Santarella engaged Hasan in conversation. The odd one out, I poured myself a cup of water from the pitcher on the table and then went to the front of the room to look at the photos of Jessie.

The first was a larger, uncropped, color version of the photo on Jessie's flyer, a simple candid shot: She was sitting on the arm of an easy chair, Coke can in hand, wearing a bright orange tank top and jeans. Next: Jessie in the black robes and mortarboard of her high school graduation, smiling and sandwiched between her mother and younger sister. Then, Jessie in an ice-blue strapless dress with a gardenia corsage clipped to it, a senior-prom photo. And then Jessie on the ice of a skating rink in a short blue competition dress, nylon-tan legs crossed at the ankle, posed as if at the end of a routine, waiting for judges' scores.

Figure skater, prom date, golden girl. Already it was starting: These photos would appear in the newspaper, if they hadn't already, accompanying the followup articles and the profiles. Television would do better; they'd have video of Jessie riding her first bicycle and coming down the stairs of her family home in her prom dress. Soon the images would become familiar to all of us. The TV stations would love them, just like they'd loved and endlessly run the footage of the kidnapped girl who'd played the harp in white dress like an angel, or the child beauty queen who'd posed and sang and danced across television screens for weeks and months after her murder.

Victimhood, followed by hagiography. There was a disturbing equation here that no one seemed to question. The photos and videos held out middle-class privilege as evidence of innocence, as evidence of merit, even. Not for the first time I had the Judas thought: Why wasn't it enough for someone to be missing, or to be murdered? Why did we need to elevate victims to a rarefied level of innocence to justify being angry over their deaths?

Movement nearby alerted me to Syed Hasan's presence. He'd come to stand behind me, looking over my shoulder at the photographic display. Well, not quite *over* my shoulder, as I'd been right in my earlier estimate of his height; he stood about five-eight to my five-eleven. But that wasn't the primary thing I noticed about the newcomer, now that he was standing: It was the cane he used to walk.

"An accident," Hasan said, acknowledging where my gaze had gone. "It's a boring story."

"How long ago?"

"Almost four years," he said. "It was late November. I'm just coming up on the anniversary, in fact."

"So it's not — ?"

17

"Still healing up? No." His smile was rueful. "After two surgeries and a permanent pin implanted in my knee, this is as good as it's going to get."

Was some kind of condolence in order, I wondered, or would that be inappropriate? Fortunately, I didn't have to make that decision; Santarella was back in the room, signaling that we were about to reconvene.

"The number-one frustration with this case," Santarella said, when we were all around the table again, "is the lack of a time and site of disappearance. That's job one for now, finding the abduction site, because I don't think we're going to make a lot of headway until we do. The second bad break: We got our first snow on Halloween morning. I don't have to tell you what that means."

He didn't: Everyone had heard of a case that hadn't broken up until a spring thaw revealed a broken knife blade or an earring on the ground.

"Another thing: Jessie was a 21-year-old white female on a campus with nearly the largest undergraduate population in America. If she were an unidentified suspect instead of an identified missing person, we'd have several thousand young women to rule out. Meaning: We're heading into a boom in tips and sightings. The vast majority will be mistaken identity and wishful thinking, but here's the thing: Somewhere in all that coal is going to be a diamond. We'll check every story out, no matter how unlikely." He turned to Syed Hasan. "Is there anything you'd like to add?"

"Not yet," Hasan said. His voice was quiet, like an actor's when he knows he has the audience's undivided attention for his monologue. "I'd like to wait until we've gathered more information."

Santarella accepted this. "Anyone else?"

Nobody spoke. Santarella stood with a faint but audible click in his knees. "Here's where we're going to start: Vang, you're going to head up the neighborhood canvass in the Como area; you've got plenty of support from our uniforms. Hadley, you've got the autopsy this afternoon. After that, I want you to light a fire under the manager of the print shop, where Jessie's body was found in the trash bin. He's supposed to be looking through personnel files for us, flagging anyone who left under a cloud, maybe of inappropriate behavior around women."

The reasoning behind that was simple: Criminals, like the rest of us, have their favored routes and pathways. Whoever had killed Jessie hadn't looked in the yellow pages for an industrial-sounding business and driven there in hopes that it would have an accessible dumpster in a poorly-lit yard. He'd seen it before. And who would be more familiar with the setup than a former employee?

"Pribek," Santarella went on, "I'm assigning you the victimology. I want you to talk to Jessie's family and her friends, learn all about her habits. Start with her roommates." Santarella rubbed the bridge of his nose. "Detective Nelson already spoke to them, of course, but he won't be available to you for follow-up questions on what he learned. He's unreachable right now. Medical leave."

Medical leave. I glanced over at Hadley, who was also MPD and would have known Nelson the best, and he was pointedly looking down at the table, not meeting anyone's eyes. With that, the facts clicked into place like a needle dropping onto a record: Nelson had a drinking problem. His perfunctory handling of Jessie's disappearance had been the last straw, and he'd been sent to rehab under the code phrase *medical leave.*

I admired the way Santarella had worked it in, saying that Nelson wouldn't be available to us for follow-up questions. It was a pretext for discreetly telling us what we really needed to know: that all of Nelson's work, the interviewing and information-gathering, was potentially compromised. Everything needed to be double-checked.

Santarella continued: "If she had one single risky behavior or one vice, it could be the key. The problem is, now that Jessie's dead, getting them to talk about those things is going to be harder. No one likes to speak ill of the departed, and we don't have the leverage anymore of saying that any one piece of information could be the thing that brings Jessie back home alive."

I nodded assent.

"Be tactful," Santarella concluded, "but be persistent."

Four

The house that Jessie Ryan had lived in, off Como Avenue, probably came into its own in the summertime. In November, though, its light-brown paint was wan, leached of color by the snow and the gray cloud cover overheard. But by May, early-summer sunlight would be caught between blades of grass in the lawn, the trees would cast greenish shadows, and the covered front porch would be a perfect place for iced tea on hot days.

Like many college students with a life in transition, Jessie'd had two homes — this one and her family home. I'd debated which to visit first. The drive out to Washington County, if delayed until late afternoon, would tie me up in commute traffic, so I was tempted to get that one out of the way first. But I'd rejected that idea. Jessie lived her daily life here; this was the place to start.

Both roommates, Kori Lindegard and Angie Eastman, were there when I arrived. Both were blond, with slightly reddened blue eyes, and both were prepared to stay out of my way. They were startled when instead I asked them to help in the search.

"This isn't a forensic kind of search," I explained. "I'm looking at Jessie's room and things to get to know her, and the best help I can have in that is someone who knew her, to tell me if anything looks out of place."

I'd done a quick walk-through to get the layout of the house. The living room was in front, morphing in an L-shape into a dining area; at the end of that room, sliding-glass doors looked out onto a snow-covered deck, abandoned until spring. The kitchen was long and galley-like, with a door at its end that led out onto the side alley, a pair of metal trash cans standing sentry by the steps. Opposite the kitchen was a hallway, with Jessie's room the first door off it.

Little took me by surprise in Jessie Ryan's bedroom. A twin bed with a sea-green down comforter, a narrow desk-dresser combination, a freestanding bookshelf. A canvas backpack slumped bonelessly against the legs of the chair, and a faux-crocodile handbag hung by its chain across the chair's back. The window blinds were up, revealing a chain-link fence and the neighbors' back yard beyond it. A family lived there, not students; a dispirited swingset stood looking cold in the winter snow. Inside her window, Jessie had hung a suncatcher, a circle of stained glass showing a moon and stars against a cornflower-colored sky.

The desk wasn't made to hold a computer; it had a narrow work surface and no tray for a keyboard. I doubted Jessie ever did any schoolwork on it; it was most likely a landing pad for cast-aside shopping bags, keys, and Jessie's phone. There were clothes draped over the chair. I sorted through them: a pair of skinny-cut pants in a fawn-colored corduroy, a black top with a rippling off-shoulder neckline, and black high heels under the chair.

"These are the clothes she wore to the party?" I asked. Angie, sitting on the bed, nodded.

"Was it typical for her to throw clothes over the chair?"

"Not really," Kori said. "Unless she was in a big hurry. Jessie kept her room really nice. And she took good care of her clothes. She had such great taste." For a moment there was a faint ripple in her face, the internal shift that means tears are threatening.

Kori regained her composure by sorting through Jessie's closet, in search of anything that might be missing. I went through the narrow single drawer of the desk. It was a mother lode of letters and notes, printouts of emails, and greeting cards; clipped magazine articles, essays, photos, and poems. I had a lot of reading ahead of me. Item after item went into my cardboard box nearby.

While I worked, I asked Kori and Angie questions they'd undoubtedly already heard from Santarella, if not Nelson. But they were patient, telling me that there had been no strange phone calls to the house, no unfamiliar cars parked out on the street. Jessie's mood in the days before her disappearance had been happy and upbeat. She'd been looking forward to their Devil's Night party and to Halloween after that.

"Let's talk about boyfriends," I said. "I'm told she didn't have a guy in her life."

Simultaneously, Angie said, "No," and Kori said, "Well, Jeremy." Then they exchanged glances, trying to reconcile the mismatch.

"Jeremy wasn't her boyfriend," Kori explained. "But she was crushing on him."

"Meaning she had a crush."

"Right," Kori said. "She was pretty stoked about inviting him to the party, remember, Angie? She mentioned it three or four times. Always like it was no big deal, but you could tell it was."

"Did he come?" I asked.

"I don't think so," Angie said.

But Kori nodded affirmation. "Yes, he did," she said, "but I think he wasn't here long. He had a girl with him."

"So he brought a date?" I said. "Meaning his interest in Jessie wasn't mutual?"

"The girl could've just been a friend," Kori said. "But I got the feeling they were together. Maybe they were holding hands or something. I don't know for sure; I wasn't staring at them."

"What's Jeremy's last name?"

"Jackson."

"What about ex-boyfriends?" I asked. "Did she have any of those?"

"She had some," Kori said, "I mean, she definitely got out and dated. If you're thinking there was one that couldn't let go, or who was stalking her, she never mentioned anything like that."

From her place sitting on the bed, Angie nodded agreement with her roommate's assessment.

"What type of guy was Jessie attracted to?" I asked.

Kori shrugged. "The usual."

"There is no usual," I told her.

"I just meant, good body, in shape, clean-cut," she explained. "Here, Detective Pribek, look at this."

Standing at the closet, Kori reached in and took out a full-length gown in a rich, midnight-blue color with silver embroidery on the bodice. A matching cloak with a hood was wrapped around it on the same hanger, and a silver Harlequin mask hung by its strap from the hook.

"It was supposed to be her costume for the masquerade," Kori said. "She was really excited when she found it in a consignment store. It's been in plastic in her closet for months."

I understood now why Jessie's failure to come home and get ready for the masquerade had set off alarms for Kori on Halloween night. This was definitely not the kind of costume you bought only to decide to go to a friend's place for beers and a *Friday the 13th* movie instead.

Done with the desk drawers, I looked through the purse, which only held a few items of makeup. The backpack held her astronomy textbook and a spiral notebook in the main compartment; a smaller side pocket held Jessie's wallet, some change, and savings card for a grocery store. "You've probably been asked this before," I said, "but have you run across her keys anywhere?"

"No," Kori said, and Angie shook her head.

When do you leave the house with your keys but not your wallet? When you're not going far. When it's cold and you're afraid of locking yourself out, like when you go out to get the paper and close the door behind you to keep the heat from getting out.

"Do you guys get a newspaper delivered?" I asked.

"No," Angie said.

"Did Jessie ever walk out to buy a paper, maybe at a curbside rack?"

"Um, not really," Angie said. "We get the movie times online."

A moment later, Kori spoke up. "You know what?" She was kneeling before the sizable rack of shoes on the closet floor. "Jessie had more than one pair of workout shoes. These are white." She pointed to a pair of Nikes.

"Meaning?" I asked.

"Jessie usually wore her black shoes at the gym." She walked over to the bedroom door and closed it partway. "I think she used to keep the gym clothes she was wearing most often back here." She indicated a bronze hook on the door, empty.

"What were they, do you remember?" I asked.

After a few seconds of musing by committee, Kori and Angie described them for me: dark Adidas sweatpants, the shiny kind, and a sweatshirt from the student store, pale yellow with MINNESOTA in russet lettering. A check of the laundry hamper found they weren't there, either.

I wrote down the description in my book, asking, "Did she work out often?"

"Oh, yeah. Almost every day," Kori said. "I almost worried about it, because she watched her weight, too. But she never looked, you know, unhealthy skinny."

I nodded. "When Jessie worked out, other than skating, what did she like to do?"

"She went to the rec center, on campus," Kori said, "usually to do yoga or the cardio equipment. If it was closed, she'd go running."

"Do you show a student ID to get into the rec center?" I asked.

"Yes. They scan it electronically."

I picked up Jessie's billfold and flipped it open. Driver's license, Mastercard, check card... here it was, the student ID.

"Okay," I said. "This is progress." I was sifting through the top drawer of Jessie's dresser, the one Kori hadn't already gone through. No surprise: It held bras, panties, stockings, socks. I don't know how it became standard to keep lingerie and socks in the uppermost drawer of a dresser, but it was true of nearly every home I'd searched.

But underneath those items I felt something else: paper. Not the high-gloss feel of magazines, but regular printer paper. I pulled the sheets out and looked.

Another unspoken American custom: keeping the pornography in the sock drawer. These photos were fairly tame by most standards: muscular, model-handsome firefighters, posed on trucks or by ladders, naked except for helmets or open turnout coats, with oiled skin and generous erections, some with smudges of soot on their cheeks for verité.

The photos didn't take up the entire page, and there was a small-print web address in the upper right corner of both pages. They'd been downloaded.

I must have let something show in my face, because Angie, sitting on the bed, said, "What?" and came to my side. "Oh my God," she said, and started laughing. "Oh my God, I can't believe it."

"Did you guys find something important?" Kori said.

"I don't think it's *important*," I said, stalling, but Kori was already at my side. She twitched as if she'd felt a static-electricity shock.

"Detective Pribek," she said, her cheeks reddening, "do you have to…" she glanced at the pile of Jessie's personal things I was going to take with me.

"No," I said. "I'll need to take them, in the very unlikely case they're relevant to something, but I'll keep them under wraps. They won't get passed around a station."

"Good, I mean — Angie, *stop laughing,*" she demanded. "It's not funny. Jessie never meant for us to see this stuff."

Chastened, Angie said, "I wasn't being disrespectful…I mean, good for her. There's nothing wrong with it."

I hadn't been lying when I'd told the girls I didn't think the firefighter pictures weren't relevant to the case. It was Kori's revelation, about Jessie's gym clothes, that interested me most, and I thought Santarella would find it important, too. For a few minutes, I sat in the car outside, making a few notes. Then I called Santarella.

"I didn't find the keys, and I didn't find a diary," I said. "But I've got something for you. The roommate says some exercise clothes are missing." I read the description from my notebook.

"Great," Santarella said. "We'll get that information out there."

"Here's the thing," I added. "Jessie typically used the University sports facility. She would have needed her student ID to get in, but it's still in her wallet. I checked."

"Hmm," Santarella said.

"Workout clothes and keys missing, nothing else," I reiterated. "I think she got up early and went running."

FIVE

The newer suburban developments east of the city were kind to trees. Where once lots were clearcut, now the spaces between homes were filled with hundreds of skinny trees, making up in number what they lacked in heft, shedding the last of their autumn foliage. The afternoon had been cloudy earlier, threatening snow again, but now, there was a little bit of yellow sun peering through. Watery sunlight, thin trees, wisps of woodsmoke: All around me, the autumn landscape was pale and fragile-looking, like flesh under a recently removed Band-Aid.

A creek bounded the development the Nedegaard-Ryan family lived on, and the bridge that crossed it was wooden, arching slightly. Underneath it, the creek wasn't yet carrying chunks of ice, nor was the current slowing. Instead, its dark waters appeared to run fast, as if realizing there was little time left to flow freely.

The house itself was handsome, with natural timbers and a stone patio, and smoke curling from its chimney. It wasn't yet sunset, but the lights of the Nedegaard house glowed a welcoming gold against the dimness of the afternoon, in a way that spoke to me of a vigil. It had been several hours since Katharine Ryan had gone to the morgue, escorted by Hadley, to identify her daughter's body.

It was Mrs. Ryan who answered the front door. She was a little taller than Jessie had been, five-foot-six maybe, her hair wrapped up behind her head. She wore a gray cowl-necked sweater that looked like cashmere over a black knit skirt and slip-on flats. Had she planned to go to work today, before getting the call from Hadley? I doubted it; her daughter had been only three days missing, and no boss in the world would have expected Katharine Ryan to report. It seemed more plausible that Katharine had returned from the morgue and dressed as if for church. Her daughter was dead; friends would be coming with food and condolences. The situation had gone from being an emergency to a set of formalities. Probably the good clothes and the gold earrings that gleamed at her earlobes helped Jessie's mother feel ready for those formalities.

"You're from the police," she said, not quite a question.

"I know you've met quite a few of us lately," I said. "Mrs. Ryan, I'm very sorry for your loss. I'm Detective Sarah Pribek. May I come in?"

There was a skittering noise on the tile of the entryway as I did. An Irish setter rounded the corner and hurried to greet me, putting an avid wet nose into the palm of my hand.

"That's enough, Luka," Mrs. Ryan said.

"Luka?"

"The girls named him. That was eight years ago; who knows why they liked it."

The Irish setter trotted off into a side room where a TV murmured. I followed him with my eyes and saw a girl sitting on the couch, knees drawn up, staring at the screen. Luka put his head on the couch cushion, as far forward as his neck would allow, and still couldn't reach her. She didn't seem to notice.

"That's Jennifer?" I asked. "Jessie's sister?"

"Jen," Katharine said. "She likes to be called Jen, if you have to interview her."

"I probably will."

Katharine led me into the kitchen. A wide window over the sink looked out onto a snow-blanketed lawn that sloped down to the treeline; the Nedegaards had no immediate neighbors.

"Would you like a caramel brownie?" she asked me. "Our neighbors brought them over."

"No, thank you," I said. "Mrs. Ryan, you've probably been over the events of the 30th and 31st quite a bit. I'm trying to do something a little different, to get a feel for Jessie as a person."

"She was a lovely person," Katharine Ryan said. "I know that's what you'd expect a mother to say. But she cared about everyone. Everyone who knew her could see that."

"That's what I've been hearing," I said. "Would you mind if I looked around her room a little?"

"No, of course not. I'll show you where it is," she said.

As she led me up the carpeted staircase, she said, "Detective Pribek, are we going to be expected to deal with the media?"

"Not as much as you did when Jessie was missing," I told her. "We're not as dependent now on appeals for help from the public."

"I wouldn't want there to be TV crews at the funeral or anything like that."

"I understand," I said, following her into an upstairs hallway. "There'll probably be a police presence at the service, but it'll be discreet, detectives in plainclothes."

"That's good," she said. "We've always valued our privacy."

We'd stopped in front of a doorway. "This is it," she said. "I'll be downstairs if you need anything."

Jessie's room was orderly and clean. There were photos of Jessie at figure skating meets, and a few framed newspaper articles about her brief career. A few ribbons were under glass. It was a room that had a headstart on being a shrine.

My search was brief; as at the Como Avenue house, there was no forensic evidence to be found here. This search went to Jessie's character and personality. I scanned the shelves, finding the books to be pleasure reading. Again, no diary. Certainly there were no firefighter photos in the lingerie drawer.

"Now, what are you? BCA? FBI?"

The man in the doorway stood about five-eleven and appeared to be in his late sixties. He had crew-cut white hair and a brushy white mustache, and pink skin so clean-scrubbed that it made hypertensiveness look healthy. His blue eyes were like an auger; I felt as though I were being inspected by Roy Nedegaard, former captain in the Minnesota State Patrol.

"Neither," I said, "I'm a detective with Hennepin County. I'm here trying to get a feel for Jessie's habits and lifestyle. Who she was."

"Who she was? That girl was the gold in our sunshine," Nedegaard said. "I raised that girl from when she was six years old, and she had a lot to overcome, you know."

I was looking over the books on the shelf. "Like what?"

"Well, her father certainly wasn't much," Nedegaard said. "It was a relief to me when Katy left him and came home. He never sent the support like he was supposed to, not half of it. I guess he figured Katy had a rich father who'd never let his girls go without anything. I didn't, of course." He paused. "It was suicide, you know, his death."

"That wasn't in the paperwork I have," I said. "It just says 'deceased.'"

"Oh, it never came out publicly. But I knew as soon as I read it that it was a one-car accident. I spent years investigating highway wrecks." He watched as I slid Jessie's high-school yearbooks off the shelf. "Among highway-patrol officers, it's an article of faith. Catholic in a one-car wreck, it's suicide."

I'd heard it before, a holdover from the days when suicides did not qualify for a burial sanctified by the Church.

"Or a wasp in the car," I commented idly. "A wasp or hornet lands on a driver or flies down clothing, it only takes seconds of distraction for the car to go off the road at fatal speed."

Nedegaard's face stiffened up as though I'd said the wrong thing, and I had. He didn't like being corrected by a cop half his age, and female to boot. In his script, my line had been something like, *Oh, that's so interesting.*

"This was November," he said finally, giving the last word emphasis. "Wrong time of year for a wasp."

"Mm," I said. "Did Jessie or her sister know about the suicide theory?"

32

"Of course not." His mustache seemed to quiver with annoyance. "I wouldn't tell those girls something like that. I mentioned it to Katy, of course."

His face was still stiff, as though he'd tasted something bad, and I decided there wasn't a lot to be gained by discreetly antagonizing him. Still holding the school annuals under my arm, I said, "Mr. Nedegaard, I'd like to take these with me, if it's okay with you." The high-school yearbooks would be a useful reference if the trail led back to Jessie's high-school years.

Nedegaard nodded, physically softening at the respect in my tone. Then he said, "You know, when they catch this guy, I wouldn't be surprised if this case starts a drive to get the death penalty back, here in Minnesota. This is just the sort of murder that could turn public opinion."

Because Jen Ryan was a minor, I asked Katharine Ryan if she wished to sit in on my interview of her daughter. She did.

"Don't expect too much," she told me, as we headed toward the den. "She's withdrawn."

"That's understandable."

"I know," she said. "What I mean is, I've had to imagine what it would be like if one of my children died before me. As a mother, if one of your kids is late coming home and doesn't call, you imagine the worst, if only for a minute. But Jen's been absolutely blindsided. I don't think she ever in a million years imagined something like this could happen."

I assured her my questions would be brief, and we went together into the den.

Withdrawn was the correct word. Katharine's younger daughter was right where I'd first seen her, sitting on the couch, her bare feet drawn up so that her heels almost touched her buttocks, her knees almost to her chest. She wore soft-looking ripped jeans, a T-shirt with many tiny horizontal stripes, and a fuzzy scarf wrapped several times around her neck. Her hair was Jessie's shade of strawberry blonde, worn a few inches longer. The Irish setter, Luka, had curled up in elliptical-shaped nap position on the floor in front of her.

"Jen," her mother said, "this is Detective Pribek. She needs to talk to you."

The girl's blue eyes shifted to me. "Okay," she said quietly, and picked up the remote and turned off the television. I was relieved to see that. I'd expected some mix of mental fuzziness and underdeveloped manners would cause her to leave the set on, requiring her mother or I to shut it off for her.

I took a seat in an armchair, angling to face her, leaving it to Katharine to settle on the couch next to her daughter.

"Hi," I said. "I'm sorry that I have to do this right now." Taking out my notebook, I said, "When was the last time you talked with your sister?"

"Wednesday," Jen said. "I was doing a paper for school and wanted to talk about *Jane Eyre*, because she'd read it."

Motion in the periphery of my vision distracted me, and Jen's eyes flicked to the doorway as well. Roy Nedegaard had come to stand in the opening. I paused in my writing. I'd planned to have Katharine here, but not necessarily a grandfather with a big, forceful personality. But I decided against asking him to leave. If he began to insert himself into the conversation, I'd deal with the issue then.

"How did your sister seem to you?" I asked.

"The same as always," Jen said in her anesthetized voice. "She was okay."

"Was anything — more specifically, anyone — bothering her?"

"I don't think so," Jen said. "She wanted to talk about the costume she bought for a Halloween masquerade. She sounded psyched." Jen wiped a stray bit of hair away from her face. Her nails were painted a sparkly crimson.

"When Jessie used to live here," I went on, "do you remember any boys she knew, or men, who gave you a bad feeling?"

"No, she just knew guys from school and the neighborhood. No one weird."

"Thanks," I said, closing my notebook. "I'll give you my card in case you think of anything else."

Roy Nedegaard walked with me to my car. I didn't expect that it was mere courtesy, and it wasn't.

"You tell Joe Santarella I'll be in to see him tomorrow morning," he said. "I asked him to keep me updated, and he hasn't called me yet."

"This case is very young. I doubt there's been anything to report yet."

"'Young' is when the trail is freshest and the breaks come fastest," Nedegaard reminded me.

Which is probably why he hasn't had time to update you. I smiled without warmth. "I'll tell him you're waiting to hear from him," I said, and got behind the wheel.

Six

At the evening meeting, it was full dark outside. The bright fluorescent fixtures inside turned the window into a glossy black mirror, as if the city outside didn't exist. We could have been in space.

Santarella, in a concession to the long day, had loosened his tie and rolled up his shirtsleeves. He let Hadley start things off, saying, "Sky, I know you've got news for us from the autopsy."

"There are some tests pending, like the tox screen, but we've got a cause of death," he said. "It's drowning."

Vang said, "Drowning?" and the same time that I said, "Really?" Hadley waved us both down, an *I'll explain* gesture. "She had a head trauma, but it wouldn't have been fatal. Jessie had water in her lungs. We don't know what kind yet. Those tests take a little longer."

I ran through the possibilities in my mind — a lake, the river, a private swimming pool — and the silence around the table suggested my colleagues were doing the same. If Jessie had been drowned in the river, there was little reason for her killer to fish her back out. A lake he might want to pull her out of, if it were too close to home for him to want her found there.

Vang said, "Let's pray for chlorine," and everyone around the table undoubtedly understood what he meant. This far north, in-ground pools were hard to maintain, a luxury item. It would narrow the search considerably: someone wealthy enough to have an in-ground pool, a relative or neighbor to that kind of homeowner, or someone with completely private after-hours access to a public or health-club pool.

Hadley flipped ahead in his notes. "The M.E. can't give us a definitive answer on rape," he said. "There was semen in the vagina, but he says it could be from prior to her murder."

He meant that we couldn't rule out consensual sex before the abduction.

"Also, there aren't tears or bruising to the vagina that suggest an assault by force. In contrast, Jessie had quite a few defense wounds elsewhere on her body — a lot of bruises and scratches. For that matter, she had some blood and skin under her fingernails that the M.E. hopes is the perpetrator's."

Vang said, "You're suggesting that she was knocked unconscious during a fight with her attacker, then stayed out the whole time she was raped."

"Yeah," Hadley said.

"I think it's likely that she was unconscious when she was killed, too."

It had been so rare, thus far, for Syed Hasan to volunteer anything that we were all quiet, simply waiting for him to speak again. He leaned forward slightly. "I think if it were at all possible, this man wanted to kill Jessie with a minimum of violence," he said. "Jessie was wrapped in sheets of high-quality fabric, which could simply be to hide her from the view of people who might look into the trash bin, thus delaying discovery of the body. But you can also read it as a protective gesture." He paused, letting his words sink in. "I'm not sure this person is at all comfortable with what he did."

"Then why leave her in a dumpster?" Vang asked. "That seems like nothing but contempt."

"Not necessarily," Hasan said. "Look at the role garbage receptacles play in our lives. Say you have someone in your home who's had too much to drink, and they're sick on your rug. That's repulsive to you, so you clean up the vomit and put it in the garbage. It's still in your house, but now it's all right, because it's in the *garbage can*. That's different.

You've compartmentalized it." He looked around at us to see if we were following him. "That's the role these receptacles play in our lives. They're where we put things that we just want to be carried out of our lives. Erased."

"What's that got to do with Jessie being unconscious when she was killed?" Santarella pursued.

"I'm coming to that," Hasan said. "The evidence is leaning toward an impulse attack on Jessie. I think it's quite possible this guy wasn't at all comfortable with what he did. If he could kill Jessie before she was awake, in the most nonconfrontational way possible, I think he'd do it. Right now, I'm guessing that Jessie was killed inside a home, probably in a bathtub."

"I'm glad you think that — the 'unconscious' part," Santarella said. "It'll be nice to tell the Ryans that for now, the theory is that Jessie didn't suffer."

After Hadley was finished, Santarella summarized what we'd learned about Jessie's exercise clothes and the possibility she'd been abducted during a run. Then Vang outlined, equally briefly, the lack of results in his neighborhood canvass.

Santarella was on his feet, pacing, an impatient general. "Pribek?" he prompted me, at last.

"Well, you stole my best material, about the running clothes," I said. "Beyond that, I learned the following about Jessie." I flipped pages in my notebook, but languidly, to illustrate the triviality of the information I'd gathered. "That she was 'the gold in her family's sunshine.' That she was a 'super friend who cared about everyone.' That she had 'great taste in clothes and loved to help friends shop.'"

I'd gotten those quotes from Jessie's friends and classmates, whom I'd contacted after leaving the Nedegaard-Ryan household. Those interviews had felt like activity, rather than progress. I told Santarella, "It reminds me of what you said about Jessie physically fitting the profile of several thousand young people at the University. Psychologically, I'm getting the same drift."

"Well, it had to be done," he said.

I went on, "The one consistent thing my interviews have turned up, including a brief talk with her sister, is that Jessie didn't seem worried about anything in the days leading up to her death. It's starting to sound like she didn't know her attacker, or at least didn't see it coming."

"That's the feeling I'm getting, too, but it's early," Santarella said. "How did the sister seem to you?"

"In shock," I said. "Not out of touch with reality, but I didn't push her too long. It might be worth a followup interview down the line if we don't catch a break and close this in the next few days." Then I shook my head, embarrassed. "Not that, uh, we'd need a stroke of luck to close."

"Noted," Santarella said, and Hadley, across the table, couldn't repress a little smile.

"One last thing," I added, "Roy Nedegaard is anxious to hear from you. Says you promised him regular updates."

Santarella's chest rose and fell with a half-repressed sigh. "He had you standing right there; why didn't he just ask you for an update? Don't answer that. I know why. He's the sort who's always got to get his intel from the top guy. I'll give him a call."

I cleared my throat lightly, getting his attention back. "I should probably go," I said.

"Right," he said, remembering my EMT class, across town. "Go. We've about covered everything."

Hadley, across the table, gave me a questioning glance as I gathered up my things to leave. He stopped short of asking, though, so I merely stood and slipped out into the hall.

SEVEN

It was nearly eleven that night when I finally returned to my Northeast Minneapolis home. A familiar white Volkswagen Rabbit was parked at the curb. Inside, the door to what had once been the spare room was open, faint light spilling from within.

Temple Lockhart, my roommate of one month, worked dogwatch. The punishing midnight-to-8-a.m. shift that wrecked the circadian rhythms of many cops didn't trouble Temple in the least. I'd seen her come home from work, drink a glass of Coke, and sleep like a stone a half-hour later. You know you have a slow metabolism when you have to speed it up to go to bed.

I paused in the open doorway and glanced in. Temple was sleeping on top of her covers, wearing sweatpants and a close-fitting, athletic gray T-shirt, headphones in her ears. Her metallic-cherry-red iPod was still playing; I could hear the faint sound of rap metal. Temple looked more like a high school student who'd dozed off during algebra homework than a cop.

It was a misperception that didn't improve much when you saw her awake. Temple was 5'4 and slender, with long light-brown hair. She looked younger than her 24 years, and a decade or so earlier, the veterans in the department, those blocky white guys with thick mustaches, probably would have complained to their sergeants about having to work with her.

Temple Lockhart had taken an elliptical path to her current career, not to mention Minnesota. The daughter of a Navy man, she'd grown up in California port cities: first San Diego, then Port Hueneme. In high school, she'd been a competitive cheerleader, then competed on the swim team. Her skills earned her a spot on the University of Minnesota women's swim team, which delighted her parents.

She hadn't declared a field of study going in, waiting for something to speak to her. Nothing did, and Temple found herself increasingly restless. The swim-team workouts, still challenging to her body, no longer engaged her mind.

Six months into her freshman year, Temple was in the student union when a representative of a nearby krav maga school was handing out flyers offering a free introductory class. Intrigued, she took one, and she followed through, showing up for the class. That was when Temple felt something that perhaps you can only experience when you're young: the sensation of picking up something that truly felt right in your hand. She was fascinated by what she was learning — a practical, self-defense-oriented martial art developed by the Israeli military — but more that that, she felt at home in the culture. Many of the practitioners were ex-military or in law enforcement. Yet they had no snobbishness about encouraging a college girl who'd once been a cheerleader.

Within months, Temple had quit swimming and was spending all her free time at the gym. She emailed friends at home less and less frequently; she had less and less time for the new people she'd met on campus. By the end of the year, Temple knew what she wanted to do with her life.

Temple's parents, thrilled when she'd been adventurous enough to go to school 2,000 miles away, didn't applaud her courage in enrolling in a police academy. Her mother's baffled queries had turned to remonstrations; then the informational materials about law schools began appearing, unsolicited, in Temple's mailbox. Suzanne Lockhart had hit on what she considered the ideal compromise: Her daughter could be a prosecutor, getting criminals off the streets from the safety of a courtroom.

"I keep trying to tell her the job isn't about the gun, that it's not even that risky, but she doesn't understand," Temple told me.

42

I wasn't quite sure I understood, either. Observing her ardor for the dirtiest, closest-to-the-ground parts of the job, I sometimes wondered if Temple was being entirely honest with herself — if she wasn't trying to tell the world, *Look at me, I'm tough,* and underneath that, convince herself of it.

Our paths had first crossed in the days when, as a new academy graduate, she'd turned up at an accident scene with her field training officer, whom I knew. But I hadn't really taken much notice of Temple Lockhart until she answered my bulletin-board notice seeking a roommate. Hers was one of three responses, and I spoke to Temple first largely because I spotted her at the gym. She'd been laying roundhouse kicks and elbow strikes into a pair of heavy bags, one in front of her and one behind, training for a multiple-attacker situation. Nearby, a parole officer had ceased his regimen of sit-ups to watch. "She's a tough little Q-tip, isn't she?" he commented to me.

In truth, the kind of hand-to-hand combat that Temple was practicing was almost never necessary on the job, but I hadn't said as much when I interrupted her workout to re-introduce myself, because I remembered what it was like to be young and zealous. After her workout, Temple went home with me to look at the spare room I was clearing out, and she liked it. Her only question was, "I don't have to leave as soon as your husband comes home, do I?" I'd assured her he was okay with the prospect of a roommate. Several days later she'd been carrying boxes up the front steps.

The change in the household had been immediate, like a light breeze on an oppressively still day. It was a relief to hear small noises around the house when I was waking or falling asleep, to see signs of life in a folded newspaper or the lingering smell of cooking even when she wasn't around.

I changed out of my work clothes, opened a bottle of Heineken and settled on the living-room couch. Temple had brought in the day's mail and set mine on the coffeetable, and behind the electric bill I could see a longer, thicker envelope with a Wisconsin postmark. That was a letter from Shiloh.

Unlike some other states and the federal system, Wisconsin didn't give its inmates access to email, so for the first time in my life, I was actually writing and receiving letters. I preferred the latter to the former. Shiloh wrote easily and fluidly, his thoughts going from mind to paper like water flowing swiftly along a downhill aqueduct. My letter-writing was like carrying water by the cupful across rough terrain.

It was tempting, of course, to open Shiloh's letter right away, but also in front of me was the box of papers I'd collected from Jessie Ryan's desk, and I reached for that instead.

Jessie's handwriting was what I'd expected, round and extroverted-looking. She'd written notes from astronomy and her two theater classes in her school notebook, and with to-do lists in the margins. There were no personal notes.

Temple's alarm chirruped, and I heard her begin to move around in her room. Presently she came out, minus the iPod, still in a T-shirt and underwear. Waving casually with two fingers, she went to the freezer and pulled out a pint container of hazelnut gelato. She dug a spoon into it even as she switched on the coffee maker and spooned ground French roast into a filter. While the coffeemaker did its work, she looked in at me.

"What are you smiling about?" she asked.

"You and your breakfast of champions," I said, "coffee and gelato."

"An alert cop is a good cop," she said.

"Alert, yes, but you get any more biochemically stoked up and you're going to be responding to scenes before the crime is committed."

"I have to compensate," she told me. "Sometimes Bent's had a cocktail or two before work and falls asleep while I'm driving."

"I didn't just hear that," I said.

Temple's partner was an ongoing source of frustration to her. A 21-year veteran in his early forties, he was married but had been rumored to take a free ride now and again with informants who were hookers, as well as free drinks from bar owners after he'd cleared their drunk-and-disorderly calls.

I'd tried to tell Temple that there are a few like him in every department, that it was more the felicity of his name, Trent Bruegger, than the outrageousness of his behavior that had earned him the nickname 'Bent Trigger.' I'd also pointed out that to the best of my knowledge, no criminal had ever fallen down a flight of stairs while handcuffed in Bent's custody.

"These are the standards?" Temple had said, incredulous, and I'd wondered if I'd become jaded.

"What are you looking at?" she said now.

"The Jessie Ryan paperwork," I said. "I'm on the task force."

"Really?" she said, immediately alight. "Can I see?"

I took the file out of the box and gave it to her. She laid out the things I'd already looked over, the summation, the maps, the witness statements, and then she looked up at me as if she'd just unpacked a Neiman-Marcus bag I'd brought home. "You've got the best job in the world," she said. "You've got to be crazy to give this up to be a paramedic."

I shook my head. "Don't start that again." It was a conversation we'd had before. With less than a year on the job, Temple was already talking about making detective. I had no doubt she'd do it — and sooner rather than later, but I didn't tell her that. One of the worst obstacles you can put in a young, smart person's path is the sense of complacency she gets from too much validation.

We read for a while in silence, then she spoke. "This is weird," she said, shaking her head.

"Which part?" I asked.

"Ryan was never alone," Temple said. "Somebody should have seen something odd."

"How do you know she was never alone?" I said.

"Girls like Jessie Ryan, they don't do anything by themselves," Temple said. "They go to the gym together. They go to the mall together. They study in groups in coffeehouses. They don't even go to the restroom alone."

45

"'Girls like her'?" I said, misquoting slightly. "You're making assumptions. That'll get you in trouble as a detective."

Temple gave me an impatient look. "Tell me you think I'm wrong."

"Okay, I don't," I said, giving in. "All accounts say that Jessie was very sociable and well-liked." I eyed the pint of gelato and said, "When you go back to the kitchen to pour your coffee, bring me a spoon, will you?"

She did, and when she'd returned, I took the pint of gelato from her and said, "So, now that we know Jessie had a lot of friends, what does it suggest to you that no one knows when she left the house, or when she went missing?"

"Maybe she was avoiding people that day. Like something was bothering her."

"Maybe," I said, "but our witnesses are saying that she was in an upbeat mood that day." I tapped my sheaf of paperwork with the end of the spoon. "This is what I think is weird. Look how everyone who saw Jessie only seems to have seen her from a distance. Even the night before she disappeared, no one reports speaking to her after about 9:30."

"You think she left her party with someone?"

I shook my head. "We considered that, but the house was packed with guests. Several people, at the least, would have seen her. I've been thinking that maybe she went to bed quite early. That at least would explain why she would be up early for a run, and early morning is the most plausible time for her to get snatched. See," I rummaged quickly and found the relevant statement, "this witness, Kelli Engle, says that Jessie was sleeping in her room at eleven-thirty p.m. But if none of our sightings of Jessie are credible after nine-thirty — they're from across the room, in dim lighting — it seems like maybe Jessie went to bed a lot earlier."

"That early? Nine-thirty?"

"Yeah, I know." I said, discouraged. "Granted, young people today aren't reading a lot of Emily Post, but who throws a party and then gets undressed and goes to bed with the living room full of people? It's even weird at eleven-thirty, come to think of it."

"But she *didn't* get undressed," Temple pointed out. "Not if this Engle person recognized her on the bed by her clothes."

I reached for the statement, but Temple wouldn't let go of it. "Well, it could be," she mused. "She could've fallen asleep in her clothes and then got up and undressed later on."

"That's not what bothers me," I said. "The thing is, Engle seems to describe a person sleeping off too much to drink — crashed out in her clothes, on top of the covers. But no one at the party saw Jessie drinking. Her roommates say she rarely drank; maybe one beer if everyone else was having one."

"What are you going to do?" she said.

I pulled at the witness statement again, and Temple let go. "I'm going to call Engle."

"At this hour?"

"No time like the present."

Temple got up to change for work, and I dialed Kelli Engle, who answered her phone on the third ring. I explained who I was, apologizing for the lateness of the hour. "You told Detective Nelson that Jessie was sleeping with her face turned away from you, but that you recognized her by her clothes," I said. "So, it sounds to me like she was lying on top of the covers of the bed, right?"

"Right," Kelli said.

"Okay," I said. "You also told Nelson that you were 'confident' the girl on the bed was Jessie. However, you also mentioned that you'd had three or four beers. Which was it, three or four?"

"I ... it was four," Kelli said. "But over three hours. I wasn't plastered."

"While you were in Jessie's room, did you turn on any lights?"

"No, but there was light from the window. The neighbors had a floodlight on their back porch, and Jessie's blinds were up."

"So it wasn't dark," I said. "Would you say, though, that it was dim?"

"I suppose," she said, a note of uncertainty in her voice.

"And did you ever walk around to look the person on the bed directly in the face?"

"No," she said, quietly.

47

A defense attorney would have torn her apart, but my purposes weren't adversarial. "Kelli," I said, "given everything, how sure are you that it was Jessie Ryan you saw in the bedroom and not someone else?"

Hesitation on the line. "I'm not so sure," she said. "Not anymore."

"Thank you," I said. "That's what I needed to know."

I flipped my phone shut, but only a second later, opened it again. My next call was to Santarella.

"I think we're going to back way up on time of disappearance," I said after he'd answered, and explained what Kelli had told me, her uncertainty about the identity of the girl sleeping on Jessie's bed.

"We thought of that," Santarella said, "and we talked to all the girls invited to that party. None of them took a nap in Jessie's room."

"I know, but have we talked to everyone *those* guests might have brought along? This wasn't a dinner party, it was a students' pre-Halloween party. The boundaries get kind of porous," I told him. "If that wasn't her in the bedroom, then it reopens the possibility that she left with someone."

"Her friends say that would have been out of character," Santarella pointed out.

"My husband says that we wouldn't have the phrase 'out of character' in our vocabulary if there wasn't a precedent for people doing things that are out of character," I countered. "We can't rule out that she left with someone."

"And changed out of her nice party clothes and into running gear to do it?"

Ouch. I hadn't factored that in. "I can't explain that one," I said, silently waving goodbye to Temple, who'd changed into her uniform and was heading out.

"Look, we'll get moving tomorrow on a complete list of everyone who was in that house, including in-and-out times," Santarella said. "It's something that should have gotten done earlier. But it's hard to imagine that Jessie left that house without a bunch of people seeing her. According to the roommates, that place was quite crowded from about nine o'clock on."

"I know," I said.

"Keep thinking about it," Santarella said. "There could be something going on here that we don't understand yet."

"I'm pretty sure of that," I said.

After we'd hung up, I went back into the living room, shuffling my Ryan papers into a semblance of order that didn't take over the whole coffeetable. I didn't mean to sit down, but did; my legs were as tired as if I'd had a six-mile run that day, and I hadn't even had a chance to work out.

When I closed my eyes, scraps of the interviews I'd done that day ran through my mind like a song I'd heard on the radio. *Jessie was a super friend. She had such great taste. Something was bothering her.* No, that last one was Temple's idea, wasn't it? Everyone I'd spoken to today had said that Jessie was happy and untroubled in the days before her disappearance, but Temple had suggested that Jessie had been upset...

In my mind's eye, I saw a slender female silhouette in a doorway, snowflakes swirling just beyond her. Then gone.

I opened my eyes as the paper I was holding fell whispering to the living room floor. I'd been asleep, just for a millisecond. The house around me was silent. I'd reached that point of personal entropy where it seemed less inconvenient to sleep where I was, on the couch, than get up and ready myself for bed.

I stood, gingerly, one foot having gone to sleep from being under the weight of my thigh. I favored it as I went into the kitchen to pour out my half-finished beer, then stood over the sink, rotating that foot at the ankle as it slowly regained full sensation. It seemed much longer ago than this morning that I'd dreamed of Shiloh at the prison.

The last thing I did before I slept was read his letter.

Sarah,

Got your last letter two days ago — two whole paragraphs. Did you injure your hand in a pickup basketball game?

Last night I dreamed about you. I was out of prison and back on the cops, and there was some kind of major disaster in the city, like a civil war, chaos in the streets. The city was really different in this dream, it was bigger — the downtown core area went on for miles, more like New York City than Minneapolis, and the buildings seemed about a thousand stories high. I should have been nervous about all this, but instead I felt good — I was back on the team, doing something important. I knew Hadley was somewhere around, and the other guys I used to work with. But in the middle of all this, I look up at these incredibly tall buildings and I see you. You're chasing somebody, running along the roofline, jumping between buildings. My first thought was *Damn, look at Sarah.* Then I got scared, I thought, *she's going to fall, she's going to fall.* And then I woke up.

Probably this is an elaborate way of saying, be careful out there. I worry about you. Don't tell me to stop, I can't.

There's nothing much going on in here, it's prison, it's always the same.

see you soon,

S.

EIGHT

By the beginning of my second day on the Ryan task force, I understood why Hadley had looked discreetly uncomfortable, like he'd been keeping something unsaid, when Santarella had mentioned Detective Nelson being left off the task force due to illness. It was clear to me that Nelson hadn't done a lot right in his preliminary investigation. Interviews were brief and perfunctory, and his report had few details. He'd done one good thing, though: He'd gotten times of arrival and departure from the few party guests he'd interviewed.

One of those people had been Jeremy Jackson, on whom Jessie had a crush, according to her roommates. Oddly enough, Jeremy had arrived at the Devil's Night party around nine and left around 9:20 p.m. This was interesting because, as I'd pointed out to Temple, no one seemed to have talked to Jessie after 9:30.

It might merely have been a coincidence. Hadn't Kori and Angie said that Jeremy had arrived with a date? But what if they'd misread the situation? What if the girl with Jeremy was a friend, and Jessie had found her affections for Jeremy requited that night? What if they'd left together? He might not have killed her, but he might have been the last to see her alive, and there could be any number of reasons why he hadn't shared that information with Nelson.

Jackson lived in the Uptown district. A little before eight in the morning, I drove past gourmet coffeehouses, bicycle sales-and-repair shops, and computer outlets to his address.

On his doorstep, Jackson looked like Kori's description of Jessie's "type": clean-cut with tousled chestnut-brown hair, good build, and sincere brown eyes. He was barechested, and the fact that he hadn't yet shaved only drew attention to his strong jawline.

"Hey," he said, stepping aside to let me in. "This is a little early for me. Sorry about the way I'm dressed." But he didn't sound genuinely embarrassed; he seemed pretty comfortable with a woman finding him in a state of semi-undress.

In the living room, I took out my notebook while Jackson went to his bedroom, then came back pulling a T-shirt over his head. "I felt really awful when I heard the news," he said, tugging the shirt down over his waist. "Did Jessie ... was it quick, the way she died?"

"We don't know yet," I said. "The autopsy was yesterday, so the medical examiner is supposed to get us findings today."

"Well, if there's any way I can help, I will," he said. "But I didn't really know her all that well."

"Still, she invited you to the party she was throwing," I said. "And you came for, by your estimate, about 20 minutes. What was that about?"

Jackson looked pained. "It wasn't a comfortable situation," he said. "Jessie didn't know I was bringing Cara."

"Why would that upset Jessie?"

"Jessie may have thought ... I mean ... " Jackson shifted his weight on the couch. "You know how it is when you haven't gone out with someone yet, but there's just this special energy whenever you're together?"

I nodded.

"Jessie and I had that. She'd lived in my dorm last year, one floor down, and then she was in an astronomy class with me this quarter. Once, I walked with her as far as the library after class, and we talked about things. She asked me what 'my girlfriend' thought about something, I forget what. She was just trying to find out if I had a girlfriend, you know? A day or so later, I ran into her at a bowling alley. She was with some of her friends, and I was with mine. We all went for beers afterward, and Jessie and I sat together, and I ended up giving her a ride back to her place." He bit his lip. "And yeah, I kissed her, before she got out of the car."

"Then what?"

"She called a few days later, to ask if I could come to the party on the 30th, and I said I would."

"And brought a date."

"I'd had a thing for Cara for a while, but she'd always had this boyfriend. Then I ran into her on campus and she mentioned that they'd broken up. I couldn't let the opportunity pass by, so I said that I was going to a party on the 30th, and I asked her to come with me. When we got there, I said hi to Jessie and introduced Cara. About ten minutes later, Jessie came back and asked to talk to me in private. We went in her room. Basically, she was upset about me bringing Cara."

I interrupted. "How did Jessie know Cara wasn't just a friend?"

Jackson said, "We had our arms around each other. I wasn't trying to hide anything." When I didn't interrupt again, he went on. "I told her that she was getting kind of possessive, given that we'd never even gone out together, and she said she thought it was clear that we were going to get together, because we'd kissed. I said, it was just one kiss, I didn't think it made us a couple. That was when she said this really off-the-wall thing." Jackson looked down at the coffeetable. "She accused me of bringing Cara because she didn't have sex with me the night I drove her home."

He held up his hands, as if fending off criticism. "I didn't even bring up sex that night. Her accusation came out of nowhere, and it bothered me, because it was like something a girl would throw at you just because she's losing an argument." He glanced at my face, to see if I'd taken feminist offense at his remark. "That sounds lousy, but sometimes girls do things like that."

"What happened after you and Jessie talked?" I asked.

"I got Cara and left. Cara didn't ask me anything. She knew what was up."

"Jeremy," I said, "I'm not here to make judgments about your dating etiquette, but when you kissed Jessie in the car, was it on the cheek, or on the lips?"

"On the lips," he said, unhappily.

"A quick kiss, or a long one?" I was starting to feel as uncomfortable as he did, but I kept my voice neutral.

"In between, I guess," Jackson said. "I feel really badly about it, seeing the way things turned out for her. I didn't mean to hurt her feelings. You don't think — " he was looking at me intently — "that this has anything at all to do with her getting killed, do you?"

I didn't know what had led to her death, so I couldn't honestly tell him what he wanted to hear. "I think," I said, slowly, "that in the normal course of events, Jessie would have been over it within a week or so. Don't pile a lot of blame on yourself."

Outside, in the car, I sat without starting the engine. My notebook was in my lap, and by the time I'd finished writing my observations down, I had a theory.

Last night, when Santarella and I had talked, I hadn't been able to reconcile the discrepancy between Jessie possibly having left the party early and her having changed into her running clothes. I'd dismissed the most obvious way to reconcile those two things, because, to rephrase what I'd said to Temple last night, who changes clothes and goes running in the middle of her own party? Particularly on a cold October night?

Now I thought I knew. Someone hurt. Someone angry. Someone young.

Jessie, excitedly awaiting the arrival of Jeremy Jackson, sees him arrive with a date. She's hurt, she has it out with him, he's unrepentant.

A thirty-year-old hosting a cocktail party would have had to stick it out for the sake of etiquette. But Jessie was young, living by the looser rules of students, and she had two roommates who were playing hostess. She could walk out on her own party if she wanted. And Jessie was a fitness buff. In times of emotional stress, she'd turn to exercise the way another woman might pull a pint of Häagen-Dazs from the freezer. And she wouldn't be discouraged by the coldness of the night outside.

Granted, the vision of it I'd had last night while falling asleep was a little off. It hadn't snowed until later, so there had been no swirling flakes behind the open doorway; that had been a little dramatic embellishment on the part of my imagination. But overall, the theory was plausible, right down to the part where, in a houseful of students, no one saw Jessie leave. I didn't disagree with Temple's assessment: A girl like that usually doesn't even go to the restroom alone. Under normal circumstances, if Jessie had simply been going out to the store for margarita mix, she was the sort of girl who'd have taken someone with her, or at least stopped to talk to three or four people before she actually stepped outside. Normally.

But if Jessie were upset, she might easily have looked out at the happy people crowding her living room — drinking, laughing, smoking — and not wanted to see or be seen by any of them. Even the most popular of young women succumbs occasionally to that nobody-loves-me feeling. This had been Jessie's turn.

There was no way she could have gotten through the front door or the sliding-glass door without being seen; those adjoined the living room and the dining area, respectively. But Jessie's room was close to the kitchen, and a kitchen is sometimes vacant during parties. People go there for more ice, for private conversations, but they don't stay long. If Jessie had timed it just right, she could have slipped out the kitchen door, unseen.

"Interesting," Santarella said, at the early task-force meeting. "It'll carry more weight if we find a girl who says she was sleeping on Jessie's bed after eleven that night."

We'd all gone around the table, sharing the ideas that a night's sleep and some time to think had brought to us. I'd been the only one to unveil a big new theory, a situation that should have made me proud, but instead I felt more than a little self-conscious.

"Still," Santarella went on, "it wouldn't hurt for you to look through our printouts of the tipline calls and pull out the possible Jessie sightings from the 30th. Who's got the tipline stuff?"

"I do," Hadley said, shuffling among the papers he'd brought to the meeting. When he'd found the sheaf of printouts, he looked at me and said, "Most of these are going to be mistaken identities, I have to warn you. Here," more shuffling, "this one's my favorite." He paused, re-reading, then summarized. "Around eleven p.m. on the 30th, a gas station attendant in St. Peter thinks he saw Jessie sitting in the cab a late-model Ford pickup truck. The gas-station guy admits he only saw Jessie through the window of the station — plus the windshield of the truck, of course — but he says it was her. There was a pit bull was sitting in the cab too, and a 'swarthy' companion was pumping the gas outside. Companion paid at the pump and never came inside the station." He looked up. "See what I mean? Come on, who says 'swarthy' anymore?"

"Well, me," Hasan said, "every time I look in the mirror to shave."

That won him an appreciative ripple of laughter, after which Santarella said, "I'm sure Pribek takes your point. When you're screening them, Sarah, be cautious. They won't all be as goofy as that."

"I will," I said, taking the printouts from Hadley.

NINE

I spent much of the day on the Jessie sightings from the 30th. Some were easy to discount, like the one from a taxi driver who thought he'd seen Jessie walking along the waterfront in St. Paul's downtown area a little after 7 p.m. I knew better. All through the early evening, Jessie had been with her roommates, making finger foods for the party, running to the convenience store for last-minute things. Others were like the St. Peter gas-station sighting, called into question by their little Gothic touches, a fearsome dog and a "swarthy" companion. And even if Jessie had gotten into a pickup truck and traveled out of town — St. Peter was about 45 minutes from the Twin Cities — why would her companion kill her in the countryside, but then return her to the Cities to dump her? Rural terrain was so much safer as a venue to get rid of a body — darker and quieter.

It took several hours of reading and follow-up phone calls before I'd isolated the three most plausible sightings.

— Around 9:30 p.m., a woman just getting off work at a convenience store turned from an ATM to nearly collide with Jessie as she ran along the sidewalk outside a bank on Hennepin Avenue, on the east side of the river.

— Between 9:30 and 10 p.m., Jessie had still been heading west on East Hennepin; this was reported by a cook on a smoke break from his job at Nye's Polonaise Room, the famous piano bar and lounge.

– Shortly before 10 p.m., Jessie was running south along the river's west bank; she was sighted by a couple out walking after a dinner date.

These three sightings fit the just-after-nine-thirty time frame. More important, they laid out a likely route for Jessie to have run.

Looking at the map, you could see it pretty clearly. Jessie emerges from her house, ready for a head-clearing run. Which way? Directly to the east were more residential neighborhoods, sleepy and pretty dark at that hour. To the southeast, the territory turned industrial, a forbidding place to be jogging alone at night. But to the north and west were well-lighted neighborhoods with stores and cafes she would have used, then the University and its surrounding neighborhoods, which Jessie would have been familiar with. If I were Jessie, that would be the direction I'd head.

I marked the spots of the three sightings on my map. Including Jessie's house as the fourth, I now had four points around which I could make a rough quadrangle with my pencil: north and west as far as the Hennepin Bridge, where I thought she might have crossed.

Granted, I didn't have a great deal of evidence for that, but I was informed by the fact that I'd been a runner in Minneapolis for years now, and I understood the role that particular bridge played in the lives of runners, cyclists, and walkers. The Father Louis Hennepin Bridge was thought to be the first bridge across the Mississippi in the Cities area, though it had been rebuilt more than once since then. The current structure was an elegant little suspension bridge, our miniature answer to the Brooklyn Bridge. It touched on Nicollet Island and was overlooked by an iconic sign advertising Grain Belt Beer. The upshot: If your run took you near the Hennepin Bridge, chances were that was where you'd choose to cross the river.

So: after that, I postulated that Jessie had turned south, where at some point she'd crossed paths with the couple on their romantic stroll. At some point thereafter, she would have turned east for home, or planned to. All the evidence we had suggested that Jessie had never gotten home.

The first and third sightings held the most promise: they both suggested fairly strict time parameters. The couple strolling after a date wouldn't have much reason to be watching the time; it'd kill the mood. But the Nye's cook, Coleman Johnson, had said he was on a break. Had he strolled away after telling a co-worker, *It's slow, I'll be right back?* Or did he have to wait for a scheduled break? Please let it be a strictly scheduled break, so he'd remember the time off the top of his head.

My hand was on the phone to call Nye's when I decided the convenience-store clerk's story was even better. She was at an ATM. An ATM meant a receipt, which would have a timestamp. Better yet, ATMs had security cameras.

On my way out, I stopped by Vang's desk.

When John Vang first took over the spot that had belonged to my partner, Genevieve Brown, he'd put up a single photo of his year-old daughter, Emmy, being pushed on a playground swing. Since then, his photographic tribute to fatherhood had grown to five pictures, three of them in a multi-picture frame.

The one that arrested my attention most often was a shot of his daughter outdoors, with her face lowered into the open petals of a purple tulip. Vang's wife was good with a camera. She'd taken the shot much closer than most amateur photographers would have dared, so that the girl's face, in profile, filled the frame. Shot so close, in such a reflective moment, Emmy looked much older than two, her face reflective and mature, lips full, skin glowing. Without any context, she could easily have been twelve or thirteen. I wouldn't have believed she were only a toddler, had I not known Vang personally.

"What's up?" I asked him, half-sitting on the corner of his desk.

"I found the girl who was sleeping on Jessie's bed," he told me. "Katya Breitland, a high-school girl from Roseville. She's five-two with blonde hair, and like all high-school girls, she has a categoric memory for what she wore when. That night, a black off-shoulder top over gray suede pants."

Gray, not tan. But it was more than good enough. In poor light, many colors seem to fade to gray.

"She ran the old 'I'm-sleeping-over-with-a-friend' scam on her parents to be able to come to the party, which is why the college-age friends who brought her didn't provide her name initially." He shook his head. "Teenage girls."

I tapped the tulip photo. "You know you're in trouble when Emmy reaches that age, don't you?"

"I'm suppressing that thought until she's about twelve," Vang said.

TEN

Natalya Karamova's convenience store was one of those that takes on the flavor of its owner's nationality: phone-card advertisements in the window suggested the buyer 'call home to Russia,' and cheese blintzes stayed warm under a heatlamp. Natalya dug through layers of detritus in her old bronze Acura to find the ATM receipt — time, 21:37 p.m. — and sent me on my way with a blintz I had to insist on paying for.

At the bank, it took one teller, two managers, and two phone calls to some unseen, off-site authority before I was finally promised the ATM's security video by the end of the day. I was relieved, getting back downtown, to find a technician still in the office who could run it for me.

The small green numbers, a time readout on the twenty-hour clock, blurred and jumped as we sped toward the half-hour mark, then slowed. Natalya Karamova approached the lens. Most people look into the fisheye mirror instead of the smaller and subtler camera lens. Karamova did neither. She looked down at the keypad. Folding her money, she stepped away, then turned directly into the path of a running figure, small, obviously female. Karamova backed up a step. The running figure broke stride but didn't come to a full stop; she dodged around Karamova and away.

Excitement jumped in my chest. The tech didn't have to be told to back it up. The figure ran backward into the frame again, and the tech froze the film at the point the jogger and Karamova nearly collided. The technician adjusted the frame by hand, moving in on the upper body, and slowly the face came into focus: the heart-shaped bone structure of her face, the now-familiar eyes and mouth. Her sweatshirt clearly read, *Minnesota.*

"That's her," I said. But what I was really thinking was, *she's real.* After all the good, close-up, posed photos I had of Jessie, this video image in unwholesome grays seemed the truest of all. We were investigating a murder, not a disappearance; yet, I felt much as though I'd found a missing person.

Outside, I paged Santarella.

At the 6 p.m. meeting, we were crowded around the city map. We were closing in on a time and point of abduction. It was a testament to the excitement generated by the video footage that Hadley, who'd gotten the M.E.'s test results, hadn't told us about them yet.

"Did she have any workout buddies? We need to find someone out there who knew her route when she went running," Santarella said.

"That's the problem; she didn't run all that regularly," I said. "Her friends say she only ran when the gym was closed. We can't count on this being her regular loop."

Santarella propped his hands on his hips, facing the map and the unfinished rectangle I'd drawn. "That argues for a crime of impulse, not a stalker," he said. "Our guy couldn't have watched her until he knew her route, then wait for her along a point, one he knew she passed five nights a week."

"If this was impulse, he must have made up his mind pretty fast to grab her," I said. "The part of the loop we've got so far isn't very big. She wasn't going for a very long run, unless she was planning to go a lot further to the south of her house than she did to the north. Which'd make the route kind of…"

"Asymmetrical," Vang supplied. "I agree that she probably wasn't going to go much further south. I think she got snatched somewhere near where your drawing stops. If she'd gone much further, someone should have seen her."

Santarella cut us off. "This might be too much theorizing," he said. "Until we have evidence to the contrary, he still might have got her within a few blocks of her house on her way back." He straightened. "Skyler, you've got some more news for us from the M.E.?"

Hadley stood. "The DNA from the blood and skin cells under Jessie's fingernails matches that of the semen the M.E. recovered," Hadley told us. "I'm comfortable calling the sex nonconsensual despite the lack of vaginal tearing."

"Because it's consistent with her being unconscious throughout," Vang said.

"Right. The other thing is, they've narrowed down the kind of water in her lungs. Definitely no chlorine, so not a pool or spa; none of the algae or microbial life-forms you'd find in river water, or lake, or pond. It's municipal water. From a tap."

"Bathtub," Hasan said, immediately.

"It would make sense," Santarella said. "If she's unconscious, it's possible he could have held her head down in anything that can be filled with tap water, but a bathtub is custom-made to submerge a body in." He cleared his throat. "If no one's got anything to add, I've got a horde of media types to face down."

His irritation wasn't genuine, though, because at this evening's press briefing, via the reporters, we were asking the public for help. The previous reports that had flooded in were unsolicited, volunteered by people interested in Jessie's disappearance and death. The large number of vague to downright silly reports were a reflection of that. Now we had a much narrower timeframe to give out, and narrower geographic boundaries; the hope was that these would bring in much more reliable Jessie sightings.

"One last thing," Santarella said. "I'm dividing up among all of you the elimination interviews with our friendly local sex offenders." He walked behind our chairs, passing out stacks of papers. "You know the drill. Get the alibi, get it checked out. See if any of these guys are limping like they were kicked hard in the balls recently, anything like that."

ELEVEN

When I was in the Sheriff's Academy, my class watched the videotaped interrogation of a man who'd broken into a woman's house at night, held a box cutter to her throat and choked her to ensure her submission, raped her, and then struck her hard across the face before leaving. The purpose of the video was to let us watch an excellent interrogator doing his thing, but I'd taken something different away from the lesson.

The rapist, at the time of his interview, had two prior offenses: one for domestic violence against a girlfriend, the other for the attempted rape of a homeless woman near a bus shelter. He'd told the interrogating detective about how he'd been through counseling in prison, where he'd been taught that his hostility toward women came from growing up in a house with several older stepsisters who had taunted and mistreated him. He'd learned that he had to "rewire" his thinking about women, and he claimed that he'd been doing well for the eleven months he'd been back in the free world.

The interview progressed, and soon the suspect was recounting how he'd committed the crime. He explained that after he'd raped the woman whose house he'd broken into, just before he'd left, he'd asked his victim if she was all right. She'd said, "Oh sure, that was *great.*" It was then that he'd hit her.

He explained it to the detective thus: "When she was sarcastic with me, the feelings I used to have, of hating women, started to come back."

No one else mentioned the case study after class, and I'd wondered if I was the only one of us stunned by his words. He'd climbed through an open window with a weapon in his hand, had choked, threatened, and raped a woman, yet honestly seemed to believe he'd had no rage toward women until this one talked back to him.

I thought of that man while I was doing elimination interviews, the routine work of visiting sex offenders and questioning them about possible involvement in an open case. I understood that even sex crimes have mitigating factors — from poor prenatal and childhood nutrition that undermines impulse control to lousy modeling of manhood by absent or violent father figures. But it would have been much easier to sympathize without hearing the mental contortions many of these men went through in convincing themselves their crimes had not really been their fault. My fourth interview of the day, particularly, was to remind me of that.

The 28-year-old parolee I was visiting lived in a southern suburb with his parents, released after serving nine years for attacking and raping a gas-station clerk, all in an apparent spur-of-the-moment rage when she'd refused to sell him cigarettes without ID. Dean Holmes interested me, largely because his MO had been one of impulse, as I suspected the attack on Jessie had been.

His address corresponded to a two-story gray house in a subdivision, with neighbors on either side and one solitary birch tree to simulate a natural setting. The front yard was more mud and melting snow than grass, as if a re-seeding project had been attempted over the summer but had not taken. A black mid-'90s Mustang was parked in the open garage. Dean's, I knew. He was mobile, which made him capable of a kidnapping in the city.

It was Dean who came to the door. He wasn't as solid as I was expecting for someone who'd committed such a physical crime. About five-nine and slender, he surveyed me with unimpressed blue eyes, and he wore a knit stocking cap indoors.

I held up my badge. "I'm Detective Sarah Pribek with the Hennepin County Sheriff's Department," I said, "Can I come in and talk to you?"

He frowned, whether in annoyance or anxiety I couldn't tell. "Does my parole officer know you're here?"

"Yes, he's been notified. May I come in?" I repeated. "I'd like to talk to you about the recent disappearance and death of a University student."

Unenthusiastically, Dean stepped aside, then walked ahead of me into the kitchen. It had a wide window facing the lawn, with embedded latticework to approximate a French window while making it easy to wash as plate glass. Dean looked morosely out at the street.

I cleared my throat. "So," I said, "what have you been doing with yourself since your release?"

"What is there to do?"

"According to your file, you haven't been working," I said.

"That's not a parole violation," he said. "I just have to prove I've been looking for work. It's not easy after the state's branded you as a violent felon."

"You are a violent felon."

"I was barely out of high school," he countered. "It was a first offense. I shouldn't have gone to jail for nine years."

A brutal and ugly first offense, but arguing with him wouldn't get me anywhere. "Dean," I said, "Are you familiar with the name of Jessie Ryan?"

He nodded, silent.

"Do you have any ideas about what might have happened to her?"

There were several things we hadn't released to the media. That Jessie's body had been wrapped in fabric, for example. If Dean were involved, maybe he'd let something slip.

"No," Dean said. "Frankly, I have better things to think about."

"What were you doing on the night of the 30th?" I pursued.

"Watching TV in my room," he said.

"Did you have a friend with you?" I asked.

He shook his head.

"So only your parents can confirm it?"

"I guess," he said.

I took out my notepad and passed it to him, along with a pen. "Write down your location and activities from about nine p.m. on the 30th through the evening of October 31st, and for each separate listing, the name and phone number of someone who can confirm you were there."

While Dean wrote, I looked out the window, thinking. There was hostility in his tone, but I wasn't sure it was directed at me as a woman as much as it was to me as a representative of the law-enforcement system that so unfairly put him away for nine years. He appeared unhappy, but not nervous. If he'd been involved with Jessie's death, he should have been nervous.

When he was finished, I saw that Dean had listed his parents as witnesses that he'd been at home all the night of the 30th. On the 31st, Dean said, he'd had a job interview and visited a chiropractor and come home around four in the afternoon.

Movement caught my eye from outside the front window.

I looked up to see a dark-blue Ford sedan slowly crawling into the mud of the Holmes yard, pulling close enough to the house that I could read a University of Montana parking sticker in the lower right corner of the windshield, though the car itself had Minnesota plates. The driver didn't look old enough to be Dean's father.

"Who's that?" I asked him.

Dean looked out the window. "Oh, that's a guy from a sexual-violence-prevention program," he said. "I get bonus points with my PO if I let him come around and 'rap' with me."

The driver got out of the car, a tall, thin man in his mid – to late twenties, wearing a Minnesota sweatshirt over gray jeans and sneakers. He moved gingerly through the mud, working his way toward the front door. Dean scraped his chair back and rose, went to the front door. I picked up Dean's account of his activities and followed.

"Hey, Steve," Dean said, letting the newcomer in.

"Hi, how've you — " He saw me and broke off. "I didn't know you had company." He was younger up close, with a high forehead, receding light-brown hair, and gray eyes.

"Oh," Dean said, negligently, "this is Detective Sarah Pribek. She's here to make sure I didn't off that University student last week."

Deliberately, I ignored Dean's disrespectful choice of verbs. "It's a formality. I'm talking to a number of sex offenders," I said. I extended my hand. "I'm sorry, I didn't catch your name."

"Steven. Steven Silverhus." As the man raised his hand to meet mine, there was a brief stutter in the movement, as if Silverhus weren't sure I was serious about shaking his hand. "I read about that girl. It's really terrible, what happened to her."

I said to Silverhus, "Dean tells me you counsel sex offenders. Are you a therapist?"

"No, no," Silverhus said. "I'm with Men Against Interpersonal Violence. It's strictly a volunteer group."

"Interesting," I said. "How'd you get involved with that?"

"I go to the University," Silverhus said. "It's a group that's organized out of the U."

This was a useful development. A psychotherapist would have required a court order before revealing the content of Dean's sessions. A lay counselor worked under no such restrictions. I nodded toward the front door and said, "Can I speak with you for a moment in private?"

Silverhus glanced at Dean and then followed me out onto the front stoop.

"Mr. Silverhus," I said, walking down the driveway toward my car, "Dean isn't a suspect, but based on a brief interview, I'd have to say he doesn't seem like he's really taken responsibility for his prior crime yet." I glanced toward the front window, but it was empty. "When you heard about Jessie Ryan's disappearance, did you have any sense of unease at all where Dean is concerned? Has anything he's said troubled you?"

"Oh, no," Silverhus said, quickly. "He's matured a lot since his crime. He's learning impulse control. I'm sure he's not responsible for what happened to that girl." He rubbed his nose with two fingers. There was a reddish mark, a shallow half-circle like a parenthesis, on his hand.

69

"What happened there?" I touched my own hand in the same place.

"Oh," he said. "I pinched my hand between a door and a frame at one of my grandfather's rental properties. I was replacing the hinges and got sloppy." He smiled self-consciously.

"I see," I said. "At the University, are you a psychology student?" I wondered how much insight Silverhus brought to his volunteer work.

"Yes," he said. "I changed my major from geology. Psychology is a fascinating field."

I took out my billfold and removed one of my cards. "You probably counsel other sex offenders, right?" I said. "If you hear anything that makes you suspicious, it's all right to give me a call. In fact, it could be the key to preventing another crime."

"I'll do that," Silverhus said, taking the card. "Sure."

TWELVE

"Six good sightings before the bridge, and none after," Temple said, looking at my map of Jessie Ryan sightings. "It couldn't be much clearer."

Beyond our sex-offender interviews, the second day of investigation had been taken up with getting confirmation for our Devil's-Night-outdoor-abduction theory, the one that the ATM camera footage had launched. Santarella's appeal for information had sparked the memories of dozens of people, who called with accounts of seeing Jessie running on the 30th. Painstakingly, Vang, Hadley, and I had winnowed them, trying to sort the plausible ones from those of the nearsighted, the mentally unstable, and the excessively helpful. We marked every sighting on the map in pencil when it came in, so that before long, the pencil marks looked like a none-too-tight shot pattern. But when the three of us were in agreement on the validity of a sighting, the pencil dot was gently erased, replaced by blue pen.

By the end of the day, we could connect the dots with a minimum of educated guesswork. My theory about Jessie crossing at the Hennepin Bridge was borne out by the new sightings, none of which were north of that point. From there, as we traced her route up to the last credible sighting, we ended up with an approximate path that Hadley said looked like an unfinished pentagon, and I thought resembled a crude, backwards-facing fishhook. Both metaphors reflected the fact that the line of blue pen stopped just east of the Stone Arch Bridge. We had no reliable sightings of Jessie east of that location, where she would very likely have turned for home.

There was a small park near the University's heating plant, close to the river. We all liked it for an abduction site, but we didn't have any physical evidence for it. Since the early hours of the 31st, it had lain under a blanket of snow. Hadley and Vang had visited it for an in-person look, and they'd talked to people who lived nearby or who worked in businesses up on the street above it. That was unproductive. The question "Did you hear anyone screaming around ten that night?" tended to earn the answer, *It's a University neighborhood. Those kids are always yelling about something.* Nobody had heard anything that had prompted them to go outside and look around.

Only Vang had heard something interesting. He'd talked to a guy who'd been walking back from a nearby convenience store and had seen a dark-colored sedan "kind of like a cop car" coming up from the park in a hurry, nearly running a red light at the first intersection. Prompted by Vang, the man had estimated that the car was only going about 35, not fast per se, but too much for a city neighborhood. Unfortunately, Vang's witness hadn't remembered anything about the license plates.

Now, Temple and I were doing what had become routine for us. We were both in the living room at around ten o'clock at night, she reading the case paperwork I'd finally set aside after a long day, me studying for EMT class. Tomorrow's class dealt with calls involving juveniles. *In contrast to the infant, the toddler has begun to develop a sense of modesty. He may resist having his clothes removed.*

"Have you thought about taking a crime-scene team out to the park?" she asked me, pursuing her earlier thought.

"Thought about it, yeah," I said. "But we've got to have more evidence for a specific place of abduction before we drag out the techs to melt away snow and look for something." *The adolescent may engage in risky behaviors due to a sense of invulnerability.*

"You'll never find anything if you don't look," Temple pointed out.

"I'm not even sure what we'd tell the techs to look for," I told her. "It's not like we know she's missing a necklace or something else she was wearing that night."

"Have you considered posting notices around the — " Temple broke off, her thought interrupted by a knocking at the front door. We exchanged looks, and my expression was probably as startled as hers. For a brief moment, I thought maybe there had been a break in the case, but that wasn't right; that news would have come via my phone.

"I'll get it," I said, getting to my feet.

"Nate," I said, surprised to see Shigawa, my EMT-class instructor, right on my doorstep. "What's going on? Is everything okay?" Though he was in civilian clothes tonight, he stood on my doorstep in the typical, slightly braced posture that I associated with his job, and I immediately thought of road accidents and bad news.

"Everything's fine," he said. "I'm not here in any official capacity. I, uh — "

I helped him out. "Do you want to come in?"

Civilian clothes or not, Shigawa wore his big, lace-up turnout boots, and he wiped the snow-dampness from them carefully before following me through the entryway and into the living room.

He stopped in the entryway. "Oh," he said. "I didn't know you had company."

"That's not company," I said. "That's my roommate, Temple Lockhart. Officer Lockhart, to you."

Temple looked up from the autopsy results she was studying.

"Temple, this is Nate Shigawa. I've mentioned him, he teaches the EMS class."

"Hey," she said, barely sparing him a glance before returning to her reading. *Big deal, another cop or reasonable facsimile,* her tone said.

His eyes stayed on her a moment longer, until I cleared my throat. "Can I get you something to drink?"

"No, no," Shigawa said. "I can't stay long. I probably should have called you instead." He paused. "Jessie Ryan's funeral is Saturday."

"I know," I said. I would be in required attendance, along with Syed Hasan, who'd expressed interest in Jessie's funeral, in observing who came and how they behaved.

"Schiller and I responded to the call when the body was found, and did the transport to the medical examiner's office," Shigawa said. "It might sound strange, but I feel involved. Do you think the family would mind if I came to the service?"

His words had drawn Temple's interest; she raised her eyes to watch us.

"I know there's a BCA agent officially handling the case," he went on, "but I came to you because I know you personally. I'm not asking to be morbid."

"I know you're not," I said, thinking. "The service is friends-and-family, but I've got Katharine Ryan's phone number in my file. I could call her."

I wasn't afraid that Katharine Ryan could possibly be sleeping early, not on the night before her daughter would be buried. I explained the situation, and she gave her blessing for Nate to come. She was sober, more than sober. Her voice was dry and soft as autumn leaves, suggesting an emotional numbness that alcohol could not provide.

When I went back out into the living room, Shigawa had moved to stand next to Temple. "I've seen you before," he was saying. "You're Trent Bruegger's partner, right?"

"Unfortunately," Temple said.

"Here," I told him, handing over the directions to the church. "It's at ten-thirty tomorrow morning."

"Thanks," he said. And then, "It was nice meeting you," to Temple.

"You, too," she said, not looking up.

When Shigawa was gone, I said, "He's a nice guy, you know."

Temple lifted a shoulder. "Probably he is."

I thought of saying, *You were kind of cold to him,* but thought better of it. Her own business, I decided, and returned to my textbook. Three pages left to read, and then I could maybe write a quick letter to Shiloh before bed.

It was only later, while Temple was in the shower, that my phone went off. It was Hadley.

"I know it's late," he said, "but this is really interesting. The DNA we recovered from Jessie's fingernails got a hit on CODIS." The national database, he meant.

"We've got a suspect?"

"No, it's not quite that good," he said. "The other case is unsolved, but now we know where our guy was two years ago. He was in Missoula, Montana, where he raped a woman and put her in a coma for five weeks with a head injury. Details to follow, Santarella says."

THIRTEEN

On Halloween night, two years ago, a waitress at a small Missoula bar called the Copper Grill had clocked out after working the 4 to 11 shift. Danielle Roback, 22, had then driven her Chrysler LeBaron to the mixed student and working-class neighborhood where she rented a studio apartment behind a single-family home.

The next morning, one of the children who lived in the front house found Danielle behind the small corrugated-tin carport where she parked her car. She was partially naked; the blood from the blow that smashed her skull had dried in her hair. She was unconscious and would remain that way during the internal examination that found clear evidence of rape. For the next five weeks, the investigation was forced to proceed without so much as Danielle's memory of what happened. She remained comatose all that time.

Other witnesses were virtually nonexistent. The young family in the front house slept early, and apparently soundly. A neighbor had heard his German Shepherd barking agitatedly, but thought the dog had scented a deer that had wandered into town. Several others in the neighborhood remembered seeing an adult figure or two, early in the evening, walking the streets in a mask or costume, and why wouldn't they? It was Halloween.

The final setback: When Danielle awoke, the last thing she remembered was asking the Copper Grill's bartender for a strawberry lemonade in a go-cup to drink on the way home. She didn't remember if she'd seen anyone in the parking lot, if she'd made any stops on the drive home, if there had been an unfamiliar car parked on the street where she lived.

Santarella had gathered a good deal of information in a fairly short time; he told us all this at the morning meeting. Afterward, he added, "I've been in touch with the detective in Montana who handled the case, and he's faxing the paperwork to us."

Montana. Where had I seen a reference to that state, very recently?

"Detective Daley lost touch with the victim," Santarella said. "She left town and didn't stay in contact; I guess she gave up hope that there was ever going to be movement in the case. But we'll track her down pretty quickly."

The University of Montana parking sticker on the blue sedan at Dean Holmes's house. The anti-sexual-violence counselor, Silverhus. I might have remembered it last night, after Hadley's call, had I not been so weary after a long day.

"Did you hear me? Pribek?"

"Sorry," I said. "What?"

"I said, when we find Roback, I'd like you to talk to her. She might be more responsive to questioning from a female detective." He held eye contact with me a moment longer, then scanned everyone assembled. "One last thing: The University's holding a vigil Friday night in honor of Jessie. It sounds like it's going to be part memorial and part anti-violence rally. I'm going to need all hands. We're going to circulate and watch for unusual behavior, or anyone who stands out." He didn't have to specify that he meant anyone male. "Understood? Okay, let's get to work."

After the meeting, I ran an Internet search, which confirmed that the University of Montana's main campus was in Missoula. Afterward, I borrowed a book from Hadley, studying it for a good ten minutes, especially the photos. Only then did I double back to talk to Santarella, privately.

"There's something I want to run by you," I said. "What would you say if I told you that while I was doing elimination interviews a couple of days ago, I talked to a guy whose car had a University of Montana parking sticker, and an injury on his hand that looks like a healing human bite?"

That was the thing I'd been checking in Hadley's book, the photos of human bite marks. Seeing them, I'd realized that I should have recognized the first time around that the red mark on Silverhus's hand was too curved to be the result of being caught between a door and frame.

Santarella raised his eyebrows. "I don't think you need me to answer that," he said. "What's the catch?"

"He wasn't a sex offender," I told her. "Just a visiting friend."

"That changes the situation," he admitted. "Where's your conviction coming from on this?"

In brief, I explained about Silverhus, including the fact that the University of Montana's flagship campus was in Missoula, and that the dark-colored, like-a-cop-car sedan Vang's witness had seen near the park sounded plausibly like a midnight-blue Ford Taurus.

Then, in my mind's eye, I re-ran the images of Silverhus. The animation with which he'd greeted Dean Holmes had diminished palpably when he'd first seen me. Later, as we'd talked about the Ryan case, he'd raised his hand to touch his face, twice. It was a classic psychological evasion gesture.

"He wasn't comfortable with me, even before he knew I was a cop, and even less so after," I said.

"Before he knew you were a cop? Meaning?"

"Meaning I think he was uncomfortable with me initially just because I'm a woman," I said. "Which is what Hasan thinks our suspect is: a scared guy who lashes out intermittently."

Santarella crossed his arms over his chest, a stalling, blocking gesture, I thought. Once you start analyzing body language, it can be hard to stop.

"Have you looked for priors on this man yet?" he said. "Do that first. Unless you find something damning, I'm more interested in you finding out what Roback has to say."

It took me an hour of electronic paper-trailing before I found Danielle Roback. She'd applied for a Wisconsin driver's license, listing an address in Clear Lake. She wasn't at home when I called, so I left a message on her machine, asking her to call me as soon as she got in. Then I went to the coffee machine. Walking back, I heard my phone ringing; I'd left it on my desk. I abandoned my coffee on a nearby filing cabinet; it was either that or risk scalding my fingers by running with it in hand, and I didn't want to miss Roback's call.

"Hey, Pribek." The voice on the other end was definitely not Danielle Roback. "Want to take a little field trip?"

"Depends," I told Hadley. "Do you let people drink coffee in your car?"

"No. No coffee."

"It's not even your personal car," I complained, "it's a department vehicle."

"Pribek, will you forget the damn coffee? This is worth giving up your caffeine fix."

We were only playing at disagreeing, but now I was curious. "Why? What do you know?"

"I'll explain on the way."

FOURTEEN

Hadley had been working at his desk when the MPD's desk sergeant had ushered back a lanky, six-foot-three kid who "wants to talk to someone about the Jessie Ryan case."

Asa Jackson was still in high school. He was a center on the basketball team, with his eye on college ball and maybe the NBA. He also worked afternoons in the shipping and receiving department of an electrical-supplies manufacturer, so he trained when he had free time, usually late in the evenings. On the evening of the 30th, that had meant going for a long, looping run through the city at nearly ten o'clock at night. That run had eventually taken him to the park just east of the Stone Arch Bridge.

"I was running on one of the footpaths when I slipped and fell," Asa told Hadley. "Not bad, because I've got pretty good reflexes. So I just kept on running. But when I got home, there was dried blood on my knee. I was surprised, because like I said, I hadn't fell hard. So I washed it off, and it still didn't hurt. You know, it didn't sting, and I couldn't see where the skin was, what's the word — "

"Broken," Hadley said. He leaned forward. "Did you tell anyone about this?"

Asa shook his head. "Why? They'da just thought I was tripping. I didn't think about it again until I heard my uncle saying that it looked like that college girl went missing from that same area. Then it made sense." In case he hadn't made himself clear, Asa Jackson spelled it out. "I don't think it was my blood I washed away."

Neither do I, Hadley had thought.

In the west, the sun was dying the pale and early death of wintertime as I stood at the east end of the Stone Arch Bridge, and the waters of the spillway were white and foamy, like agitated water rushing over a giant washboard. Behind me, crime-scene technicians were moving back and forth in the area where Asa Jackson had slipped and fallen. Hadley and I had brought him, to point out the spot as exactly as his memory would allow. Then a uniformed officer had given him a ride back home.

Now, our techs were melting snow and examining the wet asphalt underneath. We weren't hoping there'd be any blood left to find, days later, after several snows. But Jessie Ryan's keys had never been found. If they'd been in her pocket, they probably wouldn't be on the scene. But if she'd held them in her hand while running – or taken them out as her only weapon against an attacker who'd loomed from the shadows — she could easily have dropped them. It was also possible that her assailant hadn't noticed, or that in his haste to get away with her over his shoulder, hadn't stopped to pick them up.

Hadley, impatient, had walked up to a convenience store for a Coke; I hadn't wanted anything, and had gone out to the bridge, instead.

"Are you Sarah Pribek?"

I'd noticed the red-haired woman approaching and taken her for a sightseer. Now I looked at her more closely. She was perhaps five-four, slender, with red curls pinned up where the afternoon breeze could try to pull it free, and she was studying me with expectant curiosity.

"I'm Pribek," I said. "Do I know you?"

"No," she said. "But there's only one woman on the Jessie Ryan task force. It was an easy guess."

She was casually dressed in jeans and a white shirt, a chartreuse parka and hiking boots of sienna-colored leather. She didn't look like someone in the middle of her working day. I'd missed the only tipoff, a pen wedged behind her ear.

"I'm Rosamund Ross," she said.

Few journalists are the gray-headed anchorman figures we associate with the news broadcasts of the past. Ross, who'd had a sole or shared byline on all the Jessie Ryan stories, was about my age, with winter-faded freckles on her clean, pale face.

"The word is," Ross said, "that the search over there is related to the Ryan case." She reached into her leather shoulder bag and withdrew a notepad.

"Wait, you won't be needing that," I said, mildly alarmed. "Joseph Santarella, of the BCA, is handling all the media inquiries. I can give you his extension."

"I have it," Ross said. Undiscouraged, she slid the pen out from behind her ear. "But since you're right here and I'm right here, can I just ask you about the general nature of the evidence you're looking for?"

"I can't comment on that."

"Have you had a significant break in the past 24 hours?"

"Rosamund — Ms. Ross, I honestly can't speak to you unless it's completely off the record."

"Would you ever question a suspect knowing nothing you'll get will be admissible in court?" She tilted her head slightly. "I'm a reporter. When I'm on the clock, I'm on the record, otherwise it's a waste of everyone's time."

"Even so," I said, and turned my palms upward, indicating impotence.

I knew it was undignified for me to be this skittish in the company of a reporter. I'd never disliked any of the ones I'd known; rather, my paranoia was drilled into me in the Sheriff's Academy. Our lecturers had repeated it over and over: no matter how innocuous the conversation seems, if you speak to a journalist under any circumstances, even in line for a beer at the Timberwolves game, expect to be quoted or at least have your words used in print. You're not off the record until you've gotten explicit verbal agreement from them that you're off.

It was common policy for reporters' questions to be handled only by department spokespersons, captains, or chiefs, and there wasn't much of an upside to breaking that rule. At best, getting your name in print earned you the jeering of fellow officers who dislike a glory hound. At worst, you came in the next day to find that you'd let something slip that had jeopardized an investigation, a mistake that would put a black mark on your permanent record.

"All right," Ross said, flipping her notebook shut and putting it away. She turned so that her back was to the safety railing and leaned against it on her elbows, looking very much at ease. "Are you from out West?"

Few people, if any, picked that up, particularly on such short acquaintance. "New Mexico," I admitted, curiously. "Why'd you ask?"

"Accents are a thing of mine. Linguistics was my minor, in school," she said. "Plus, I'm from Arizona. I came out here for school and never left." The wind kicked up slightly, and she shook hair off her face. "My first fall here, that's all people wanted to talk about: how awful the winter was going to be. They love finding out you're a Westerner." She adopted the voice of a schoolyard bully. "Yew've never spent a winter here? Yer gonna wish yew *were* dead!"

I smiled. I knew what she was doing; it was rapport building. I couldn't help but find it a little disarming, even while I knew it was deliberate.

Her blue gaze sharpened. "Looks like your guys found something."

I turned and saw Malik, one of the two crime-scene techs, waving an arm, trying to get my attention. He was holding up a plastic bag, but the last of the day's sun glinted off the metal inside it, a shape about the size of a key ring.

FIFTEEN

"Steven Silverhus doesn't have any priors in Minnesota or in Montana. But he was a college student in Missoula at the time of Roback's rape, just like he was living here when Jessie Ryan was killed."

It was shortly before 9 a.m., at the early meeting. I was pitching what I'd learned last night to Santarella, who was surveying me tiredly over a pint of convenience-store orange juice. We were all underslept after a late night. We'd gotten confirmation yesterday evening that the key ring was Jessie's. Between it and the blood on the ground, we had our abduction site. So we'd immediately started interviewing — in some cases re-interviewing — people who lived or worked nearby.

Now I was recounting how I'd met Silverhus, how he'd acted, and the odd mark on his hand. This was mostly for the benefit of Vang and Hadley, who hadn't been around when I'd told those things to Santarella the first time.

I went on: "His car is a dark-blue Ford Taurus, and we have a witness account of a 'dark-colored' sedan driving up from direction of the park on the night of Jessie's abduction. That, the Montana connection, and his injuries are what I have to go on so far. I've got a call in to Danielle Roback, but I haven't heard back from her yet." I stopped there. "What do you think?"

Santarella scratched one of his thick eyebrows. "You told me this guy did something unusual, like unpaid social work...what was that again?"

"A volunteer group. Men Against Interpersonal Violence."

Santarella tapped his pen against the table. "That's the part I don't buy," he said. "Why would a guy with these kinds of feelings about women join a group of guys who feel just the opposite?"

"To resist those feelings," Hasan said.

Everyone turned to look at him.

"He may hope that these meetings will keep him safe from acting out what he wants to do," Hasan explained. "Depending on how self-aware he is, he may not even realize that's what he's doing. He may have convinced himself he believes in this group's goals."

"Suggesting that the abduction had little to no planning," Vang said. "That when he saw Jessie, he just snapped."

"Right," Hasan said. "Danielle Roback was raped on Halloween. It's possible that the approach of that anniversary was stressful for Silverhus."

"You mean, the very act of feeling guilty and upset about raping one woman two years ago may have led this guy to do something worse to a second girl?" Vang said.

"I think it's possible," Hasan said. "I'd really love to see this guy up close."

"Well," Santarella said, "you've got everyone's interest, Pribek. Do you have any ideas where you'd like to start investigating this man?"

"I do," I said.

About 20 years ago, a sociology undergraduate at Boston University left a late-night study session at a friend's house. She never made it back to the apartment she shared with her boyfriend, a Ph.D. student in psychology. Instead, she was carjacked, raped, and murdered, her body abandoned at a construction site.

Her boyfriend, Robert Donovan, made the news two years later, when he visited his girlfriend's murderer in prison. He also publicly forgave the man, a 24-year-old recidivist who had been abandoned as a child by a drug-addicted mother and had grown up largely in the juvenile penal system.

Partly because Donovan and his girlfriend were white while her murderer was black, his gesture drew widespread public reaction, from civil-rights and prison-reform leaders to feminist groups to crime-victims' lobbies. Some applauded Donovan's ability to forgive; others called talk radio shows to say that he was all but spitting on his girlfriend's grave.

Donovan's fifteen minutes of fame passed, but he went on to create a campus group called Men Against Interpersonal Violence. Its stated aims were to promote research into the underlying social causes of sexual violence and to reposition rape as a men's issue as well as a women's one. Today, there were seven chapters on campuses around the East and the upper Midwest. Most functioned as part support group for men whose partners had been victims and part activist organization, doing volunteer outreach and counseling with sex offenders.

Several years ago, Robert Donovan had taken a professorship at the University of Minnesota, and for that reason, Donovan himself led the Minneapolis chapter. When I'd called him, I'd only mentioned to him that I wished to discuss the Jessie Ryan case. He'd agreed to make a little time for me after his Adolescent Psychology class, which ended at noon.

I have to admit something here: None of the Web articles on Donovan and his cause had included a photo, but I expected someone bearded, perhaps with graying and thinning hair, maybe underweight, or overweight but just around the midsection, the badge of long hours spent at a desk.

But the man who met me at his office in the University's Elliott Hall was built like a hockey defenseman, and he had a heavy shock of dark hair which wasn't showing any grays yet. When his eyes met mine, as he leaned out to open the door for me, his gaze was almost like a physical touch. He had pale-blue eyes with a darker ring around the iris, and there was a direct focus in them I didn't associate with scholars. If Donovan had been introduced to me as someone from Quantico, instead, I wouldn't have been surprised.

His door wouldn't open all the way. Looking around, I saw what impeded it: a stack of books. "Sorry," Donovan said, and his voice was the low rumble that his deep chest suggested. "I keep hoping my office will reach critical mass and implode, preferably when I'm not in it, and then they'll have to give me a new one in which I can start fresh." He moved a similar stack of books off the chair so I could sit down.

"Wouldn't that be a crushing loss of important reference material?" I asked him.

Donovan shook his head. "It's up here," he said, tapping one finger against his temple. "I'm blessed, or cursed, with a nearly photographic memory."

Whether or not it was egotistical of him to share it with a stranger on two minutes' acquaintance, I believed him when he said it.

Donovan took a seat behind his desk. "What can I help you with today?"

I took out my notebook. Though I wasn't sure I'd need to write anything down, it made a good prop; it flattered people who needed to feel they are officially helping the police in their inquiries.

"I was hoping," I said, "that we could talk a little bit about your group and the different motivations that might lead a man to join it."

"Detective Pribek," Donovan said, "are you suggesting that a member of Men Against Interpersonal Violence might be a suspect in the Ryan murder?"

That was fast. I'd meant to start him in generalities, gradually working my way around to Steven Silverhus. Like arcing electricity, his thoughts had leapt over all that and arrived at the point.

"Is there a reason why you'd ask that?" I countered.

"I thought you were coming to talk about the offender who killed Jessie Ryan," he went on. "Now you're here asking questions not about the psychology behind the Ryan murder, as I'd expected, but about members of my group."

"It was a fairly broad and open-ended question."

"But a revealing one," Donovan said. "Believe it or not, this is not the first it's been suggested to me that a man might join the movement against sexual violence to repress urges he won't face directly in therapy." He picked up a pencil, held it by both ends. "I tell you what, give me a name and maybe we can do a little quid pro."

"I'm really not in the quid pro business," I said. But almost immediately, I realized that we'd have to talk about Silverhus eventually. So what if we got there early? Maybe this was a good thing; maybe he'd already sensed something wrong with Steven Silverhus.

I said, "I need to stress, first of all, that no one is a suspect at this time."

"But you have a person of interest?"

"We're a little troubled," I said, carefully, "about similarities between what we know about Ryan's murderer and someone involved in the work you're doing. But I can't mention a name until I have your word that you won't mention my visit to him. Not only could that jeopardize the investigation, it could be unnecessarily troubling to him, should he be eliminated from suspicion, say, tomorrow."

Donovan's mouth made a crooked line of suppressed amusement.

"Did I say something funny?" I said.

"The latter part, about sparing your suspect personal anxiety. You'll have to forgive me, but I've had a lot of dealings with police in my day, and very few have impressed me with the compassion they bring to their work."

Half the cops I knew would have used the old line about saving their compassion for the victims of crime, but I didn't want to be forced into playing the role of the reactionary cop. I said instead, "Do I have your word not to speak to him?"

"You have my word."

I had to trust him. "Then please tell me what you know about Steven Silverhus."

"Steve?" His face registered mild surprise, and I saw that I'd been wrong, earlier. He hadn't had Silverhus in mind.

I pursued that: "Were you thinking of somebody else?"

"No," Donovan said, shaking his head slowly, "not at all. About Steven, he's studying psychology here, and before that, he was at school in Montana. He's been in the group for about six months and felt strongly enough about the work that three months ago he started counseling a couple of first-time sex offenders."

"I know that much," I said. "What I'm wondering about is what led Steven to get involved with this work in the first place. Did he have a close friend or female relative who was a crime victim? Or was it something else?"

Donovan said, "I think it'd be a violation of Steven's privacy to get into that."

I gave him an incredulous look. "I'm sorry, I thought we were doing 'quid pro' here. You've told me nothing yet I didn't already know."

"I know, but there are certain things that — "

"Are you a practicing therapist, Dr. Donovan?"

"I have a limited one-on-one practice, yes."

"Is Steven one of your patients? I think it'd be *fascinating* if you were sending out a man with admitted sexual issues to counsel sex offenders."

His lips thinned slightly. "No, Steven is not one of my patients."

"Good," I said. "Then attorney-client privilege, I mean — "

"Attorney-client?" he echoed, eyebrows raised.

Goddammit. I felt my face heat. "Therapist-client privilege, I mean, does not apply here. You can tell me anything you wish to."

Donovan smiled, but there was a hint of irony in it. "I can, but am not obliged to. You can certainly use the legal process to compel me, if you have what a judge finds to be adequate reason, but I doubt you're there yet. Until then, I feel that I've built a rapport with group members that I'd be irresponsible to tear down without a good reason." He paused. "Maybe if you could tell me a little more about why Steven is of interest to you … "

Oh, no you don't. He'd already gotten me to give him Silverhus's name on the promise to exchange information, and then reneged on it. He actually thought it was going to work twice. I said, "I'm afraid I can't discuss the details of an ongoing investigation."

He spread his hands. "Then it seems we are both restricted by the demands of our fields."

I could have invoked Jessie Ryan's name, and the way she'd been found, in a dumpster, like trash. But I wouldn't use her memory like that.

"Right." I stood and laid my card on his desk. "If you're ever ready to cooperate, you know where I am."

It's strange how things work out sometime. If, on getting back to the parking garage, I'd immediately gotten into my car, I wouldn't have had a second encounter with Rob Donovan. But instead, I went up to the roof and paced for a good five minutes. I couldn't remember the last time a witness had punked me out like that. Occasionally, on the stand, a defense attorney caught me flatfooted, but that was nothing personal. Donovan wasn't supposed to have been the enemy.

I could have rattled his cage by warning him that if he went back on his promise not to tell Silverhus I'd been asking questions, I'd have him charged with obstruction. But even in my anger, I'd sensed that Donovan wouldn't take back his word once he'd given it. The fact that I couldn't simply dismiss him as a man without integrity made me feel even more humiliated.

Come on, we're burning daylight here. Stop indulging your feelings and get back to work.

I went to the stairwell and headed down to where I'd parked. I was just unlocking the door when Donovan came up behind me. "Detective Pribek."

I turned, my feet braced as if for a fight. He stopped a careful six feet from me. "I feel badly about how our conversation went."

Donovan's tone was conciliatory, but I didn't soften. "If you've come after me for a personal apology, I'm not concerned about my feelings. I need information. That's all."

"I know," he said. "That's why I followed you." His gaze cut away, to where a student was walking to an old Subaru. "Listen, sometimes guys join the group without giving a clear reason for their interest. Obviously, I'm not in the business of making them justify their interest in working for the greater social good, but personally, I find it curious." He paused. "Sometimes they can't bring themselves to say it right away, but it often transpires that some kind of unhealthy interest in pornography is the underlying cause."

"Was that the case with Silverhus?"

He shook his head. "Steven never explained, and it would be irresponsible for me to speculate. But I gave him my card and my cell number and told him to call me if he ever needed to talk about anything. He's only used it once."

Donovan crossed his arms in front of his chest, body language that indicated discomfort, but he went on: "I lead a group of recovering sex addicts," he said. "Steven called me during a meeting, but I missed his call because I always turn off my phone. The message he left just said that he really needed to talk to me. That was all. But this was on the night of the 30th. That's the night Jessie Ryan disappeared, isn't it?"

"Yes," I said. "Dr. Donovan, this could be very important: at what time did he call you?"

He rubbed his jaw. "The meeting is between nine and ten p.m. I should say, too, that when he finally called me back the next day, he explained that he'd been in crisis because his grandfather had just been diagnosed with cancer." He added unnecessarily: "It's a plausible explanation."

"When you say that he called you 'back', do you mean he called you twice? Or was there a call from you in between?"

"As soon as I heard his message, I called him. He wasn't answering his phone."

"When was this?"

"Ten-thirty or a little before."

The timing fit. "Dr. Donovan, can you get me the exact times of those phone calls, his and yours?"

He looked away for a moment.

I said, "I'll be discreet about your involvement. I won't tell Silverhus I've been talking to you unless I have to."

"It's not about me," he said. "It's about whether you're sure you're going down the right road here. Nobody deserves this kind of attention from the police when they're innocent."

"I can't know whether he's innocent," I said, "until I do go down this road a little ways."

"I can get you the times." He reached into his coat. "They'll still be in the log of my phone."

He thumbed the keypad briefly, his face tipped down toward the screen. Nearby, someone unlocked their car with a remote opener, the electronic chirp amplified by the hard surfaces of the garage.

"Nine forty-one," Donovan said. "That was the first call. I called him back at 10:19 and got no answer."

I didn't say what I was thinking, which was, *Oh God, perfect.* At nine-forty he first sees Jessie, wants to trail her, calls his mentor for help resisting that urge. By 10:19 it's too late; Jessie is in the trunk of his car.

"Thank you. That helps a lot." I unlocked my car door.

"About before," he said, slowly, "I meet some cops now and again who think I'm their adversary, because of what I do. I didn't mean to take it out on you."

"Forget about it," I told him, meaning it. He'd more than earned my goodwill.

SIXTEEN

Before I went back downtown, I did some driving. Purposeful driving, though.

Location: It's said to be the first rule of real estate. The same is true of any sophisticated crime. Purse snatchings can happen on the street, but if you want to commit any sophisticated, time-consuming crime and not get caught, you need a place to yourself.

We'd been thinking of the Ryan case as a murder and a sex assault. But first of all, it had been a kidnapping. Which meant the kidnapper had needed a place to take Jessie. It was highly unlikely that she'd been assaulted anywhere outdoors; the risk of being caught was too great. Plus, we now believed that she'd been drowned in a bathtub. You couldn't carry one of those around in the backseat of your car.

If Silverhus was our guy, where had he taken Jessie? He lived with his grandfather; I'd confirmed that matching his address from the U of M online student directory against that listed for Niels Silverhus, his grandfather. That house was on Portland Avenue, and while it was a wealthy neighborhood, the houses stood shoulder-to-shoulder, no acreage, no outbuildings. I didn't believe Steven had brought Jessie to his grandfather's home unconscious and sneaked her up the stairs over his shoulder.

But Steven himself had given me a hint: he'd told me he'd caught his hand in a door at one of "my grandfather's rental properties." A search of property-tax records had turned up the information that

95

Niels Silverhus owned two properties. If both were occupied, that ruled them out as well as places for Silverhus to have taken his victim. I'd find that out later. For now, it wouldn't hurt to drive by each of them and see how much privacy they offered.

The first property was in St. Paul, only two miles from where Niels and Steven lived.

I'd driven by the St. Paul house first. It was a simple one-story suburban place with an unattractive margarine-yellow paint job. There was a melting mound of snow, about two feet high, in the front yard that might have been the remains of a snowman — the snowfall that had covered up Jessie's dropped keys had been the first of the year, and snowmen sprang up in the wake of first snows in neighborhoods with children. From its low stature, this one looked like it was about at the right stage of decomposition for a six-day-old snowman. Perhaps that could be a new forensic specialty: snowman dating.

I went up the front steps and rang the doorbell, intending to ask the tenant if there had been any sign of trespassing on the property, any unusual noises at night. A dog barked from somewhere inside, but no one answered the bell. Before I left, I checked the mail in the unlocked mail box, getting a name off an electric bill: Thomas T. Jones. I left my card wedged in the screen door, with a handwritten note asking him to call me at his convenience.

His convenience because I already knew it wouldn't be profitable. In this neighborhood, houses were fairly close together, offering little privacy. Plus, I now knew there was a vigilant dog on Jones's property, the one that had barked at the sound of my footsteps.

This house wasn't the place.

Niels's second property was at a considerable distance from the first: in Victoria, to the southwest of the Cities. I followed a winding county road until I found the address. It was a modest house in a moon-white color similar to that of approximately half the houses in the upper Midwest countryside. I'd grown up with the colorful, rustic architectural styles of the Spanish and Indian West. The Midwestern reliance on white paint and red brick sometimes wore on me.

The detached garage that stood behind the house put this property's construction at sometime in the early – to mid-20th century, when architects still looked at the garage as the heir to the carriage house, something to be kept separate from the home. It was also two stories, the upstairs meant to be a workshop for the man of the house, or perhaps attic-like storage space. The land surrounding the two buildings wasn't fenced, so it wasn't clear to me where the property line lay. In the center of the loosely-defined "yard" were a clothesline structure and a weather vane, tiny icicles hanging off both.

The front walk, unshoveled, was treacherous; I was glad for my solid winter boots. The steps, likewise, had a scrim of ice on their surfaces. At the door, I rang the bell, but once again no one was home. I went back up the walk to the mailbox to find the renter's name, as I'd done in South St. Paul. The box, though, was empty; it seemed the mail hadn't been delivered yet.

Could the place be unoccupied? I studied it. The blinds of the front and side windows — all the windows that were in my line of sight — were down. There were no wisps of steam escaping from vents on the roof. You usually saw at least a little steam rising from any heated building in midwinter. The colder the weather, and the bigger the buildings, the more prodigious the clouds. I sometimes drove into the basin of downtown St. Paul on frigid mornings in mid-January, where the Capitol and its surrounding buildings appeared to steam like the remains of a massive fire, white clouds rolling up toward a heartlessly cold blue morning sky.

Here I saw nothing, and that was odd: People turned the heat down when they were going to be gone all day, but almost no one turned it off. It was just as costly to heat a home up again in the evening as it was to leave the thermostat at a low temperature, with the added unpleasantry of having to come home to a very cold house.

Beyond that, I thought, the South St. Paul house had given me clear signs of occupancy: the dog that had barked from inside; the melted-down snowman on the white lawn. This house didn't display those signs of being a home, at least not on the outside where I was allowed to be.

If it wasn't currently rented, what did that mean? Steven would know it was unoccupied. And it was out in the countryside. That made it an ideal place for Steven to have taken Jessie.

This was going to take more looking into. I crossed the road to where my car waited, then swung in a wide U-turn back toward town.

SEVENTEEN

"Okay," Syed Hasan was saying, "the most useful thing I've learned on the job is that you can't identify and deal with serial rapists and lust murderers if you look at their crimes as a freak anomaly in human behavior. Because they're not. Human behavior is a continuum."

Hasan, his wife Natalie, and I were in a downtown bar with a excellent happy-hour menu. Hasan was expanding on the approach he brought to his profiling work, presumably more for my benefit than Natalie's. I assumed Natalie had heard most of it before.

"Every woman who's ever taken a boyfriend's shirt and kept it even after the relationship is over understands the impulse to take trophies," Hasan continued. "Every man who's ever enjoyed having a sex partner's panties in his desk drawer while none of his co-workers guessed it knows the power of a totemic object. And if you've ever been infatuated with someone who drives a certain kind of car, and then started to see that make and model and color of car everywhere, then you understand obsession. At least a little bit."

He leaned back, ceding the conversation to me or to his wife, but neither of us took up the thread right away. I lifted my glass and drank, instead.

Earlier, I'd succeeded in reaching Thomas Jones, the tenant of the house within St. Paul city limits. He told me what I'd been expecting to hear: that he hadn't been away on vacation, and that there had been no signs of any trespasser on his rented property. But the tenant of the Victoria house was proving harder to track down, and so when Hasan had invited me out to meet Natalie, who'd arrived from D.C. that morning, I'd been more than receptive.

Had it not been for Hasan rising to his feet, I wouldn't have immediately recognized Natalie Singh-Hasan when she'd entered the bar. I think I'd unconsciously been expecting someone petite and soft-spoken. I knew more than one man with a high-powered law-enforcement career who'd married someone small and soft, an artistic type or an academic in the humanities, working in a field far from the ugliness of criminal investigation.

But Natalie Singh-Hasan was five-ten, and less radiant with impending motherhood than electric with intelligence. She had thick, dark hair pulled back into a knot held with two sticks, and her dark gaze was friendly but piercing. Like Hasan, she was trained in psychology, and she had a subspecialty in linguistic analysis.

She wasn't, however, FBI. She was British; they'd met when Hasan was assigned to the FBI legal attache in London.

"I was quite delighted to come to the States, when Syed was reassigned," Natalie explained to me. "This is the big leagues. If you want to be in film, you go to Los Angeles, and if you want to play country music, you go to Nashville. If you work in crime, you want to go to America. You lot have the best crime in the world."

"I keep trying to tell her that we just own more guns and have more open space to hide in, but she doesn't listen," Hasan put in.

He and I were drinking beer, while Natalie had mineral water. It was she, however, who was most enthusiastically attacking the homemade tortilla chips we'd ordered, and was ignoring the milder pico de gallo in favor of the hot green salsa.

"What kind of work here can you do here, without citizenship?" I asked her, nudging a triangular chip into the salsa.

"I can't be a part of a government agency, like Syed is," she said, "but any number of those agencies can hire me as a consultant. And I can lecture, at the National Academy or somewhere else. But I'm on my holidays right now anyway, because of the baby."

I nodded. I couldn't speak. My tongue was on fire from the salsa, which I eased with an infusion of cold Rolling Rock. I couldn't imagine how Natalie ingested it so easily. Clearly, the Hasan firstborn was going to have a love of hot foods.

Though I could have spent all evening learning about Syed and Natalie's criminal specialties, and the paths that had led them there, eventually they turned the conversation to me. I'd explained about Shiloh's situation to Hasan earlier, privately, and he'd understood it to be a sensitive point and not asked further questions. Now, however, both he and his wife wanted to know what had led me to the Sheriff's Department.

"Were you an adrenaline junkie from an early age?" Hasan asked. "That's a fairly common profile."

"The short answer is yes, but that wasn't exactly what led me to police work," I said. "In fact, I was resistant to the idea, at first."

"Resistant?" Natalie repeated. "You mean, someone else was urging you?"

"Right. I lived in a mining town, on the Iron Range," I said. "At the time, I was friendly with an older guy who served weekends on the town's citizen-patrol program. My life was going nowhere, and he saw it and suggested cop work. I wasn't having any of that, not at first."

I told them about my life at twenty, working in the cleaning and maintenance shop of a taconite mine, drinking my weekends away, until one hot summer night, around two in the morning, I'd heard a disembodied female voice scream right outside my bathroom window. I'd stuck my head out the window and seen nothing, called to her and gotten no response. Unable to let it be, I'd gone outside, flashlight in hand, and searched all over for the source of that scream. I never found it, but by the morning, had decided what I wanted to do with my life.

"But how did you explain it, the screaming woman? Do you think it was just a drunk, clowning around after a night of overindulgence?" Natalie asked.

"It didn't sound like that kind of a scream," I said, slowly, thinking. If I tried, I could still call up the sound of it, despite all the years in between. "It sounded like distress. But there was nothing in the morning papers about a crime or an accident. Nor on the grapevine, and this was a small town."

"Small enough that you should have found something, if you went out looking?"

"Probably," I agreed.

"Do you suppose you imagined it, then?" Natalie asked. "I mean, if you hadn't heard it, it sounds like you might have done something else with your life. It was either the heavy hand of fate, or your subconscious mind giving you a nudge."

"I'm not sure if I'd be a cab driver today, if I'd been soundly asleep by midnight that night," I said. "I might well have come to the same decision about police work a week later."

Neither of them would let me buy the second round. Hasan had turned quiet, content to listen to us. Natalie entertained me by explaining the differences in sentence structuring in upper-class and working-class British speech. I told her about the difficulties of casting footprints and tire prints in snow with sulfur, which had to be heated on a camp stove at the crime scene, and which could ignite if you let the temperature get too high.

EIGHTEEN

With no interesting field trips to edges of the metro area, Friday crawled past. It required several database searches before I found the person who currently paid the gas and electric bills on the house Niels Silverhus owned out in Victoria: a woman named Martha Ann Washington. When I called the number that was on record with those utility companies, she didn't answer, but a pre-recorded voicemail message was current; a smooth, cool voice identified her as 'Marty' Washington. I left a message asking her to call me.

The rest of the day was taken up with routine follow-up on the reports that were still coming in on the Jessie Ryan tipline, calls that were well-intended, but amounted to nothing. Toward the end of the day, around the time when I was about to pack up and head out to EMT class, Vang and Hadley came in, together. Whatever they'd been doing, they'd been outside long enough to trail a bit of winter cold behind them.

"What's up?" Hadley asked me. "We were just coming to see if you wanted to pick up a sandwich and a cup of coffee before the memorial."

"Memorial?" I repeated, and then, "Oh, hell. I forgot." It was the public event at the University, the one Santarella had told us about yesterday morning. And it clashed, again, with EMT class.

It was on the tip of my tongue to ask Vang and Hadley if they could cover for me, pick up the slack my absence would create. I wouldn't have, except for this: Monday and Wednesday nights were lectures, while Friday nights were skills lab. Whereas I could easily make up for not attending lectures with thorough reading, lab exercises were graded, and missing tonight's was going to hurt my overall class grade.

But Santarella had been clear on this, yesterday morning: *I'm going to need all hands.*

"Sure, a sandwich sounds good," I said, trying to squelch the de-stabilized feeling that always accompanies plans falling through. I reminded myself that I'd told Santarella that I couldn't miss very many classes, but I hadn't said I couldn't miss *any*. I was on top of the material; I'd survive missing one lab.

While Vang made a quick phone call to his wife, checking in, Hadley leaned casually against my desk and said, "You were in a big hurry to get out of here on Monday and Wednesday night, too." He inspected his thumbnail for dirt that wasn't there and then said, "Monday, Wednesday, and now Friday. That sounds like night school to me."

"You got me. I *knew* you were a detective."

"Mid-career education, for a cop, usually means someone's got their sights set on a management position. Lieutenant, maybe even captain. I didn't know you were that ambitious."

"I'm not," I said. "I'm downwardly mobile. It's an EMT class."

"You're leaving cop work?" He looked more than surprised; he was perplexed.

"Yeah," I said.

"Can I ask why?"

Was he taking this personally? It didn't fit with what I knew of Skyler Hadley's live-and-let-live character. But before I could say anything else, my phone rang. Hadley and I both looked at it, and then he stepped back, giving me some privacy as I answered.

"Detective Pribek, this is Marty Washington," a woman's voice said. "You called me. How can I help you?"

"Right." I sat down at my desk again; I'd stood to talk to my colleagues. "I'm trying to confirm that you're the tenant at — " I read her the address.

"Yes, that's my home."

"Is it a primary residence? You live there?"

"Of course I live there," Washington said. "As do my husband and son. Why would anyone rent a home and not live there?"

"I assume you wouldn't, but I needed to be sure. In the past week, have you and your family been on vacation or otherwise away from the house?"

"Detective, uh … "

"Pribek."

"Pribek. My husband and I are a working family. We spend long hours in the city. But we do live in Victoria, and we haven't been away on vacation. May I ask about the reason behind your questions?"

This was tricky: I didn't want her to realize that her landlord's grandson was under suspicion in a major crime. As Donovan had pointed out, I owed Silverhus discretion until I knew more.

"I'm sorry, but I'm afraid I'm not at liberty to share details about this investigation," I said.

Marty Washington hesitated a moment, then said, "Detective, I'm a member of the alternative press here in Minneapolis. Without sounding confrontational, I'm pretty sure I can make a few phone calls and find out what you're looking into. It might be easier for you if you were simply straight with me about it. Not to mention that if there's a threat to my family, you have an obligation to tell me."

Marty Washington being a member of the media only gave me greater reason to be discreet, but I could sympathize with her concern for her family. "I'm sorry," I said, "I don't mean to worry you. I'm simply looking for unoccupied properties in your area that might have been trespassed on as part of the commission of a crime. If you and your family are living in your home, there's virtually no chance your place was involved."

"Oh." She sounded appeased. "Well, the answer is, we live there. But if anybody *has* been trespassing on the property when we're not at home, I'd appreciate a call about it."

"I'll keep that in mind," I said. It wasn't quite a promise. "Thanks for your help."

After hanging up, I chewed on the end of a pen for a moment, hoping I'd handled the situation as well as I could have. The safety of the Washington family came before Silverhus's right to discretion; I understood that. But Jessie had been kidnapped and killed at night. I just couldn't see any possibility that she'd been brought onto the Washington property while the family was on site. Not to mention, Silverhus was still just a suspect, not a sure thing.

"Ready?" Vang's voice came from behind me. "Skyler's so hungry he's about to start raiding random desks for snacks."

"Right," I said, standing and wrapping a blue-and-gold scarf around my neck. "Let's go."

NINETEEN

Jessie Ryan's vigil began at 6:30, a time when classes would have broken, but early enough that many students would still be on campus. We arrived at the big, snowy quad at the center of the East Bank campus a little after 6, all of us still in plainclothes. That wasn't unusual; we were detectives. But this evening, even the symbols of authority we usually wore in the open were covered up — badges, shoulder holsters, guns. The university's campus police, in uniforms, would provide what crowd control was needed. Our job was surveillance, and if we weren't exactly undercover, we were being discreet.

What we were looking for wasn't easy to sum up: a man who didn't quite belong, a man who seemed to be enjoying this a little too much, privately reveling in his notoriety, anonymously mingling with those who his actions had shocked and outraged.

At one end of the quad was a plaza and stone steps, where the organizers had set up a microphone stand and speakers and a big, blown-up, cardboard-backed photo of Jessie at a rink, in her blue competition dress and white skates. Volunteers passed out white candles to the crowd. Down at ground level, several of the organizing groups had set up tables, offering informational leaflets about safe-ride and campus escort programs and rape prevention.

"Look," Hadley said, next to me, his breath clouding on the air. He tipped his head in the direction of the tables, and we all saw what had drawn his attention. Men Against Interpersonal Violence had a table set up, and the man who stood behind it was immediately recognizable despite wearing a hat and parka against the November evening cold.

"Is that him?" Hadley asked me.

"Yeah," I said.

Both Hasan and Santarella leaned past me to get a better look at this man who was our only valid suspect. Santarella shook his head. "Dammit," he said. "He's volunteering."

We all understood what that meant. Silverhus's position behind the informational leaflets immediately called into doubt any conclusions we might have drawn about him turning up here. He had a perfectly legitimate reason for being at Jessie Ryan's public memorial.

"You know what?" Santarella said. He turned his back to the table, facing us instead. "Let's make this work for us. Vang, go talk to him. Just introduce yourself, ask for a pamphlet, make nice. Don't spend more than a minute or two, then move on."

Vang understood. "You want to lay some groundwork," he said. "You're thinking I can introduce myself now, and maybe in a day or two, we can get him to come downtown and talk to us by appealing to his status as a psych student and unofficial expert in this kind of thing."

"Right," Santarella said.

"Will do."

Santarella looked at Vang, Hasan and me. "Let's spread out," he said. "You know what we're looking for."

Except we didn't, not really. The watchword was "anyone suspicious," but who was that? The relatively rare male face among the females? Not exactly, because that was the whole point of Rob Donovan's group, to tell the world that men cared about violence against women. An older man among young students? No, again; people pursued degrees at midlife, and besides, the memorial was open to the public. The vague idea was the five of us were here to watch, listen, and to follow our gut instincts about suspicious demeanors, unusual behaviors.

Vang was across the quad, making contact with Silverhus. I watched him but stayed mostly out of view. A girl in a bright magenta parka gave me a candle and lighted it with a long-barreled safety lighter.

The program got under way, half a memorial and half an educational event. As a young woman took her place in front of the microphone and began reading statistics about violence against women, I scanned the watchers in the crowd. Predictably, the majority were young and female. Pretty, too, I observed: like characters from Hans Christian Andersen in their pastel parkas and fur-trimmed Sorels, their skin glowing from the cold and the ambient light, their eyes large and sober, pupils dilated as only those of the young can. It wasn't long before I did see a familiar face, but not a suspicious one. It was Temple, dressed in street clothes. I made my way over to her.

"Hey," I said. "What brings you here? Showing support for the cause?"

"Not really," she said.

I looked pointedly at the white candle she held. "You've got a funny way of showing it."

She looked down at her candle as well. "This is the problem in a nutshell, isn't it?" She paused. "America loves to break out the white candles for its dead girls, but at the same time, it doesn't give them even a day of self-defense training." She looked around at the young women surrounding us. "Think about how many hundreds of hours these girls have spent in the gym doing cardio or on a yoga mat. You think any of them have spared even two hours learning to throw a knee or elbow to good effect?" She glanced up to read my face. "You're going to tell me I'm blaming the victim, aren't you?"

"No," I said. "I'm going to tell you to walk with me; I'm supposed to be circulating and keeping an eye on things."

Temple fell silent; our boots crunched the snow underfoot. A older woman, possibly a professor, replaced the first at the microphone. I didn't listen to what she was saying, still thinking about Temple's words.

My young roommate expressed herself rather forcefully; I'd gotten used to that. Besides which, her own obsession with martial arts was a strong reaction, if not an overreaction, to an overprotected youth. But was she, at core, wrong? If Jessie had had the same fixation on fighting and self-defense that Temple had, would she be alive today?

If Temple were attacked by the same man, off-duty and without her service weapon, would her skills save her?

This was dangerous territory. As Temple had pointed out, people were quick to use the phrase *blaming the victim.* But I couldn't help but think back to my own youth. I had hardly been overprotected; my childhood was different from Temple's in many ways. But what I was remembering, specifically, was my self-defense training, back in high school P.E. class. It had consisted of listening while a lecturer in front of a chalkboard told a roomful of girls how to jab for an attacker's eyes or stomp down hard on his instep. We never practiced these moves. I could think of no other discipline in which physical skills weren't physically taught.

If Jessie Ryan had been typical, she'd grown up on strong female role models, with vampire slayers and warrior princesses on the TV screen. America gave its daughters heroines who could singlehandedly beat up five men, played by actresses with perfect abs and stunt doubles. It sold them "Chicks Kick Ass" and called it empowerment. At the same time, it barred or steered them away from contact sports and told them it was abnormal and wrong for a girl to get in a fight, a behavior that was shrugged off as inevitable in boys.

The fact that young women like Jessie reached adulthood without ever learning the first thing about practical self-defense was only half the problem, I reflected. The other half was that men like the one Jessie Ryan had fatally met on Devil's Night could take it as a given that she hadn't.

Across the quad, Syed Hasan caught my eye, snapping me out of my thoughts. He raised his eyebrows: *Anything?* I shook my head.

The next person to mount the stairs and take the microphone was Jessie's younger sister, Jen Ryan.

Jen unfolded a piece of paper and began to read a letter to her sister. She talked about how much she'd been looking forward to the one year they'd both have on the U of M campus, like the year they shared in high school, when Jessie was a senior and Jen a freshman. She talked about how she would never be able to help her sister with her hair and dress on her wedding day, and how she'd already been planning to hide her sister's shoes or her lipstick as a prank, and how all that would never happen now. Her voice began to shake. The crowd rustled and murmured, their sympathy palpable.

I looked over at the Men Against Interpersonal Violence table. Silverhus's attention was riveted on Jessie's younger sister. But then, everyone's was.

Jen finished her letter without crying, at least not outright, and descended the steps. The moment was too sober for applause, so the assembled people just watched her go, candlelight flickering off their chins and cheeks, breath clouding on the air.

As Jen reached her family, and was enfolded in her mother's arms, the rally's organizer took her place in front of the microphone again, clearing her throat to make closing remarks.

Beside me, Temple asked quietly, "So? Did you see anyone in the crowd who struck you the wrong way?"

I hesitated, then said, "No." For now, our theories about Silverhus couldn't go any further than the confines of the conference room.

But when Temple was looking up at the steps, not at me, I let my eyes stray to Silverhus again. He didn't notice me. Nor was he paying attention to the speaker. He was watching intently as the little Ryan-Nedegaard family moved off, heading home. At least, at that distance, you'd say that Silverhus was watching the whole family. But I felt a shiver of unease, knowing it was possible that his attention was a little more narrowly focused.

It was impossible not to see how much Jennifer Ryan looked like her older sister: slender, attractive, red-gold hair. And we'd also known that Jessie's killer might be here. I hoped we hadn't made a mistake in allowing the victim's younger sister to be front and center at this memorial.

TWENTY

It's just another dream. I am at the closet, finding something to wear to Jessie Ryan's service. At the back of the closet is a black dress I wear only to funerals. I pull it out. It's wool. It'll be warm enough for when I'm standing by the grave.

"Not that one. That's for private occasions," Shiloh says.

"I'm going to a memorial service."

"But you're doing so for work. Wear your black suit," he instructs me. "There are things that need to be kept separate." Shiloh comes to stand beside me, laying his hand on the small of my back. "You were wearing that dress the night we met."

"I remember." We had met in an airport bar, about twelve hours after I'd buried my father.

"You left scratches on me," he says, his voice low, mouth close to my ear, one hand stroking my spine, all the way down to my lower back.

"Shiloh, stop, I can't do this now." I feel the beginnings of dampness between my legs, not a remnant of my shower.

"Will you wear that dress to my funeral, sweetheart? Promise me you will."

Of course, I woke up.

Wintertime looks brighter in small towns, where there are more open fields, blanketed with unbroken snow, to reflect the sunlight, and wider expanses of sky to shine cloudless and blue. On this ten-degree morning, the sun was almost blinding as I drove Syed Hasan and myself out toward the Wisconsin border, where Jessie Ryan had grown up and was to be buried.

Syed had been waiting for me outside the apartment building where the Bureau was housing him and Natalie, wearing a sober, dark suit and sunglasses against the glare we'd encounter driving east, against the morning sun. I said, kidding him, "You look like a real Fed at last."

"So do you," he said, stepping off the curb. I was wearing the dark suit that Shiloh had urged me to wear in the dream. Then he noticed the car. "Your private ride?" he asked.

"Yeah."

On a normal weekday, I'd have checked out a motor-pool car. But going downtown to make that exchange had been too big a hassle for a Saturday morning when I had to get appropriately dressed for a funeral and pick up a colleague and still be out near the Wisconsin border before ten. So I was driving my 1970 Nova, my first and only car, the one I'd bought with savings from my phones-and-filing job on the Iron Range years ago.

"Don't get your hopes up that we're going to see anyone suspicious at the service," Hasan said on the drive, looking out at the snowy fields.

"But you're making a point of coming along," I said, surprised.

"I know," he said. "I get restless when I'm cooped up too long with witness reports and diagrams, maybe I can blame it on that." He shrugged. "It's not that I'm *sorry* I'm coming along, but I was discussing the situation with Natalie last night, and increasingly I'm inclined to think that if this guy's the type to act on those kind of impulses, he did it last night, at the public memorial. He's probably smart enough to realize that the funeral's a smaller venue, and he's more likely to stand out as someone who shouldn't be there."

"Unless we're wrong, and he knew Jessie a lot better than we think," I said.

"Right," he said. "If he's an old high-school friend who'll fit in, he might take the opportunity to attend. Whether we recognize him from his behavior, though, that's another story."

I eased up on the gas, steering the Nova off the highway and onto a side road. "If he does come," I asked, "what's he getting out of it?"

"A couple of things," Hasan said. "The funeral is the last event planned, so it's his last 'get-together' with Jessie. He might also enjoy mixing unrecognized with her friends and family, getting a contact high off their grief."

I spotted the church just in time, and steered the car up a steep driveway.

Shiloh once told me that architectural and ecclesiastical history are linked, with churches often representing the finest engineering work of their era. The Lutheran church that the Nedegaard-Ryan family attended did not follow in that tradition. Perhaps fifty years old, it had a windowless A-frame front with a metal cross at the peak of the roofline. No smell of incense or mystery clung to its interior, but rather a community-center smell of aged carpet and lemon dusting wax. Jessie's casket, black with bronze trim, rested on the podium, a spray of lilies and carnations behind it.

Hasan and I split up; we would sit toward the rear of the sanctuary on either side of the aisle, the better to observe those seated ahead of us. Jessie's family occupied the front row: Roy Nedegaard stiff-backed in his dark suit, Katharine wrapped in dove gray, and Jen looking slight and pale in a black cowl-necked dress.

The rows beyond that were almost exclusively young and female: a small crowd of Jessie's girlfriends, from high school and the University. I'd seen a few of them entering and taking their seats, and noticed that Jessie's friends were wearing a ribbon pinned to their dresses or shirts, the small folded-over-on-itself kind people wore for breast cancer research or some similar cause. Theirs were black, which surprised me a moment. Of course, black was traditional for funerals, like an armband, but at the same time I would have thought that Jessie's friends would have chosen a bright color for a memorial ribbon in celebration of life. The following rows were mixed in age and gender; older people and married couples, most likely friends of Katharine Ryan and Roy Nedegaard.

I scanned the rows toward the back, spotting Nate Shigawa, nearly unrecognizable in a dark suit. He'd taken a seat in the very back row, a respectful distance from the family and friends who had known Jessie well. I considered taking the space next to him, in his pew, but then settled on a spot two rows up, with a slightly better view of the front.

A prayer opened the service, then a hymn, then the scripture readings, a sensitively tuned microphone on the lectern transmitting the thin crackle of the Bible's pages.

"Do not fear those who kill the body but cannot kill the soul. … Are not two sparrows sold for a penny? Yet not one of them will fall to the ground apart from your Father. Even the hairs of your head are all counted. So do not be afraid; you are of more value than many sparrows."

There was a small commotion from the front row, which resolved into the sound of soft, feminine sobs. For a moment I couldn't place their source, but then I saw Jennifer Ryan, bowed over like a tree under too much snow, her shoulders shaking. Her grandfather shifted and started to put him arm around her, but Jen wormed away before he could touch her. Then she slipped from her place in the front pew and hurried down the side aisle. Roy Nedegaard, red-faced, twisted to watch her go; Katharine Ryan laid a hand gently on his arm, stopping him from following.

I was sitting on the aisle; it would be a small and unobtrusive thing for me to get up and go after her. I barely knew this girl, true, and the grief she was experiencing wasn't something that could be eased with a few kind words. Even so, I rose from my seat.

It wasn't hard to guess where Jen had gone. Across the narthex from the side aisle she'd gone down was an open doorway; it led to what most churches call a bride's room. I looked inside, but what I saw there made me stop short. Jen was indeed inside. She sat at the small vanity, weeping aloud.

But she wasn't alone. Nate Shigawa had pulled up a chair close to where Jen was sitting and turned it around backward, straddling it. On the seat back, he'd crossed his forearms, then rested his chin on them. He wasn't saying a thing. He wasn't touching or patting her. He was just sitting nearby, letting her cry.

Nate's posture reminded me of the way big dogs watch humans in moments of distress, as if to say, *I don't know what's bothering you, but I'm here to help.* It was all that was needed.

Only four years separated Shigawa and I, but there are times when the space between generations breaks open along a very specific line, like a seismic rift in the earth. It had opened now, with Jennifer Ryan and Nate Shigawa on one side, and me on the other. Any comfort I could offer Jen would be stiff and superfluous, so I withdrew before either of them could see me.

At the end of the service, something unusual and lovely happened. Six young women rose and came forward. I recognized Jessie's roommate Kori among them, and all the rest were girls whom we'd interviewed in recent days.

As they took their places, three on each side of the casket, I stiffened involuntarily, imagining they wouldn't bear up under the burden. They seemed so slight. Not one of them was over five-foot-six. But they lifted Jessie to shoulder height, and then slowly began to move, down the aisle, and everything was all right.

Except, of course, that it wasn't.

TWENTY-ONE

Mortality.

As a cop, you hear a lot about the moment you recognized that you could die on the job. Of course, most officers don't have that pulp-novel experience. You know: *I stared down the barrel of the gun and saw my own death in its empty black eye.* I hadn't, either.

For me, death became a real thing when I was in the Sheriff's Academy. We'd already had the speech on how dangerous the job could be; a veteran deputy told us about his partner's fatal shooting at a simple domestic-violence call, and I'd nodded seriously with my fellow students, and afterwards commented to a friend about how *That was a hell of a sobering story, wasn't it?* I'd thought I'd really meant it. But that wasn't the moment when the prospect of a premature death became real. That came about a week later.

I was at the range, getting a little one-on-one tutorial on shooting from one of the instructors. Guns didn't faze me. I'd already done some shooting with a .40 caliber, blowing holes in a paper target. But then, the instructor had wanted to show off one of his favorite weapons. It was definitely nothing he used on the job: a Desert Eagle, a powerful, powerful machine. When he fired it, I was wearing adequate ear protection; it was in my sternum, instead, that I truly felt the Eagle's booming.

After he was done utterly tearing up the paper silhouette of a human, the instructor casually turned to me and started to say something. No, he *did* say something, I just don't remember what it was. I didn't hear any more than the first couple of words: "What a lot of people don't realize about a gun like this — " and after that my brain was frozen.

This is what I had realized: I was standing perhaps sixteen inches away from him. All he had to do was point that Desert Eagle at my face, and pull the trigger, and my life would be over. I probably wouldn't even have time to finish wondering what the hell he was doing before it would be all over. The idea that I could die without even realizing I was going to die, I think, was what chilled me so badly.

The instructor went on making the point he was making; I kept my eyes on his, behind those yellow protective lenses, and nodded seriously, but I had no idea what he was saying. There were people walking around Minneapolis with loaded guns like his. There was no way to know who they were. In a few weeks I'd be a sheriff's deputy, and it would be my job to approach those people, confront them, arrest them.

The gunnery instructor kept talking, but my mind just kept on its morbid train of thought. I knew the killed-in-the-line-of-duty scenarios. It wouldn't matter how carefully I'd learned my job; the call would probably be routine and not seem dangerous. Maybe the shooter would be someone suicidal, or delusional, or maybe just desperate not to go back to prison. He wouldn't even see me, not as a person. It wouldn't matter to the shooter that I wasn't very old and I'd never seen the ocean and I had steak marinating in my refrigerator for the end of my shift. I'd just be an obstacle to his continued freedom, and he'd raise his gun and fire at point-blank range and my life would be over.

Shiloh had always been more articulate than I was, and he'd put it better. Early in our relationship, during one of the wide-ranging conversations we used to have, he told me about visiting the Vietnam memorial in Washington.

"I'd heard a long time back that the average age of the combat soldier in Vietnam was nineteen," he'd said. "For the first time, I understood what that really meant for them to die at that age. 'Sorry, kid, that's all you get. No more Saturday nights at the drive-in; no more church on Sunday morning. No more great movies, or bad TV. No more sex, no marriage, no kids, no grandkids. No more life for you. We know it's a lot to ask, but we didn't want Vietnam to have a communist government.'"

TWENTY-TWO

There was another ten-minute service at the cemetery, a high field with a view of the river. Hasan went to the graveside, but I'd driven up the hill a short way, to scan with binoculars for someone else who might be watching at a distance. I saw nothing, no answering glint of sunlight off glass. Down at the gravesite, the crowd was beginning to break up. I watched the silent-movie action of Hasan shaking hands with Roy Nedegaard and Katharine Ryan, saw their breath clouding on the air, and imagined the words of condolence.

Hasan said nothing when I picked him up again. I prompted him. "Did Jessie's family see anyone they thought was out of place?"

"What? No, they didn't," he said.

"You asked them specifically, right?" I said. Normally, I wouldn't have checked up on him, but his tone was distracted, and that worried me.

"Yes, I asked," he said. "Just a minute ago."

Another silence. "Are you okay?" I said, finally.

He sighed and said, "We're going to need to stop for cigarettes."

"Cigarettes?" I said, and I couldn't keep the surprise out of my voice.

"I know," he said, running a hand through his thick hair. "I don't really want to start again, but … "

"I have a wild guess here," I said. "You're thinking about the wisdom of bringing a child into the world that ate up Jessie Ryan in twenty-one short years."

123

Hasan rewarded me with a smile. "I'm living a cliche," he said, "but yes, you broke the code. Natalie is hoping for a daughter. I used to say, 'I just want a healthy child,' but now, I want a son." He closed his eyes, rubbed the bridge of his nose, opened his eyes again. "And Natalie's going to wring my neck if I start smoking again when she can't."

"Natalie too?"

"Oh, yes. We both smoked like chimneys when we first met." His dark eyes had a faraway cast; he was revisiting old fond memories. Then he straightened up and said, "I tell you what. Let's back-burner the cigarettes, just for now, but I'm really not ready to go back to work yet. Do you know someplace quiet, where we could just walk for a while?"

It was still twenty-five degrees out, at most. A park wasn't going to do.

"Yes," I said. "I know a place."

The wooden floors of the Minneapolis Institute of Art were a better fit for my dress shoes than the icy sidewalks outside the church had been. Despite this being a Saturday, the museum at just after noon was hushed and quiet, except for the soft feminine murmur of a tour guide's voice from another room.

"I wouldn't have guessed you'd be into art," Hasan said.

"I'm not," I said. "Honestly, when I look at Renaissance paintings, a lot of them look like the artist had a shoebox full of human figures and just dumped them headlong into the frame."

Hasan chuckled. "I can see what you mean," he said. "The ideas those painters brought to composition aren't really the parameters that artists use today."

"My husband, Shiloh, is the one who likes art. He brought me here, when we were first dating," I explained. "Let me show you something."

Hasan followed me to a small, narrow side room, where the light was a few degrees dimmer, and where the Asian drawings on silk and paper were housed. "These are Shiloh's favorites."

124

Hasan studied the long vertical illustrations of steep mountainsides, low habitations and trees, and waterfalls, all depicted in very fine black lines.

"Interesting," Hasan said, quietly. There was no one else around, but the museum's high-ceilinged hush seemed to encourage low voices. "Did it trouble you at all, to be involved with a man who was drawn to pictures without any human figures in them?"

Until that moment, I'd only thought of the Asian silks as "nature scenes." I'd never recognized the underlying implications.

"I'm ashamed to say that I never thought about it like that," I said. "You're right, though. That's Shiloh all over. He's hard to know. Doesn't seem to need anyone very much."

Hasan studied a pale-bluish scene of a cabin half-hidden by bristling trees. "You must have been somewhat proud," he said, "being the rare person who was invited inside."

"Proud? Nervous, maybe," I said. "Right after he showed me these drawings, he asked me to point out something that particularly appealed to me. I was afraid that nothing would, and he'd trade me in for a more educated girlfriend."

"But you found something."

"Under pressure, yes, I did." Again, I said, "I'll show you."

Standing in front of Tissot's *Les Rois Mages en Voyage,* Hasan surveyed the painting for a long moment before asking, "What is it about this one that you liked?"

"The light," I explained. "It reminds me of the light in New Mexico."

"You grew up there?"

"Yes."

We walked the museum's rooms a while longer, and though Hasan seemed reflective, he didn't speak again about his unborn child or the fears that Jessie Ryan's funeral had spurred in him. It appeared we didn't need to; just being in the museum had a calming effect. I thought I understood why: For very intelligent people, agnostic or atheist, as I suspected Syed Hasan was, a museum could be more like a temple than an actual place of worship.

Over coffee in the small cafeteria, I asked him about it. "Did you and your family attend any kind of religious services when you were young?"

"A mosque? No." Hasan had been graceful in supplying the exact term; I hadn't wanted to make assumptions about his religious background. "My parents were very secular. I've been in mosques, of course. My grandparents were observant."

"Is your family originally from Saudi Arabia?"

"Pakistan," he said. "Of course, if you go far enough back, the family line probably leads to Arabia."

When I spoke again, I chose my words carefully: "It can't always be easy," I said, "having that ethnic background in post-September 11th America."

"You have no idea," he said, and his gaze dropped momentarily to his cane. He smiled, with a touch of rue. "Sometimes I think I should have taken Natalie's last name. If I could just sign 'Singh' to everything, instead of 'Hasan,' my life would be a lot easier." He clarified, "I've always suspected that my family has a touch of Punjabi blood. A lot of Arab Pakistani families do, and people often mistake me for East Indian."

What Hasan was saying was interesting, but my mind had gone back to something else, the way he'd glanced down when he'd said, *You have no idea.* I also remembered that in my first, cut-short conversation with him, he'd said his accident was four years ago, and that the anniversary was coming up late this month. Late November in 2001 would have been just two months after the attacks on the Twin Towers and the Pentagon.

"Syed," I began, "a minute ago, when I first brought up September 11th, you looked at your cane."

Immediately, he knew where I was going: "You're profiling the profiler."

I put up my hands. "I'm sorry, I — "

"No." He was unperturbed. "You've clearly guessed, and it's not a huge secret. This — " motioning down to his leg, " — wasn't an accident. It was human-caused."

"You were attacked."

"Outside a bar in D.C.," he said. "Natalie was traveling for her work. She'd just gotten back on the road after all the restrictions on travel started to ease up. I'd been working tons of overtime — we all had — but things had just slowed down enough that night that I was able to get out of work by ten, and I went to a bar to unwind."

I frowned. "Didn't the fact that you were drinking alcohol clue anybody in that you weren't a devout Muslim?"

"One would think so," he said, slowly putting a dry emphasis on every word. "But when I left around eleven o'clock, two guys caught up with me a block away from the bar. Smashed up my ribs and leg pretty good."

"I'm so sorry," I said. "Were they caught?"

"Never."

"Syed, I'm so sorry," I said again, feeling the inadequacy of the words.

But he was shaking his head. "I don't dwell, Sarah," he said. "The only reason I tell people it was a car accident is that in my line of work, I meet new people every month, if not every week. I just don't want to tell the story to every single new acquaintance." He paused there, watching the counterwoman pouring sugar from a one-pound sack into a smaller glass container. "Four years in, even I'm getting a little bored with the story."

I took that to mean that he didn't want to talk about it further with me, either. I turned my attention to what was left of my cappuccino, at a loss for where the conversation could go from here.

Hasan wasn't, though. "Earlier," he said, "you asked me if I saw anyone out of place at the funeral, or at the burial, which I didn't. But what about you? Did you see anything that struck you as odd?"

"Other than the pallbearers?"

"That they were female?" he said.

"Yeah. Pallbearers are almost invariably male relatives. We know Jessie had male cousins. And then there's the grandfather. He was very involved in her life."

Hasan shrugged. "It's unusual," he said, "but it's not suspicious."

"I didn't mean it was," I said, and then asked myself, *So why'd you bring it up?*

He was staring out the window. "Maybe it was fitting," he said. "Jessie never got to have bridesmaids. Her bridesmaids were her pallbearers, instead."

TWENTY-THREE

Danielle Roback had agreed to meet me at a diner in New Richmond, Wisconsin. It was a bright cold Sunday, the day after Jessie Ryan's funeral, and even though this was official business, I'd once again taken the Nova.

The diner had no off-street parking. Curbside, I wedged my car between a new white Ford pickup and a battered old Silverado and got out, locking the door out of city habit. The plate glass windows of the diner held two signs, one advertising "Today's Sandwich's" and the other urging the re-election of the city administrator. Inside, forced-air heat circulated sluggishly, touching the skin like a caress. I took off my parka and hung it on the rack by the door.

"Go ahead and seat yourself; that's how we do it here," a waitress said from behind the diner counter. I scanned the tables. No one matched Danielle Roback's description of herself: 5'3, 105, shoulder-length brown hair. I took a seat by the window, where I could watch the street outside as well as the front door, and waited. Without a jacket, my shoulder holster was clearly visible; Roback would easily recognize me.

She came in about six minutes later, nodded recognition, and came to join me. The waitress, told I was expecting someone, had left two plastic-laminated menus and two glasses of water with pebbly machine-made ice floating in them.

Roback's hair was a little more than chin length, and her face was thin, almost vulpine. There was something wary in the way her brown eyes surveyed me.

129

"Thanks for meeting me," I said. "I'm hungry, so I'm eating. Please have whatever you like."

She asked the waitress for a garden salad, nothing to drink, she'd stick with water. I'd had only coffee and juice for breakfast and was tempted to give in to the day's special, an open-face hot roast-beef sandwich with whipped potatoes on the side. Instead I ordered the grilled cheese sandwich with black coffee. It's hard to maintain an aura of professionalism when you're eating like a farmhand just in from the field.

"This is about what happened back in Missoula?" Roback said, when the waitress had gone. She knew it was; I'd told her on the phone. She was just giving me an opening.

"I know you were very forthcoming with Detective Daley, back in Montana," I said. "I'd just like to hear it again."

"Did he attack someone in Minneapolis? Is that why you're here?"

"There's a potential link," I said. I was hedging; there was nothing tentative about a DNA match. "It's important that you not share that with anyone just yet."

We hadn't released the Montana angle to the media. It was a big piece of the puzzle, and if the perpetrator knew we knew it, he'd be a lot less complacent. We didn't want to spook him.

Our food arrived, and Roback told me the story. While it was a little more detailed than what I'd gotten from reading the file, it wasn't more helpful. The memories she'd regained in the interim lay closer to the stranger's blitz assault, but not close enough. She now remembered driving home, and there was one snapshot-memory of her own hand holding her car key and locking the driver's door. But of the attack itself, nothing.

"I'm sure you talked to Detective Daley about the men you'd seen around," I said. "Customers at the bar, men in your neighborhood. Given time to reflect, is there anyone you didn't mention to him that you now feel you should have?"

"I'm sorry," she said. "There isn't."

We were silent as the food arrived. Afterward, I said, "I'm going to show you some photographs, and I'd like you to tell me if any of these men look familiar to you."

I took them from my bag and laid them on the table: A City Hall custodian who'd amiably posed for the Polaroid I'd wanted, a mug shot of a convicted burglar from St. Paul, and the driver's license shot of Steven Silverhus.

It didn't prove much if she picked out Silverhus. They'd lived in the same town at the same time. But if he did look familiar to her, I'd know that they'd crossed paths frequently enough for her to remember him. Therefore, that he'd seen her more than once.

Danielle leaned forward to examine them.

"Sorry," she said. "I don't think I've seen any of these guys before."

"It's okay," I said. "Let me ask you something else that might help us: When you lived in Missoula, was there anything different about your appearance?"

She thought. "My hair was blonde. I used to color it."

"Regular blonde, or did it have a red tint?"

"It was reddish," she said. Her hazel eyes locked onto mine, understanding dawning in them. "You do have a second victim."

That wasn't a question, so I didn't answer it. After a second, she went on: "After the attack, I cut my hair very short, and I dyed it dark brown for a while."

"Why?"

"I was ... I didn't like to think he could recognize me," Roback said. "Detective Pribek, the worst thing about what happened to me is that I never remembered any of it. Some friends have told that I was lucky not to have been conscious throughout it, but they didn't understand." She speared a cherry tomato on her plate. I noticed she hadn't eaten much of her salad.

"When I woke up, I didn't know what had happened to me. Detective Daley had to tell me. It had been under investigation for weeks. Everyone who I knew, knew. Everyone except me." She raised her eyes, watching as a pair of men in trucker caps made their way to a table in the back. "When I couldn't remember anything, I realized that I could go back to work and be serving this man a drink, and not know it was him. He could be watching me and thinking about that night and enjoying the idea that I didn't recognize him. So I left town, and when I did, I changed the way I looked, too. If I ever crossed paths with this guy again, I didn't want him to recognize me on the street."

Notwithstanding the attention I had to give the sometimes-slick roads, the drive back to Minneapolis gave me ample time to think.

Steven Silverhus had left Missoula about seven weeks after Danielle Roback had been attacked. Not days afterward, but nearly two months. He had never been identified as a suspect. His name appeared nowhere in the Montana detective's files. He wasn't running from imminent arrest. Instead, the way he'd abandoned his life in Montana made me think of something else.

I'd been involved in more than one rape case in which a young college woman was the victim. In several cases, the girl had dropped out of school and moved home within months of the crime. None of them had been identified by the media; it wasn't notoriety they were fleeing. The impetus for their flight had been purely emotional: College life was ruined for them. Reminders were everywhere of how wrong their first foray into adult life had gone, and they sought security and support by moving back into the family home.

Silverhus's decision to leave Montana reminded me of those cases.

The phrase, *went out into the world to seek his fortune*, doesn't appear much outside fairy tales, but it seemed true of Silverhus's move to Montana. He'd struck out at 20 to become an independent adult. Why Montana? Maybe Steven had remembered it fondly because of the summers he'd spent there with his grandfather. Otherwise, he had no connection to Missoula, no family or friends already living there. I thought that might have been the very thing that appealed to Silverhus.

Missoula would have been all his idea. Then he'd left so abruptly he hadn't bothered to finish the semester at school.

I believed that Missoula was ruined for him because of what he'd done to Danielle Roback there.

We still hadn't been able to make a link between Silverhus and Roback. Silverhus had worked on a landscaping crew, so it was possible he'd worked at a house on the same street where Roback had her little rental. It was also possible that he'd stopped in for after-work beers at the Copper Grill, where Roback had worked. Whatever it was, he'd most likely seen her repeatedly. His need for this woman had built up over a period of days or weeks. It was Danielle Roback who had been the template for Jessie Ryan. That was why I'd wanted to make sure she'd looked the same — slender with auburn-blonde hair — when they'd both lived in Missoula.

Somewhere even further back on the vistas of Silverhus's life was yet another female, with similar coloring and a similar figure. Maybe she was a grade-school teacher, or a girl a few years older than he, whose red-gold hair had caught the sunlight when she stood on the playground, and Stevie Silverhus had watched, unaware that the sight of her was like molten metal being poured into a mold he'd never be able to break.

But of ten boys watching a girl on the playground, about six or seven would grow up to marry someone like her. Two or three would have repeated failed relationships with someone like her, for various reasons too stunted to be able to commit. Perhaps one might grow up to be pathologically shy, satisfying himself with a rich fantasy world prominently featuring women like her.

None, statistically, should have grown up to drown her in a bathtub.

Santarella called me while I was still on the road back. "You're coming downtown aren't you, this afternoon?" he asked, after a quick, terse greeting. "I thought you might've forgotten we're meeting, even though it's Sunday."

"Didn't forget," I said. "But don't pin your hopes on me. Roback didn't give me anything. She wanted to help, but she just didn't remember anything useful."

"Mm, that's too bad. But Vang and Hadley have been busy, looking into Silverhus's background."

"Is it interesting?"

"Parts of it," Hadley said. "He'll run through it once we're all here."

TWENTY-FOUR

There are parts of America — New York City or Los Angeles chief among them — where celebrity isn't particularly uncommon; in contrast, there are places where the coin of celebrity shines a bit brighter. In Minnesota, there were few people who wouldn't find the name of Niels Silverhus at least vaguely familiar.

The Silverhus family had roots in St. Paul that went back to before statehood. Their butcher shop operated for nearly a hundred years, finally closing and being razed in 1958. The Silverhus name could be found on various property-tax records; it was engraved on tombstones in the city's cemeteries. The *Pioneer Press* recorded that a police sergeant named Silverhus was wounded in a Prohibition-era shootout with a handful of gangsters up from Chicago. But by and large, the Silverhus family was a pale-blue-collar clan whose lives were, while hopefully pleasant, without distinction. Until Niels.

You can see a picture of him in a St. Paul tavern, hanging over the bar amid the rest of the sports memorabilia. The picture was taken in Squaw Valley, in the Californian alps, at the Olympic games in which Niels competed. In the photograph, Niels stands on his cross-country skiis, his body rail-hard, his hair thick and dark. He exudes vitality. The black-and-white tones of the photo do little to suppress the ruddy patches that exertion and cold air have brought out in his pale skin. Niels had competed in the biathlon, the event that combines cross-country skiing and rifle shooting, however odd that combination might sound to 21st-century ears. Niels did not win an Olympic medal, but he came back a hometown hero no less.

After Harvard, Niels returned to Minnesota. With the exception of a few years at the Mayo Clinic in Rochester and six months lecturing at a medical school in the then-Soviet Union, Niels spent his career in the Twin Cities. He didn't invent any surgical techniques, but he was more than once the doctor who first performed a groundbreaking procedure in Minnesota, gaining a reputation as one of the Cities' finest medical talents. By the 1970s, he had a house on Portland Avenue, seats at the symphony, and season tickets for the Vikings.

He was also a member of a rapidly dwindling tribe. Migration and low birth rates, as they did to families across America, had reduced the Silverhus presence in St. Paul to just four souls: Niels and his wife Julia, their son Kevin and daughter-in-law Mary-Anne. Then the family increased by one, when Mary-Anne gave birth to a son.

Five years later, tragedy: Julia Silverhus had a fatal stroke, and by the end of that year, Kevin and Mary-Anne were killed in a wreck when a truck jackknifed on a snowy section of Interstate 94. The last two survivors of the Silverhus family were the noted surgeon Niels and his six-year-old grandson.

Steven Mark Silverhus had been born 25 years ago, at a now-defunct St. Paul hospital. Of the interim years, there are only the expected, unrevealing records: Steven attended the city's elementary and then secondary schools. He had no criminal record in his youth, although he was named in a complaint when he was fifteen years old. Around ten o'clock on a summer night, a neighbor had found Steve Silverhus standing in the bushes alongside his house. On the other side of the lighted window, the man's teenage daughter, already in her nightdress, was painting her toenails. Silverhus had explained that he was walking home when the urgent need to urinate had overtaken him; he'd slipped into the neighbor's bushes without even paying attention to what was happening behind the nearby window.

The officer that responded to the justifiably angry homeowner's call had advised that the only charge which would stick was trespassing; he counseled a talk with the boy and his grandfather instead. No charges were filed, and Silverhus was never again caught in such a situation.

At 18, he graduated solidly in the middle of his high school class. He didn't go to college right away. Instead, at the age of 20, Steven Silverhus moved away from the Twin Cities, to Missoula, Montana. He enrolled in classes at the city college and found work on a landscaping crew. A year and a half later, Silverhus withdrew from school in mid-semester and moved back to St. Paul.

In St. Paul, Silverhus moved back in with his grandfather, who hadn't slowed down much; to this day, he had practicing privileges at Hennepin County Medical Center, and he worked as an editor for a line of medical textbooks. But he'd also invested some of his considerable income in real estate, buying a pair of houses, one in South St. Paul and one in Victoria, which he rented out. His grandson Steven became his property manager and handyman.

The two houses had, between them, recorded five prowler calls in the past two years.

Niels Silverhus's neighbors spoke of Steven in the code words of guarded pity: Steven was "taking a little longer to find himself," they said. He was "bright enough," and "seems like a nice kid."

None of them blamed Niels for Steven's failure to detach from the family home. Niels was busy, they said, and he could be blunt and impatient in his speech, but no one had ever heard him speak a harsh word to his grandson, nor disparage Steven behind his back. Despite his grueling surgeon's schedule, he'd taken the boy to the cabin in Montana every summer, where the boy had first developed his interest in rockhounding and fossils. Niels had also, it was said, initially staked Steven in his attempt to build a life in Montana. And when Steven decided to return to school, Niels paid his tuition at the University of Minnesota.

When Hadley was finished with the summary, Santarella rubbed one hand flatly against his cheek, tired, thinking. Finally, he spoke. "I want to bring this guy in."

His words surprised me. We didn't have anything more on Silverhus than we did yesterday night. He'd had a legitimate reason to be at the public memorial and rally, hadn't been at the private funeral, and then I'd come back from Wisconsin without any fresh evidence.

Hadley put it into words: "What's changed?"

"Ticking clock," Santarella said. "If we keep developing him as a suspect, it means talking to people he and his granddad know, and pretty soon someone's going to mention it to one of them."

He was right. Vang and Hadley had asked for discretion from the neighbors and others we'd talked to, but too many times we'd seen those kind of promises forgotten as soon as the front door closed behind us.

Santarella went on: "We can't arrest, but we might be able to get him talking if he thinks we want to use his insights as a lay counselor to sex offenders. Vang did the groundwork for that at the memorial."

"I'll call him," I said, already looking in my notes for his phone number.

"No, not you, Pribek. I'd like Vang to contact him and to do the interviewing."

I looked up. I was the one who'd developed this suspect, who'd laid the foundation for what we now knew.

"You said Silverhus seemed intimidated around you, and probably afraid of women overall," Santarella explained. "If this is going to be a friendly interview, at least to start, we need a neutral interviewer."

"In other words," Hadley said, "not a nearly six-foot-tall Amazon or a scary brother from the street like me, but — "

"A nice Asian boy," Vang finished.

Santarella cut us off. "Yeah, I know," he said. "We all hate it when considerations like this come into play. But to get him talking, I'd use a Martian, if I had one on my team." He jutted his chin out at me. "Pribek, hand off the number to Vang; Vang, make the call. And then, everyone get some rest."

TWENTY-FIVE

Santarella had second thoughts about keeping me out of the Silverhus interview entirely. Instead, I was going to watch with the rest of the team behind the one-way mirror, until we decided Vang had gotten everything he could from the soft approach. Then I was going to go in and unsettle him.

We were all assembled behind the mirror — Hadley, Hasan, Santarella, and me. Both Santarella and Hadley leaned forward as Vang ushered Silverhus in. I'd forgotten how tall Silverhus was, as tall as Shiloh, but with the rounded shoulders of a man whose ego will not properly support that kind of height.

"The traffic wasn't too bad on the way here, I hope?" Vang asked, taking a seat in front of the table.

"It was fine," Silverhus said.

"So you drove here," Vang commented. It wasn't a casual question; it would be important later.

"Right," Silverhus said.

"Well," Vang shuffled papers, "I've just got some formalities for you to sign off on," he handed a sheet across the table, "saying that you're here willingly to help us with our inquiries and don't want a lawyer present."

Silverhus scanned the page in front of him. Vang added an extra reassurance, like a spoonful of sugar. "I spoke to Dr. Donovan about your work with Men Against Interpersonal Violence," he said. "He vouched for the work you're doing there, and I almost felt silly bringing these papers in. They're just a formality. It's a lawsuit-happy era, you know."

Silverhus initialed and signed.

Vang opened by talking to Silverhus about his life. Some of it was meant to put him at ease; other parts filled in questions we had about Silverhus's background that we couldn't get from the neighbors. He characterized his long tenure in his grandfather's house as more for Niels' benefit than his own, saying that before his grandfather was diagnosed with prostate cancer, he'd had various other health problems. Vang sympathized and allowed how he and his wife had gone through a similar trial with his wife's grandmother.

As we watched, Silverhus relaxed by degrees, responding to Vang's mild demeanor and nonthreatening questions. He stretched out his long, thin legs under the table, and his hands began to move expansively in the air, like a sea creature responding to a quickening current.

Vang drank a little coffee, sat back. Then he said, "I'm curious — it's sort of a professional curiosity — about the work you do for Men Against Interpersonal Violence."

Silverhus nodded, amiably. His relaxed posture suggested that he felt this part of his life could only serve to draw suspicion away from him.

"What's the appeal of joining a group like this?"

"The polarization of the sexes hurts everyone," Silverhus said. "It's not just a woman's battle to fight. The way that drinking and drugs and pornography undermines healthy, loving relationships is everyone's problem."

"He's reading straight from the script," Hasan murmured, and Santarella nodded. It was textbook rhetoric.

"So you don't have a personal attachment to this cause?"

"No."

"What does your girlfriend think about you being involved with this kind of work?"

Silverhus smiled weakly. "I'm not really seeing anyone right now. I'm too busy with schoolwork and work and taking care of my granddad."

"Sure, I imagine you are," Vang said. "Well, it's interesting work you're doing. Sometimes I think we in police work could stand to work more closely with lay experts like yourself. Tell me, when you first heard about Jessie Ryan's disappearance, did you have any insights into the situation?"

"What kind of insights?"

"Insights into what kind of man might have done this." Vang paused. "Did any of the details speak to you?"

There were several things that we'd kept out of the news accounts of Jessie's abduction and death, including the bolts of brown velveteen that her body had been wrapped in. If Silverhus was to spill one of those details, this was where he'd do it.

"I thought it was terrible," he said, "what happened to her."

"You go to the University, like she did," Vang commented. "Did you ever meet Jessie Ryan?"

"No."

No uncertainty there. It was probably the truth.

Vang said, "What was it about her that you think attracted this man to her?"

"She was very pretty," Silverhus said. "I can see where a man watching her would have romantic feelings about her."

"Romantic," Vang echoed. His tone was nonjudgmental, but there were unspoken questions behind it: *Romantic like hitting someone over the head with a blunt object is romantic? Like leaving her in the garbage is romantic?*

"Salacious," Silverhus amended, shifting in his chair.

Vang leaned forward. "Do you think the man who killed her feels remorse?"

"I, I don't know," Silverhus said. "I didn't spend that much time thinking about the incident. I've read some of the news stories, though." He bit a thumbnail. "You have DNA, right?"

"That's right." Vang's voice was neutral. Santarella hadn't spoken publicly about the DNA findings, but anyone who watched TV could have guessed that our techs retrieved some. It didn't hurt anything for Vang to confirm what Silverhus had guessed.

"How, uh, can you follow up on that?" he asked.

Next to me, Santarella leaned forward. This was a red flag: Silverhus wanted to know what we knew, and what tools we possessed that might catch him.

"When we develop a suspect," Vang said, "a judge can give us a warrant to take a DNA sample that we can match up."

"But you'd need pretty solid evidence, before you could get a warrant like that, right?"

"Depends on the judge," Vang said.

Behind the glass, Santarella cracked his knuckles, a surprisingly loud sound. "I've heard enough. Pribek, go on in there. Shake him up."

"My pleasure," I said.

Hasan winked at me as I got up to leave. A vote of confidence, I thought, pleased.

Outside, I took a moment to pour a jolt of fresh coffee into my cooling cup, then scooped a manila folder off the desk and went into the interrogation room.

I had to admit that dressing for work was more fun than usual. To best intimidate Silverhus, I'd pulled from my closet a black leather jacket I rarely wore, plus a pair of ankle boots that Shiloh had bought me, with solid heels that took me to six-foot-one.

"John, what *am* I going to do with you? You said you weren't going to start without me," I said to Vang, closing the door behind me, my voice a few decibels above its normal speaking volume. Something told me Silverhus wouldn't like loud women.

Vang turned to look at me, but I only saw it peripherally. I was watching for Silverhus's reaction, and he didn't disappoint, the feminine lips falling open slightly. He recognized me.

"I thought we agreed that I was going to handle this solo," Vang said, an edge of dislike in his voice for his brash female partner. "We're just about wrapped up here."

I ignored him, speaking to Silverhus. "You remember me from Dean Holmes' place, don't you? Sarah Pribek."

Silverhus shook the hand I extended with reluctance. I pulled out a chair and sat down. "That mark on your hand is healing up nicely," I said. "Did you tell John about that, how you pinched your hand in a door, got a strange-looking injury, just around the same time that Jessie disappeared?"

"Excuse me," Silverhus said, politely, directly to me, "I would really prefer to just deal with Detective Vang."

"Would you, now?" I said, staring at him until his eyes slid away from mine. "This isn't a bank, Mr. Silverhus. You can't back up in line to get the teller you want. Besides, I bet I know some things that you didn't share with John." I opened up the manila file I'd brought with me. "You made a phone call on the night of the 30th, to Rob Donovan's cell phone."

I tilted the file so that John could pretend to be seeing this information for the first time. "Check out the time," I said, lowering my voice.

Vang looked up at Silverhus. "You didn't mention that," he said, a note of surprise in his voice. "You called Dr. Donovan only minutes before we believe Jessie was attacked."

"I can explain that," Silverhus said. He was anxious not to lose the support of Vang, his Officer Friendly. "My grandfather was only diagnosed with cancer a day earlier. That was what I was calling about."

"Odd how you didn't make any reference to that in your message," I said, "and how you chose to reach out to an expert in deviant sexual psychology."

"Dr. Donovan is the only therapist I know," Silverhus said. "I had his business card."

"And he called you back a little after ten o'clock," I said, "and you didn't pick up. What were you doing, Steven?"

Silverhus's face hardened in discomfort. "Detective Vang, I thought I wasn't a suspect here."

Vang said, "I'm not sure I ever said that, Steven." But he and I exchanged a quick glance. This was dodgy legal territory.

"You've got the right to stop answering questions," Vang went on, "but if you stop the interview and lawyer up at this point, it's going to look pretty bad. It would really help us, to eliminate you as a suspect, if you could tell us where you were and what you were doing the whole evening of the 30th."

Silverhus exhaled shakily. "The 30th? I was at home with my grandfather. I believe I went to bed early that night."

I believe. He was hedging, one of the signs of deception.

"I see," said Vang. "And your grandfather will bear that out?"

We didn't have to worry about it. A detective was already on his way to the Silverhus home, to talk to Niels about the events of the 30th. We couldn't wait for Steven to get home from this interview to tell his grandfather what he'd told the police, allowing the two of them to coordinate their stories.

"Sure, he will," Silverhus said. "Although, I don't know, he might have been asleep early, too."

Vang sighed, made a disappointed face. "That's not terribly useful to us." He thought. "You know what would help here? If we could just take a look at your car."

"My car?" Silverhus said.

"Right," Vang said.

Then Silverhus smiled. It wasn't the reaction I was expecting. Nerves, perhaps. He said, "It's kind of a mess."

"We hear that a lot," Vang said, reassuringly.

Silverhus had left his Ford Taurus on the fifth floor of an open-sided parking ramp that reminded me of something a child would build with an erector set; when we got out of the elevator, I could see my breath clouding on the air. I touched the place on my hip where my handcuffs rode. If there was any physical evidence at all to support the idea that Jessie Ryan had been in Silverhus's car, we were going to arrest.

Vang did not speak, his hands in his pockets; Silverhus had quickened his pace. From nerves, or eagerness to have this behind him? I had to wonder why he would make this offer, if he had anything at all to hide. We'd expected to have to push a lot harder for this agreement.

Silverhus unlocked all four doors so that Vang and I could look inside. Other than a folded newspaper on the passenger seat and an empty styrofoam cup in the cupholder, the car didn't seem to be the mess he'd said it was.

"We're going to need to see the trunk, too," Vang said to Silverhus, as I got out my flashlight and began to run it over the gray upholstery, finding nothing.

"Oh, the trunk?"

Was that unwillingness I heard in Silverhus's voice? Was he going to refuse? I didn't stop in my inspection, but kept an ear cocked to follow what Vang and Silverhus were saying.

"That's what I meant when I said the car's a mess." Silverhus's voice drifted back to me. There was a muffled pop, audible through the backseat, of the trunk's latch being released. "I was driving two nights ago, and I saw an injured dog by the side of the road. Some kids had shot at it with a BB gun. I picked the dog up and took it to the pet ER."

Now I did stop working, leaning back to see the two of them. Silverhus had swung the trunk open, and Vang was looking down into it. What I saw on his face had me scrambling to my feet, to come around and see what he was seeing.

The hard fuzz of the trunk's upholstery was almost universally covered with a tacky, brown-cherry scrim of dried blood, clearly enough to have thoroughly soaked in. There was no way a technician would be able to separate out human blood in all that the dog had shed.

God almighty. Whatever I'd been expecting to find in the car, it wasn't this.

"Yeah, the poor guy bled a bit, unfortunately," Silverhus said. "I haven't even tried to clean it up yet."

We had thought we were smart, running a good cop-bad cop shuck on this young man, chasing him around the interrogation room like a pair of sparrows harrying a hawk. Maybe he'd even been scared of us, maybe he still was, but he wasn't defenseless. Since the night he'd had Jessie Ryan unconscious and bleeding in his trunk, he'd foreseen this moment. He'd planned for it. There was no doubt in my mind that Silverhus had made sure the veterinary staff saw his face and recorded his name. And I had no doubt that Silverhus had gotten rid of the gun after shooting the dog.

Vang, his voice dull, asked for the name of the veterinary hospital and the date, and Silverhus willingly gave him the details. "You're more than welcome to check, I think the vet on duty was named — "

I cut him off, moving in to stand inches from his face. "You are not okay here, Steven."

Silverhus blinked and backed up a step.

"You've made things much, much worse," I said. "You're twice the suspect you used to be, because you had to get clever like this."

"Sarah," Vang said, wearily. "This isn't helping."

TWENTY-SIX

The room where Nate Shigawa's EMT-Basic Certification class was held was little different from most classrooms I'd been in: whiteboard instead of a chalkboard up front, and overhead, the banks of fluorescent lighting that drained the life from nearly all complexions. However, instead of the classic single-unit chair-desks, the kind with the writing surface soldered to the chair's arm, we had long banks of tables with rolling stools. Which I appreciated, as this setup both felt more dignified and provided generous space to write.

By habit, I had chosen a place at the end of a table near the back, in case I needed to slip out and take a call. My phone was set to vibrate, not ring, but it was in my coat, close to my side. I wanted to be able to feel it, should it alert me to a call.

Shigawa had drawn an inverted triangle on the whiteboard, with NEONATAL RESUSCITATION written in red letters below. The triangle mapped the steps involved in getting a newborn to breathe, descending from the simple and least invasive to the most advanced. Because I'd done the reading, and thus seen the diagram already, I was finding it hard to stay locked onto Shigawa's lecture.

No, that wasn't the real reason. I couldn't stop thinking about Silverhus's ruse.

Vang and I had checked out his story, of course. At a St. Paul veterinary hospital, a young woman had led out a barrel-bodied black Lab from the kennel in the back. His stomach was shaved and seamed with stitches, and his gait was an awkward, mincing run that spoke of healing internal injuries. But the dog's unfortunate encounter with Steven Silverhus hadn't dampened his faith in the human race any; his eyes were bright, as if the visit from Vang and me, instant new friends, was the highlight of his day. The veterinarian's assistant had assured us that she remembered the man who'd brought the dog in, that he'd even called the next day to ask after the Lab's condition.

The St. Paul detective who'd gone to talk to Niels had reported back to Santarella that the elder Silverhus has said he'd gone to bed early that night and though he thought his grandson was home, but couldn't swear to it. That wasn't very helpful to Steven. Not only did it exactly bookend what Steven had said — *I think I went to bed early* — but it was a classic evasion. Sleep was the simplest and most private of activities; no one could be expected to show ticket stubs afterward, or produce eyewitnesses to it.

"Pribek." Shigawa's voice cut into my thoughts.

"Mm?" I raised my eyebrows, hoping to signal polite attentiveness. Had he seen from my face that my mind was wandering? It was hard to tell sometimes with Nate, whose voice always had a sharp ring of authority, at least in the classroom.

"Run a theoretical with me: You've helped to deliver an infant on scene; when it failed to breathe on its own, you succeeded in starting respiration through bag-and-mask ventilation. While waiting for transport to hospital, the mother asks you to clean off her baby. What do you do?"

That was easy. "Politely decline," I said. "Explain to her that the residue of the birth is actually protecting the infant."

"'Residue of birth'?" Shigawa repeated. "Is there a more specific name for that?"

That one was harder. I rummaged mentally through half a dozen mnemonics before coming up with *springtime*. "The vernix," I said. "The adipose coating that was protecting the baby's skin from softening with exposure to amniotic fluid."

"Good," Shigawa said. "Thank you. Chantal, could you tell us … "

After class, I'd only gotten as far as the entryway of the building when I felt my cell vibrate. I stopped where I was, in the small space between the two sets of doors, and fished out my phone. Santarella was calling.

This was good timing; a few moments earlier and I'd have had to endure Shigawa's disapproval as I ducked out of class. Turning my back to the trickle of fellow students making their way past me and outside, I pressed Connect. "Joe?"

"You're not going to believe this," Santarella said. "I'm having a little difficulty with it myself, but Steven Silverhus called me an hour ago. He says he's willing to give us a blood sample for DNA."

"Are you serious?"

"I am, and apparently so is he," Santarella said. "I need a detective to walk Silverhus through the process. Vang's daughter is sick and he's taking her to the doctor tomorrow. Can you do the honors?"

"I'm up for it," I said. A gust of cold air swirled through the entryway as the doors swung shut behind Chantal and Kim, and I tugged my coat tighter against me. "Do you have any idea where he's coming from on this?"

"Not a clue, and I'm too dead on my feet to speculate," Santarella said. "We'll talk about it tomorrow."

I mused on this new information on the short drive home.

What was Silverhus playing at? He'd gone to such lengths to keep us from finding anything in the trunk of his car. The trick with the dog's blood hadn't been subtle, but it hadn't needed to be. The burden was on us to prove to a judge that he was a viable suspect, to get warrants for an arrest or a property search, and Silverhus had neatly knocked us back down to circumstantial evidence. Any physical evidence in the park had been washed away, and whatever had been in his trunk had disappeared under a flood of canine blood.

Having successfully fended us off, why the hell would he turn around and make such an amazing offer? Was he playing chicken with us? It reminded me of movies in which the unlikely driver with contraband in her trunk smiles innocently at the traffic cop and says, *You can look in the trunk, officer, if you really think that's necessary,* and disarmed by her serene confidence, the cop loses interest and waves her through the checkpoint.

It wasn't going to happen here. If Silverhus thought we wouldn't go through with the test, he'd learn differently tomorrow.

TWENTY-SEVEN

It was 1 p.m. when I pulled up in front of the tall, regal house that Niels Silverhus owned on Portland Avenue. Technically, escorting Steven Silverhus through the blood-draw process didn't obligate me to pick him up at his home, but I'd wanted to see where grandfather and grandson lived, apparently alone. It wasn't a mansion, but it was sizable. Like most of its neighbors, it had been built close to the turn of the twentieth century. Three stories tall, its roofline was so steep no snow could stay up there; the front was painted a creamy elm green, a reminder of summer in the approach of winter. A glassed-in sun porch ran the whole length of the front.

When Steven Silverhus came out, he was dressed in the most wholesome, bland way possible: clean blue jeans and a knit Henley shirt, a mid-thigh length, pine green outdoorsman's jacket with a hood, and hiking boots. It was hard to imagine him as anyone's murderer.

I'd called him at eight that morning, and he hadn't backed down from his promise to Santarella. He had, though, mentioned that he had things he needed to do in the morning and wanted an afternoon appointment, so I'd set one up at the BCA lab at 1:30 p.m.

I'd never done this particular procedure before. I understood my role in it, which was simply to observe the blood draw and sign off on the chain-of-custody forms, so that later no defense attorney could challenge the provenance of Silverhus's DNA or claim contamination.

The phlebotomist's lab was a small room. At the center was a chair with a fold-out armrest on either side, and on the shelves behind that, a choir of tubes with variously colored stoppers. A dull tapping of rubber-soled shoes announced the entrance of the phlebotomist. She looked about 16, with blonde hair pulled back in a ponytail and wide-set blue eyes. Her name tag read *Mandy*. I half-expected it to say *trainee* underneath, but it didn't. Even so, I thought that she must have been very recently certified.

"You can sit down and put your arm up on the table, that's good," she said to Silverhus.

He obliged her, and began to push up his sleeve. The knit shirt had ribbed cuffs, and he had a little difficulty getting it up past the elbow, where the muscle of the bicep began to bow outward. He smiled apologetically at Mandy.

"Is that far enough?" he asked.

"That's okay," she said. "It's better, if you're having blood drawn, to wear something with short sleeves. You can always wear a jacket over that if it's cold." She picked up a disinfectant wipe and tore open the outer packaging. "Okay, make a fist."

He did and she swabbed the pale, soft crease of his inner elbow with disinfectant, then busied herself with the equipment of needle and Vacutainer.

I'd been to the blood bank and donated enough to know that often people look away during a draw. Silverhus didn't. He watched intently as the needle bit into the spongy pale flesh of his inner elbow. He seemed comfortable with Mandy, too. Perhaps it was her youth and diminutive build that set him at ease.

The tube began to fill with dark, venous blood as Silverhus watched. When Mandy pulled the needle free and taped down a cotton ball over his arm, he made a little sound, not quite a sigh, of relief. Without wanting to, I understood how he felt. There are few instincts so universally shared as the desire to keep your blood inside your body.

Mandy and I signed off on the chain-of-custody paperwork, as Silverhus pushed his sleeve down to the wrist again, the movement fastidious.

"I need to get home," he said to me. "I'm worried about my grandfather."

"Sure," I said. "We've just got some forms to deal with here."

"So," I said, when we were on the road, "I was thinking last night that this seems like a sharp turnaround. You seemed almost offended yesterday, when you asked Vang if you were a suspect in Jessie Ryan's death. Now it seems like you've embraced the idea."

"I'm just cooperating," Silverhus said. He settled his arm stiffly on the armrest and stared straight ahead, as though he were watching television through the windshield.

"More than cooperating," I said. "We hadn't gotten around to asking you for a DNA sample yet. That was your idea." *Gotten around to asking* was my euphemism for the fact that we didn't have enough evidence for a warrant. "So why? Why volunteer?"

"Because I'm trying to help," Silverhus said. He was studying the naked winter trees, not looking my way.

When I'd pulled up outside his grandfather's house, just before he got out, Silverhus said, "I'd like to get a phone call, when you get the results of the DNA test back and I'm officially ruled out."

I dropped my hand to the parking brake and searched his face for something, maybe an inkling of martyred anger. But I couldn't read him.

"That's an odd request," I told him. "If you know that you'll be exonerated, because your DNA won't match what we got from Jessie, why does it matter to you when the test results are back?"

"My grandfather has been upset by all this," Silverhus said. "It's just for his peace of mind."

Then he touched the crook of his elbow, as if he wanted to worry the tape and cotton ball Mandy had applied. A smile flickered and failed to stay in place on his lips, like a neon sign with a faulty tube. "There's no hard feelings about this," he said. "I don't hold a grudge."

He didn't look back at me as he went up the front walk.

A pall settled over the remainder of my afternoon. Since Santarella had called me late last night, I hadn't had a lot of time to think about the ramifications of what Steven Silverhus had done. Now, though, the implications were beginning to close in: Either Silverhus was innocent, or he was delusional. The latter was a tough sell: if he had killed Jessie, I could see him blanking the whole thing out of his memory afterward, convincing himself it was a nightmarish fantasy, even a bad dream.

But could he do that and go on to cover his tracks the next day, injuring the Lab with a BB gun, making sure the veterinary ER staff remembered his name? Could he have wiped it out of his memory more than a day later, only after methodically covering up his crime? I didn't believe that. That was the kind of contorted hypothetical that lawyers tried to sell juries. Juries rarely bought those arguments, as well they shouldn't.

I was considering going down to the main floor for a head-clearing cappuccino when I spotted Syed Hasan, waiting at the elevators. When he saw me, he tipped his forehead toward the closed double doors and asked, "On a break?"

I nodded confirmation.

"You want to go for a short walk, then? I'm stepping out for a smoke."

"A cigarette? Oh, Syed." My dismay at his lapse was only half-feigned, but he just laughed.

On Third Avenue, city maintenance workers were hanging greenery from the lampposts, bushy evergreens with red ribbons. I watched them as Hasan bent his head down, all his attention on the flame he was holding to the tip of his cigarette. Then he tipped his head back in that posture common to all smokers and exhaled the first prodigious lungful of smoke.

"Did you see today's *Star Tribune*?" he asked me.

"Just the front page. Why?"

We began to walk at an unhurried pace, heading by unspoken consensus toward the river.

"Jessie's grandfather, Roy Nedegaard, had a piece on the op-ed page today."

"Was it about a return to the death penalty in Minnesota?" He'd mentioned that to me the day he'd watched me search Jessie's bedroom.

"That, and he called for more life sentences for first offenders in serious but non-homicide felony cases, like rape or kidnapping. He called it a way of preventing recidivism," Hasan said.

"What'd you think?"

"It's a fairly common stance for family members of crime victims, particularly young victims," he said, tapping a bit of ash off the end of his cigarette. "'My granddaughter's dead; if only we'd passed enough laws this wouldn't have happened.' It's not perfect logic, but it's understandable." He thought a moment. "Also, usually I'd say that he's making a leap if he's taking as a given that Jessie's killer has committed a prior felony. But we know he has."

"Roback," I said.

"Yeah. But since no one was arrested and charged in that case, tougher sentencing wouldn't have helped here."

"Wait, does Nedegaard know about Roback?" It was a detail we were keeping from the public.

"No, though he probably would if he had his way. He's been calling Santarella regularly, implying that his retired-peace-officer status means he should get more information than we'd normally give out to family members."

"But Santarella isn't doing that."

"Oh, hell no. Nedegaard probably wouldn't tell the media about Roback, if Joe asked him not to, but eventually he'd have to tell one of his old pals in the State Patrol, maybe more than one. They'd tell a couple of people, and eventually it'd be public."

We walked for a short space without talking. Then I asked, "What did you do today?"

"Chased down an anonymous phone call," Hasan said. "A confession."

"No kidding?" I said. "What was the story there?"

"He got us a little excited. He either had inside information or he guessed about Jessie being wrapped in fabric. I kept him on the line long enough to get a trace and we found him. But he wasn't the guy. He had a history of psychiatric hospitalization."

"Doesn't rule him out," I said.

"He's in poor health, too," Hasan added. "Even a girl of Jessie's size could have knocked him over with one push."

We'd stopped halfway across the bridge. Hasan took a last drag on his cigarette and pitched it into the river.

I leaned against the railing. "This is what I've been thinking about," I said. "I've been trying to figure out why Steven Silverhus would make this big gesture, coming in to give DNA."

"Excluding the obvious, you mean?" Hasan said. "That he's innocent?"

I chewed my lower lip. "Not quite excluding that. Say he *is* innocent. Why not wait for us for ask him for DNA?"

"Offhand, I'd say nerves. Being a suspect in a major case is frightening, and he wants the glaring spotlight to move on." Hasan paused. "That's what I'd say if I felt certain he were innocent."

"You don't believe he is," I said, pleased to have my private conviction confirmed.

"I can't know, but I saw him yesterday in the interrogation room. He was scared of something," Hasan said.

"I thought so, too," I said. "I just can't reconcile everything else I know about him, especially the stunt he pulled with the dog, with his willingness to give blood." Then: "I'm being paranoid, right? You're going to tell me that criminal masterminds are few and far between, and murderers rarely hide forever."

"That's been my experience," he said. He watched a city maintenance truck, its bed loaded with holiday greenery, trundle slowly onto the bridge. "I wish we knew a little bit more about Steven's family. I've done just a little bit of looking around online, trying to find out more about Niels, things other than what's in his official biography."

"And?"

He shrugged. "He's got a little of that old-fashioned medicine-man hubris. He still calls his receptionist his 'girl,' and he had a reputation for being rude to nurses. That didn't really surprise me; he's just a product of a particular era." He frowned. "I didn't learn anything at all about his personal life. That household seems so insular; just the two of them. Niels's wife is dead, Steven never married, and the generation in between them is gone."

I waited, not sure of the significance of that.

Hasan said, "Under those circumstances, people get into really symbiotic relationships, unhealthy symbiotic relationships. Niels has already supported Steven financially and materially into his 20s, and Steven doesn't seem to have thrived as a result of it."

No, he seemed more like a frail hothouse plant, drooping under an onslaught of steam and a lack of fresh air.

I said, "Are you suggesting that growing up in his grandfather's shadow gave Steven a raging psychosis, to the point where now he's attacking women?"

Hasan shook his head. "Crimes this serious, it'd have to be more than that. It's frustrating, but often there's no one thing you can identify that pushed a guy like Steven over the edge. If," he said, backpedaling, "Steven really is our guy."

In my mind, there was very little doubt.

Hasan concluded, "I just wish we had someone else in that household to approach, someone who might break away from the circled wagons and give us some information."

"We'll crack Steven," I told him. "One way or another."

TWENTY-EIGHT

The ringing of my cell phone roused me from sleep the next morning, only ten minutes before my alarm would have done so. For a moment, my drowsy mind wouldn't differentiate the two sounds, and I tried ineffectually to switch off the silent clock radio by my bedside, before seeing that the face of my cell phone was flashing.

"Pribek."

"It's John," Vang said. "We just got a heads-up about a disappearance near the University. I'm told it looks like a pretty clear-cut abduction."

"Where?" I said.

About a half-mile from the Twin Cities campus is a cluster of apartment buildings that students probably call romantic and their parents likely find shabby. The buildings were tall and thin, the back sides laddered with a wooden system of catwalks and diagonal stairs that served as a fire escape and rear porches, the central courtyard shaded through the summer with elms. In the hot season, air conditioning would take the form of roaring electric fans and ice cubes you rubbed on the back of your neck, so they'd drip down your shirt. But in winter, like now, the heat would be adequate. Heat was one thing Minnesota landlords knew better than to stint on.

At ten after seven, the temperature was hovering at around five degrees, and the cold had brought out the colors in the city landscape the same way that cold water brings out the redness of a swimmer's lips and the darkness of her eyelashes. The Nova's engine — there'd been no time to check in downtown and switch to a motor-pool car — had barely begun to put out heat from its vents when I was waved into the parking lot by a uniformed officer.

The real action was around the back of the building, where about half the parking spaces were. All of the rear lot was cordoned off with yellow tape, and just inside that perimeter stood Vang, Syed Hasan, and a middle-aged woman with a heavy hunter's parka over her bathrobe and cinderblock-solid boots on her feet, her makeupless face reddened by the morning wind.

All three were watching the action surrounding an unoccupied parking space, where two crime-scene techs were circling and photographing something at ground level that could have been a strange outdoor art exhibit.

Lying in bright white, fresh snow was a small black handbag, its mouth open like a hooked fish, and near that, a single cigarette with sodden skin. All around these items were footprints in a tight clustered pattern, pointing every which way, like an Arthur Murray diagram of dancers having a shared grand mal seizure. Between the footprints were Morse-Code-like spots and splashes of blood.

"What's the story?" I asked Hasan, as Vang began talking with the woman in the parka and bathrobe.

"A student with a work-study job in a dorm kitchen was leaving for work around six-fifteen and saw all this." He gestured to the trampled and littered snow. "Unfortunately, he approached and picked up the purse to find the ID, so the scene isn't pristine anymore. Anyway, the bag and the driver's license inside belongs to a Cydney Ann Perrin, twenty years old. The student went to her apartment and talked to Perrin's roommate. That's her," he turned to point to the woman Vang was talking to. "Maureen Rand. Apparently, Cyd — the roommate says that's what everyone calls her — works on a janitorial crew at the University."

"Is that work-study, too?" I interrupted. "She's a student?"

"No, she's just employed by the U," Hasan said. "She'd probably just come home when she was attacked right outside her car, lost a bit of blood, was put back in her own car and taken somewhere. That's what it looks like." He sniffled, his nose reddened by the wind and the cold. "I'm guessing that we're going to have three crime scenes: this one, a point where he transferred her to his own vehicle, and the place she was ultimately taken."

"Where's the student who reported it?"

"Downtown. We could've taken a statement here, but we need elimination fingerprints, because he touched the purse, plus a cast of his shoes to compare against the ones we take here."

"We'll hope it stays cold a while longer," I said.

"For the casts," he said. Apparently he'd been at enough wintertime crime scenes to know about the difficulties of making shoe – and tire-print casts in the snow, particularly as the sun's warmth begins to soften the structures.

"Let me show you something," I said, and led him to the edge of the parking lot, keeping my progress slow and glancing discreetly back to make sure the uneven, snowy ground wasn't giving him trouble with his bad leg. Where the parking lot ended, a hillside ran down to the railroad tracks, thick shrubbery and finally, the Mississippi.

"See how there's no natural or manmade barriers between the apartment complex and the river or the tracks?" I said. "When I was on patrol, I responded to a lot of prowler and suspicious noise calls around this neighborhood. Never very sophisticated crimes, just people going around trying doors and tugging at windows."

Homeless people liked to sit and fish and drink down by the river, and trains rolled through all the time, carrying those who still, in the twenty-first century, jumped freights to get around. Those weren't crimes, of course. Homeless people were more often victims than criminals, but some were mentally ill, and some were strong. It was possible that Perrin's abduction was a simple crime of opportunity: someone walked up from the river, thinking to try windows until he found one open, and saw Perrin and her car, instead. It would explain why he'd taken her somewhere in her car.

"Another thing about Perrin," Hasan said. "The roommate says she has a baby. Rand watches him while she's at work."

"Oh, Jesus," I said.

We weren't to the apartment yet when Vang came out onto the front step. He had a photo in his hand, and turned it around to show us.

In it, Cyd Perrin sat in a hospital-nursery rocking chair, a newborn infant wrapped in a blanket at her chest. She was slender, and her red-gold hair fell to a little past her shoulders. My hope that her abduction wasn't related to Jessie's began to melt away.

"How tall is she?" I asked Vang.

"Five-one," he said.

We shared a moment of silence. Then I said, "This is the same victim type as Ryan and Roback, and the same MO as in Missoula. Roback was blindsided after work, just after getting out of her car. We need to find Silverhus."

Hasan watched a crime-scene technician delicately spraying snow print wax into the ridged basins of tire and shoe prints. The wax, which was a bright, arterial red, made the whole process look even grimmer.

"We can't arrest," Vang said. "We don't have any more evidence than we had yesterday, and that wasn't enough for an arrest, plus he's cooperating."

"I know," I said, "but this is an emergency. If Perrin got off work at four in the morning, he's only got a few hours on us. She could still be alive. Santarella can make the judge understand that."

"I agree," Hasan said. "Plus, the fact that Silverhus is cooperating isn't everything. In the absence of blood-test results, which we don't have yet, he's not exonerated. We've got to call Santarella." He sniffled again; the cold was really getting to him. Then he added, "We should talk about how you're going to handle him, if you get the go-ahead to bring him in. I've got some ideas."

Vang already had his phone out, but hesitated with his hand over the keypad when he saw Hasan looking directly at him.

Hasan said, "You've got the best rapport with him, John."

Vang nodded.

"For the kind of interview I'm thinking about, you should be the primary, with Hadley to back you up. We're going to need two married guys." Hasan turned to me. "That means we're not going to be able to use you this time. Sorry."

"Whatever you need," I said.

TWENTY-NINE

Vang spoke to Santarella; Santarella got our warrant. By late morning, I was in the same observation room that I'd been in two days ago, Santarella and Hasan again beside me. It was unlikely that I'd be called in to put pressure on Steven Silverhus this time. As Hasan had said, this was going to be Vang's show, with Hadley as backup.

For now, they were letting Silverhus sit behind the table, waiting. Vang and Hadley were letting the tension build. Silverhus's head was bowed forward, giving Santarella and me a good view of the beginnings of a bald spot. Silverhus looked almost as if he were praying. I doubted he was, but clearly Silverhus was the type to internalize his fear. Some men would be tapping their feet, jittering, unable to keep still. But Silverhus looked like an android that had been powered down.

Since he was giving us so little to observe, I turned my attentions to the notes Vang had handed off to me. Maureen Rand had given Cyd's life story to Vang, and I wanted to familiarize myself with it.

Cyd Perrin's story wasn't an uncommon one: the small-town girl, a little wild, who'd turned up pregnant in her last year of high school. She'd grown up in Morris, Minnesota, a farm town that was also home to the smallest University of Minnesota campus. Her father, Donald Perrin, was a farmworker and a shade-tree mechanic; her mother had died when Cyd was four years old. Cyd and Donald were very much a family of two.

By high school, Cyd was not averse to a few beers on Friday night or a joint when one was being passed around, and her grades were not the stuff of which bright college careers are made. But she had no criminal record and held down regular part-time jobs. The summer before her last year of high school, Cyd had secured a coveted summer job at a resort on Lake of the Woods. For her lodging and a small wage, Cyd worked at the boat-rental outlet, renting and refueling fishing boats, selling bait and tackle. She came home tanned and healthy, and, it became clear in mid-September, pregnant.

The father was never even listed on the birth certificate; that's how it was. Cyd settled for a GED instead of a diploma, studying at home. It was probably no small topic of speculation around town why she'd chosen to keep the baby: She had few prospects, and there'd never been much money in the family to start with. Donald Perrin and his daughter weren't churchgoers, so religious objections to abortion didn't seem to be the issue. Whatever it was, Cyd kept it to herself.

When her son Daniel was six months old, Cyd moved the two of them to the Twin Cities. Her father had an old friend and high-school classmate there, Maureen Rand, who was willing to have mother-and-child roommates. Divorced and childless, Maureen took to Daniel as though he were a godson.

Cyd sought shift work that would let her have days free to care for her son, and found it on a University janitorial crew with 9 p.m. to 3 a.m. hours. Daniel was sleeping through the nights by then, but Cyd nonetheless ran chronically short on sleep. But she was young, Maureen said. She was resilient.

Maureen also said that Cyd wasn't above having a beer on Friday or Saturday night to relax, or bumming a smoke from a friend, but that was all. Her partying days were behind her. She had no time for dates and had mentioned no men angling for her attention of late. The greatest risk in Cyd's life seemed to be the late hours she kept, and it seemed that last night, that risk had become reality in a terrible way.

At last, the interrogation-room door opened and Hadley came in, followed by Vang. Silverhus raised his head and looked at them with pale, uncertain eyes.

"I gave you guys blood for your DNA test just yesterday," he said. "I don't understand why I'm here. I've been cooperating."

"The game changed today, Steven," Vang said. "You know why, right?"

He was firing a good opening shot right out of the gate. Perrin's disappearance wasn't in the news yet. If Silverhus said anything like, *Because of the new girl missing,* he would incriminate himself.

But Silverhus merely shook his head. Vang glanced at the mirror, the briefest indication that he was thinking about those of us who were watching. He pulled up a chair and sat down.

"You're here because we need your help, Steven," Vang said. "The Twin Cities have been my home since I was born, just like they've been yours. His, too." He indicated Hadley, who was standing against the wall, at a distance Silverhus would find non-threatening.

"Something really bad is going on in our hometown," Vang said. "I want to show you a few pictures and tell you about it." He laid a photograph on the table between them. "Do you recognize this woman?"

Silverhus leaned forward, and I thought I saw his posture stiffen in reaction. But he shook his head. "No."

"Her name is Danielle Roback," Vang said. "Someone hit her on the head and raped her while she was unconscious. She was in a coma for five weeks."

Silverhus blinked. "I thought you said this was about the Twin Cities."

Vang had said nothing about Roback being from out of the area. Silverhus hadn't said the word *Montana*, but he'd come close to making a bad misstep. It was subtle, but Vang's face registered that fact. I knew he'd circle back to it soon, when it was time to tighten the net.

"He's good," Hasan said quietly, and Santarella nodded agreement. I agreed, too, but I also felt the smallest bit of jealousy. *Relax, will you?*

167

I told myself. *Pretty soon you won't be a cop at all; there's no need to compete with your colleagues for validation.*

Vang took out another photo, set it on the table. "Do you recognize this woman?"

"Of course," Silverhus said. "That's Jessie Ryan."

"That's right," Vang said. "She was hit on the head too, and also raped. This time the guy drowned her afterward."

Silverhus stared down at the table.

Vang laid a third photo on the table. "This is Cydney Perrin," he said. "She's been missing since early this morning."

"Only two weeks since Jessie was killed," Hadley noted.

"This is escalating, getting worse," Hadley said. "The first victim was in a coma for five weeks, but survived. Jessie Ryan died. She was drowned by her attacker."

"Why are you telling me all this?" Silverhus asked.

"Because things like this tend to get worse," Vang said. "They don't get better until someone is strong enough to say, 'I need help, this has to stop.'"

Silverhus said, "I don't know anything about Jessie. Or the girl in Montana, or some girl who just got killed this morning."

Vang tilted his head. "I didn't say anything about Roback being from Montana, did I?"

"You didn't," Hadley said, stepping forward from his place on the wall. "Neither did I."

Santarella made a soft grunt of satisfaction. But I pressed two knuckles against my lips, because I'd heard something else in Silverhus's words: Cydney Perrin was dead. He'd just said so: *some girl who was killed this morning.* None of us knew whether she was dead; he hadn't gotten that idea from us.

In the interrogation room, Silverhus was scrambling to cover up for recognizing Roback. "Well, I...I lived in Montana awhile. Maybe the case was in the news. I just didn't recognize the name at first."

"Well, then, let's talk about Danielle for a minute. Not the details. The broader picture." Vang leaned forward. "Let me ask you something,

Steven. Sex with an unconscious woman behind a carport in the middle of the night: Whose idea of a love life is that?" He let that question sink in. "I don't believe any boy thinks, growing up, that that's what his future is going to be like. Nobody wants that."

Hadley, too, leaned in: "I just got married six months ago. It's a scary thing, standing up and promising to love and protect one woman for the rest of both your lives." He indicated Vang. "John's married, too. Got a little girl, two years old, to look after."

Vang nodded.

"It's hard to be a lover, a husband, and a father," Hadley continued. "It starts with being a man. And being a man is difficult, I won't kid you."

His voice was hypnotic. I almost felt myself sway where I stood.

"I think you've wanted to be that kind of man all your life, Steven." Hadley came around to sit next to Vang, facing Silverhus. "But what you did to Danielle and Jessie, that's not how a man treats a woman. These were both good women who didn't deserve it."

"And now, there's Cyd." Vang tapped the photo. "Did you notice the baby in the picture? That's Daniel, her son. He's going to grow up and try to be a man, too. He already doesn't have a father. Can you imagine how much harder it's going to be for him if he doesn't have a mother, too?"

"I grew up without parents," Silverhus said. His voice was barely a murmur.

"That's right," Hadley said.

Beside me, Hasan was leaning forward, one hand gripping his cane in what was probably an unconscious gesture, completely locked onto what was happening behind the glass.

Vang said, "Steven, do you think your parents would be proud of you today? Do you think your father would?"

Silverhus's eyes were glassy with unshed tears.

Vang's voice was gentle: "It's not too late to start being a man. You can start with Cydney Perrin. Do right by her. Tell us where she is."

To my left, the door to the observation room opened, letting bright hallway light spill in. A uniform stood in the gap. "Agent Santarella?"

Santarella put up his hand sharply as if stopping traffic: *Not now.*

"Lab's on the phone for you. Said it's urgent."

Santarella looked over at the officer, then he rose to a crouching position and slipped out of the room like a moviegoer trying not to disturb other patrons.

I turned my attention back to the tableau on the other side of the glass.

"What do you think your father would want you to do, right now?" Vang was saying.

A single tear fell over Silverhus' lower eyelashes and onto his cheek. He wiped at it, saying nothing. Vang and Hadley didn't speak, either. They were at the tipping point now, letting the silence work. They knew better than to push their arguments too far.

Then the interrogation-room door opened, and I saw Santarella come in. I stiffened in shock and felt Hasan do the same; it was the worst possible time for an interruption.

"I'm sorry," Santarella said, "but I'm going to have to cut this short." To Silverhus, whose wet eyes had gone to him as if for salvation: "You're free to go."

Next to me, Hasan's shoulders sank heavily in disappointment. But in the interrogation room, relief ran through Silverhus like a current. He got to his feet. Hadley and Vang were both silently telegraphing Santarella the same message: *What the hell?*

At the door, Silverhus turned. "Was it the DNA? I have a right to know if I've been exonerated."

Santarella nodded. "Yes," he said. "You are no longer a suspect."

You've got to be kidding me. I turned from the window and grabbed for the door, barreled out of the observation room, and joined them just as they were coming out. Silverhus started a little when he saw me — it was clear he'd had no idea I'd been here all along — and then whipped his head away, so I wouldn't see his tears. He moved down the hall in a quick shamble, like a bear in a hurry.

"There's got to be some mistake," I said to Santarella. "He was an inch from confessing. We all saw it."

From the look on Hadley's face, he'd made the exact same point just before I arrived. Santarella turned to glance at Silverhus's retreating form as it disappeared around the corner. Then he said, "I'm sorry, but he didn't do Roback and he didn't do Ryan. The DNA is from a different suspect."

"That can't be right!" I said. "He knew Roback was from Montana without being told. He was *crying*, for God's sake."

"His grandfather, a respected surgeon, vouches for him on both nights," Santarella reminded me. "Roback didn't pick him out of a photo lineup. There's no physical evidence to link him to either case."

"How do you explain the business with the trunk of his car?"

"Maybe he's telling the truth about the injured dog."

"You've got to be fucking kidding me," I said, forgetting etiquette. "What about Perrin? We don't have DNA on her yet. We don't even have *her*. We can still hold him on those grounds."

"But the similarities to the Roback and Ryan cases were all the reason we had to suspect him in Perrin's disappearance. Once that link was disproved, what legal grounds do we have to question him?"

I shook my head. "There's too much evidence pointing to him. Mountains of it, practically."

"Pribek!" Santarella said. "I. Couldn't. Hold. Him." His throat was constricted. "Since the early days of DNA evidence, defense attorneys have tried to tear it down. They suggest the technology is unreliable or the results are inconclusive. Our forensic scientists have spent decades refining the procedure so that it's unassailable. Every day, they stand up in court to tell juries that DNA does not lie, it doesn't change its testimony, it doesn't take sides. Juries need that spelled out for them, but I didn't expect to have to explain that to a detective."

I swallowed. "I know. I'm sorry. It's just — " I looked at Hadley and Vang for support, but saw that they'd given up on this fight.

"Don't be sorry," Santarella said. "Just put Silverhus behind you. We've got a lot of work to do on Perrin."

It was a little more than an hour later that the police outside of Hastings called. A towboat captain had reported sighting what looked like a female body caught in a semi-submerged treefall in the Mississippi. He wasn't quite right about it being a corpse. When the water patrol reached her, Cyd Perrin was alive.

THIRTY

"I brought a lot of photos, all you might need."

Cyd's father, Donald Perrin, had a face that was benevolent even in its grief, round, with a brushy walrus mustache. He was wearing dark, new jeans and a quilted parka vest over a flannel shirt, a ball cap that he took off and held in his hands intermittently. He'd recently arrived after a half-day's driving from Morris. I was keeping him company in the corridor of the Hennepin County Medical Center.

"I don't think we'll be needing photos any longer," I said. Photos, of course, were for a missing-persons case. Cyd was now very much accounted for; she was down the hall, fighting shock, hypothermia, exposure, and a head trauma. The doctor had made it diplomatically clear that he didn't hold out a lot of hope for her. It was also clear that her father Donald had heard no warnings whatsoever in phrases like *very guarded condition*. That was probably for the best. Humans are wired for hope; it's a palliative in times of terrible pain. Sometimes, though, it's a relief that can't last.

"This is her with the baby at Christmas," he said. "This is an older picture. She's at the boat rental place with her friends from the Lake."

Cyd had her back to the camera, a nearly-naked back except for where the strings of her bikini top came together, and the top edge of her low, faded cutoffs. She'd turned to look at the photographer, laughter in her eyes.

"This is her with the baby on her last birthday." She was feeding the baby a little bit of white frosting off the tip of her index finger. "March, that was."

Please stop. "Mr. Perrin, since Cyd isn't missing anymore, I don't think we'll be needing photos."

"The news won't want 'em?"

"No, sir." Not unless Cyd died, in which case they'd want to illustrate stories about her. I didn't think Perrin needed to hear that. "Mr. Perrin, when you heard Cyd was missing, was there anyone you thought of, even for a minute, even though you later told yourself it was ridiculous? Like former boyfriends or men from Morris?"

"Sorry, I didn't, Agent Pribek."

"Detective Pribek," I said. "It's Mr. Santarella who's with the BCA. I know we're hard to keep straight." I slid the photos back into the envelope he'd brought them in.

"I heard that you all think it's the same guy who killed that girl on Halloween."

Devil's Night, really, but I didn't correct him.

"So that means that it's nothing to do with Cyd's past, it's just about how she looked?"

"We really don't know yet," I told him. "Had you heard from Cyd recently?"

"Not in person."

"In person?"

"Not over the phone, I mean. She wrote me a postcard."

"Does she do that often?"

"Yeah, she likes to find funny postcards in shops. Ones with black-and-white photos from the '40s or '50s, and funny captions. Some of them, the humor is kind of…salty, I guess you'd say, like nuns doing stuff that's out of character, but she's never been a prude about things like that." A smile shifted his thick mustache. "I raised her myself after her mom died, and after about the first year I stopped trying to watch my language. I used to tell some off-color jokes, so we're pretty relaxed about that stuff."

I nodded. "What sort of things does she write about?"

"Nothing much. Neither of us are big writers." he thought. "She has this code for telling me how things are going. She draws an old-time elevator monitor, you know, the half-circle kind with an arrow to show which floor the elevator's at?" He looked to me to be sure I was following. "Well, hers have words where the numbers would go: Great, Good, Fair, Poor, Don't Ask. She calls it the Mood Elevator."

His face tightened, and his eyes began to shimmer glassily. Without speaking further, he rose heavily and walked to the men's room.

The evening news had identified Cyd erroneously as a student: *Second coed missing.* They'd fix that soon enough, but it wouldn't make a dent in the excitement over her disappearance. Her resemblance to Jessie Ryan was clear to anyone who put their pictures side-by-side.

My stomach growled, and I realized I was hungry. More than hungry, ravenous. Keeping vigils did that to me. Strange, given that there was nothing to them but sitting and standing around. Someone had changed the station on the television set to a cable-news channel, where several experts were debating whether a war-crimes trial of Saddam Hussein would be seen as legitimate by the rest of the Middle East, or whether it would ultimately hurt the legitimacy of the new Iraqi government.

I got up and headed for the cafeteria. Vang was coming to relieve me later, but that was so I could go to class. If I didn't eat now, there wouldn't be time until I got home.

Should I wait for Donald Perrin to emerge from the restroom and try to get him to eat something? No, he'd say he wasn't hungry. Nobody could eat during a vigil in an ICU. Except cops.

THIRTY-ONE

"**D**etective Pribek."

Rosamund Ross, who'd spotted me moving a tray down the assembly line of the cafeteria offerings, was better dressed today, wearing a chestnut-brown blazer over a white shirt and wheat-colored trousers. The boots were the same sturdy leather ones, a wise choice in winter. She had a pen over her ear.

"Any news?" she asked.

"You'd have to ask Perrin's doctor," I said, studying a basket of muffins. "You probably know what I know."

"How long before they get forensic evidence back on the car?"

That stopped me short. "What car?"

"An officer spotted Cyd's Buick on a river frontage road about a half-mile from her apartment building," Ross said. "They've already towed it to the BCA lab."

I shook my head. "I always feel smart when I have to get this kind of news from a reporter. No offense."

"None taken," she said. Then: "A half-mile. That'd be a convenient distance for him to park his vehicle, and walk to her place for the snatch. Is that the theory?"

"Since I just heard about the car from you, I can honestly say I don't know what the theory is." I didn't add, however, that there were certain conclusions you only needed a map to draw.

"Mmm," she said. "Listen, can I buy you a cup of coffee?"

177

"No need," I said, "but I wouldn't be averse to company. Provided everything's off the record."

"Yeah, that's fine," she said.

We proceeded through the line. I ended up with a plate of spaghetti and meatballs and a garden salad, with black coffee; Ross had a blueberry muffin and a machine-dispensed drink that advertised itself as French Vanilla Cappuccino. She was a fan of the much-maligned carbohydrate.

"I thought," I said, as we took a booth by the window, "that you didn't talk off the record. How'd you put it? 'When I'm on the clock, I'm on the record'?"

Ross looked wry. "Yeah, that always impresses sources the first time they hear it. But it turns out, you never get to know anyone if you don't do a little OTR."

What she was really saying was a friendly acquaintance with me might pay off someday, a day when I'd trust her enough to speak for attribution.

"Well, I'm a low person on the totem pole," I said, cutting a meatball in half with my fork. "By next spring, I'll be an EMT. I'm not worth cultivating."

She looked at me appraisingly. "Burned out?"

"No, I just want to save lives. Sounds corny, I know."

"It seems like no one could have saved Jessie or Cyd," Ross said. "By the way, I should be above this kind of excuse-making, but it wasn't me who called Jessie Ryan a 'coed' several times in that story last week." Her mouth had tightened in distaste, which I thought I understood; it was a dated term, both sexualized and frivolous.

I raised my eyebrows. "If 'coed' wasn't your idea, how'd it get in there? On rewrite?"

"A copy editor made the replacement," Ross said, breaking apart her blueberry muffin with her hands. "So, when I get to work the next day and ask her why she put this word into my story without giving me a phone call first, she says, 'We don't make phone calls when we're just replacing a word with a synonym. *Coed* is just a word for *female student*.'"

Ross took a deep breath. "So I tell her, 'That's odd. We do a story on tuition hikes, the women we talk to are *students*. The women's basketball team is on a winning streak, the players are *student* athletes. Then, one of them gets murdered, and all of a sudden she's a *coed*.'

"That's when she contradicts her own argument about synonyms and says, 'It's more compelling.' Her exact word, 'compelling.' So I lean over and run a Web search on her own computer, on the word *coed*. I show her all the links that come up, to soft pornography and grade-B slasher movies, and I tell her, 'Does this make you wonder, just a little, what we're *compelling* readers to think about?'"

Ross smiled, as if she were happy to be getting to the worst part. "It turns out, the copy editor is here from Ohio State on an internship. She's 21 years old, and the next thing anyone knows, she's crying in the women's room because a 'veteran reporter' bitched her out."

I winced in sympathy, for which of them I wasn't quite sure.

"'Veteran reporter' is what the copy chief called me, in the meeting that was called to 'handle' this issue. I'm 27 years old, for God's sake, six years older than her. They're making it sound like I turned a 16-year-old intern over my knee and spanked her." Then she shrugged. "Probably you didn't need to hear all that, but I wanted you to know that *coed* wasn't my idea, because you're a woman. I figured you'd get it, where maybe the guys on the task force wouldn't."

When I got back to the waiting area on Cyd's floor, Donald Perrin had dozed off, his head canted over awkwardly onto the edge of his chair. For that reason, when my cell rang, I caught it as quickly as possible.

"It's me," Vang said.

His voice sounded tense and harassed — well, for him — and I immediately knew this wasn't going to be news I wanted to hear.

"My daughter's pretty sick and I'm taking her over to the after-hours pediatric clinic," he said. "Sorry, I'm not going to be able to get over there right away to spell you."

Isn't that why she has two parents? I thought, but held my tongue.

Vang seemed to read my mind. "I'd let my wife do it, but she's been dealing with this all day. She was pretty relieved to see me walk through the door. I can't turn around and go right back out. It's been a thing between us, the extra hours I'm working because of this case."

"I understand."

"I'll call Hadley. If I can't raise him, I'll come in as soon as Emmy's down for the night."

"Okay." But I looked unhappily at the industrial black-and-white clock on the wall. *As soon as Emmy's down for the night* probably meant after eight, maybe close to nine — much too late for me to get to EMT class. Not good.

There was no question, though, of me leaving before someone else arrived. If Cyd regained consciousness at all, it might be brief. One of us had to be there to hear what she might have to say.

"I'm really sorry," Vang said.

"I know. Just don't keep me here all night."

"I won't," he assured me.

The rest of the evening passed in a slow blur. Donald Perrin refused to go to his daughter's apartment and rest. Maureen Rand came by the hospital, the baby on her hip. Syed Hasan, not Hadley or Vang, arrived at 9:26 p.m., but by that time I was feeling a tired, giddy fatalism that made me stay a while longer and keep him company. We watched the late news together. Jessie and Cyd's photos ran side by side, overtly linking the two crimes. The doctor came out to talk to us, but refused to get any more hopeful about Cyd's chances. It was as if we were slowly living through her murder.

Murder was, indeed, what it was. Cydney Perrin died at four in the morning. I volunteered to attend the autopsy. "I won't argue," Hasan said, when I met him in a hospital corridor at 7 a.m. "Right now, I just want to go back to the apartment, have a shot of whiskey, kiss my wife, and go to sleep."

Lying on the medical examiner's table before the examination began, Cyd looked better than most of the murder victims I'd seen. Her head wound didn't show, and her body was otherwise unscathed. She looked as though she could have been lying on a riverbank, her hair stiff with dried river water, merely unconscious. She looked as though a kiss might awaken her.

I thought that whoever had killed her would have liked that. He might find her more lovely now than she'd been in life.

THIRTY-TWO

An investigation like the Perrin one is basically an expanding circle — a widening gyre, a poetry lover would say. It helped that Cyd had been kidnapped from where she lived: The apartment complex was Ground Zero. While I caught about five hours' sleep at home, Hadley and Vang interviewed everyone who lived in Cyd's building; they also reviewed several weeks' worth of 911 logs for calls from the city block on which the complex was located.

By early afternoon, they were in the war room with Santarella, Hasan, and me. Hadley explained that they'd been looking for the same thing in both the interviews and the logs: reports of suspicious vehicles or loitering strangers. There was nothing like that in the 911 calls; they were mostly domestic disturbances, noise complaints, and one case of chest pains.

But one neighbor, a woman who lived alone, had been troubled by the same car parked across the street on two consecutive nights: a dark sedan with a man's head clearly visible. Under Vang's careful interviewing, the woman said she felt "reasonably certain" the silhouetted head she'd seen was masculine — "you just know, you know?" — and that the sedan was an older, plainer kind. "It wasn't a rich person's car, like a Cadillac. It was something like a regular person would drive." She couldn't venture a guess as to its make, and Vang, wisely, didn't insist that she try.

After they were finished, I spoke briefly about the preliminary results of Cyd's autopsy. Santarella had the information already; I'd left him a voicemail message in the very early hours, just after the M.E. was finished. Now, for the benefit of Hadley, Vang, and Hasan, I reiterated what I'd said then: that Cyd's head injury was serious enough that she would have needed hospitalization to recover from it under any circumstances, but cause of death was shock and exposure from being thrown into the frigid Mississippi waters.

Nobody had anything to add to that. After a moment, Santarella spoke. "What about the father of the baby?" he said. "Do we know anything about him?"

Lately, he had adopted a way of sitting with his elbow on the table and his chin propped tiredly in his hand. It didn't convey confidence in whomever he was listening to at the time. I opened my notepad to support my assertions.

"Donald Perrin doesn't know who he is," I said. I'd been the one to talk with him and with Maureen Rand, the roommate. "He says that when Cyd found out she was pregnant, she just said she didn't want the father in the baby's life, and Donald left it there."

"We're going to need more than that," Santarella said. "I want to know who this guy is and where he's living lately."

Hasan spoke up: "The baby's father doesn't match the profile for these crimes."

Santarella's brows rumpled. "How do we know that without even knowing who he is?"

"The guy we're looking for is so scared of women he couldn't rape Jessie while she was conscious. Or Danielle Roback. I don't think that man would have been able to have a summer romance at a resort. And if he's already had consensual sex with Cyd, why does he need to follow her here and smash her head and have non-consensual sex?"

"Do we know for sure the sex in Lake of the Woods was consensual?" Santarella countered. "What if it wasn't?"

Hasan's mouth was a thin line, which wasn't lost on Santarella. "Look, I get that you're skeptical," he said. "I probably won't buy it either, but first I gotta see it up close and kick its tires. Meaning I want to put a name and a face to this guy. Pribek, you got this ball rolling. You might as well follow up."

That meant tracking down Cyd's circle of friends from the Lake of the Woods resort, all of whom had presumably dispersed to their homes and college campuses around the Midwest. Which meant first I'd have to track down the place's human-resources director. Who probably also had gone elsewhere, since the resort would be closed for the season. All this when Hasan was most likely right about the murderer not being the baby's father. Fantastic.

"Will do," I said, pleasantly.

But it wasn't long after reviewing my notes that I realized there might be an alternative to hunting down Cyd's companions from the lake resort. I went out into the hallway to make a quiet phone call.

"Mr. Perrin, it's Sarah Pribek again," I said. "This probably isn't the last follow-up question I'm going to have for you, but it'll be a simple one."

"Anything you need," he said.

"If you could pick one person you'd call Cydney's best friend from home, who would that be?"

"Oh," he said, slowly, "I'd say Gabrielle Murray. Do you want that phone number?"

"Sure," I said. "Can you text it to my phone right after we hang up?"

"I'll do that."

THIRTY-THREE

By six that evening, full dark, the promised snow was falling. By seven-thirty, I was in a family restaurant near the University, sitting across a booth from a young man of about 5'5 with sandy-brown hair, quick blue eyes, and fingernails that weren't clipped quite short enough to hide the grease underneath them. This was Cyd Perrin's best friend from high school, Gabriel Murray, who I'd carelessly assumed was a "Gabrielle."

Gabriel had been driving down from Morris when I'd reached him on his phone, the better to lend moral support to Donald and help with arrangements to take Cyd's body home. When he'd arrived, he'd taken a room at the same hotel near the University that Donald was staying at. Hungry from the drive, he was eating a full dinner of steak, home fries, and mixed vegetables. His good appetite had given me license to order a slice of pie along with my cup of coffee. I'd already led him through a little bit of getting-to-know-you small talk, learning that he was an auto mechanic and wasn't married, had lived in Morris all his life and wasn't planning on going anywhere else. Well-bred, Gabriel had wanted to know similar things about me, and I'd told him I was from New Mexico and had "backed into" police work after about a year at UNLV.

On the surface, it was hard to tell that Gabriel Murray's best friend had died. His eyes weren't reddened, and he was composed and calm. But numb shock can carry you through for a while, the first days after a death. And some people are stoics, plain and simple.

"You know," I told him, "when Donald gave me your name, I thought you were a girl. That was sloppy of me. I work with a lot of guys and I've always gotten along with them. I don't know why I assumed Cyd's best high-school friend would be female."

I wasn't saying that to poke gentle fun at myself; it was throat-clearing for the subject I needed to bring up next.

"What I'm saying," I continued, "is that I know guys can be good confidants, just like women can. Was your relationship with Cyd like that? Did you talk about things, or were you the kind of pals that just hung out?"

"We talked about things," he said. "Not all the time, but when there was stuff to talk about, we did."

"When Cyd came home from her summer job pregnant, I imagine that qualified."

"Oh yeah," he said, dryly.

"What was her demeanor like when she came home?"

"She seemed her usual self," he said. "I should mention that Cyd didn't know she was pregnant until she'd been home a few weeks. When she did find out, her attitude was, 'I know I screwed up.' That's what she decided to tell her Dad. I was the first person she told about the pregnancy, so mostly we talked about how she was going to break it to Donald."

"Sounds like she really trusted you," I commented. "Did Cyd tell you the baby's father's name?"

"Yeah, it was George."

"You're sure of that."

He nodded. "The last name, I can kind of estimate."

"Estimate?"

"I don't remember it outright. Is it okay if I give you the closest thing I remember?"

I nodded. "It'll give me something to go on."

"It was something like Percheron."

My notebook was open at the side of my plate. I wrote "*George Percheron,*" the quote marks reminding me the last name was an "estimate."

"What else did Cyd tell you about him and their relationship?"

"He was from Louisiana and came north every year for resort work. He did maintenance on the boats," he said. "Cyd said he had a sexy accent and played the guitar and had a 'certain something-something.' She said she'd have advised a girlfriend not to get involved with a guy like him."

"But she didn't take her own advice."

"No," Gabriel said.

"And she never contacted him about the pregnancy."

"No."

"You're a man. How'd you feel about that decision, the decision to cut him entirely out of his kid's life?"

"I thought it was a *great* decision," he said, cutting a neat slice off his steak. "This guy already had two kids by two baby mamas back in Louisiana, which is where he lived most of the year, and according to Cyd, he didn't have enough money to support *those* children." He studied my face, checking to see if I found him too judgmental. "Look, when I have kids, I'm not just going to support them; I'm going to *raise* them. Why should I get bent out of shape about this guy's father's rights?"

It was a question that didn't demand an answer, which was good, because I was still thinking about the first part of his response: two kids with two baby mamas. That clearly indicated an active, consensual sex life. That didn't line up with our suspect and his smash-from-behind, rape-and-run MO. Hasan had been right.

"You sound like you've already spent some time thinking about marriage and fatherhood," I commented. "What about Cyd? Did you ever think of her that way?"

"Lots of people ask me that, or her about me," he said. "We aren't like that. I mean, weren't. We both loved barbecue; we both followed the Packers. We had a lot in common, so we were pals."

It sounded like a better basis for marriage than that of many couples I knew, but I understood what he was saying. I flipped my notebook closed, indicating the formal part of the interview was over. While

Gabriel finished his dinner, and I switched to decaf, we talked about American muscle cars and their most common mechanical problems. Eventually, I turned the subject to his life in outstate Minnesota and why he'd chosen to make his adult home there, instead of striking out to see the world.

"Why should I leave?" he said, lifting a shoulder. "I like where I grew up. I like small-town life."

When the check came, I reached for it but was too slow. "I got it," Gabriel said casually, moving the folder out of my reach.

I frowned. "This was official business. Let me."

"No, I got it." His tone was pleasant but very direct, suggesting that he was a man and I was a woman, and this was the natural order of things. I sat back, mildly surprised and a little charmed. I couldn't remember a time when a witness had picked up a check for me, much less a young man on a mechanic's pay. Cyd Perrin, I thought, could have done a lot worse than to have seen Gabriel Murray as more than a friend.

Thirty-Four

Gabriel Murray had been close; the man he loosely identified as "George Percheron" turned out to be Georges Bergeron. I learned that from the HR director at the Lake of the Woods resort, whom I finally reached on the phone. After that, using various government databases, I'd learned that Bergeron had a minor criminal record, a disorderly conduct charge that stemmed from a bar fight. He'd never, though, lived in Missoula. About two weeks before the attack on Danielle Roback, he'd appeared at a court hearing in Shreveport due to nonpayment of child support, and his current address was in Bossier City.

That satisfied Santarella. "If we had to, we could've gotten a buccal-cell swab for DNA from the baby and run a parentage index," he told me. What he meant was that a cheek-cell swab, resulting in DNA from Daniel Perrin, could have told us if Daniel was the biological son of the unknown man who'd left DNA on both Jessie Ryan and Danielle Roback. "I just didn't want to go that route, asking the grandfather for consent, even though a cheek swab is painless."

He yawned and rubbed the heels of his hands against his cheeks. "I should have bowed to Hasan's superior knowledge in the first place."

"Syed's smart," I agreed, "but I think you were right. It had to be checked out."

❖ ❖ ❖

That Friday, the widening gyre of our investigation continued to grow, as we interviewed and re-interviewed those who'd known Cyd. Her friends characterized her as goodhearted but wised-up. Definitely not naive, they said. It was hard to imagine her falling for a strange man's ruse to gain her trust.

In late afternoon, more results from the medical examiner's office came in, and we met a half-hour earlier than usual to go over them. Cyd's tox screen was negative; she had no poisons in her system, no alcohol or drugs. The DNA matched that of Danielle Roback's attacker and Jessie Ryan's killer. We were three-for-three. No one was surprised; we'd already had to operate on that assumption.

Hadley, though, had unexpected news.

"It's not part of official procedure yet," he told us, "but one of the technicians at the lab is interested in antibody profiling," he said. "You all know what that is?"

Santarella, Vang, and Hasan nodded, but I had to half-raise my hand and shake my head, outing myself as the only one ignorant.

Hadley looked at me, then at Santarella, and said, "You mind if I fill her in? It'll be re-runs to you guys."

Santarella nodded as much as he could with his chin in his hand.

Hadley turned back to me and said, "Basically, it's an alternative to DNA profiling — a way of proving or disproving identity, using the antibodies in your system. Think of it like your skin. By the time you die of old age and you're on a slab, your body's been banged around a bit. You'll have a few wound scars, maybe a surgical scar, maybe tattoos. It's probably safe to say that by death, the sum total of markings you have on your skin is unique to you."

"Gotcha," I said.

"Well, your immune system does the same thing, knocks around getting exposed to stuff and making antibodies, and you don't even have to be very old before you have your own antibody signature. No two people get exposed to the same things in the same amounts, so everyone's walking around with a different set of antibodies. In fact, statistically speaking, it's unique. With me so far?"

I nodded.

"What makes antibody profiling useful is that unlike DNA, you don't need cellular material to do it, or even blood; antibodies are in all the bodily fluids. In fact, antibody profiling predates DNA testing in a sense, because the old blood-type tests we used to do on blood found at crime scenes — you know, 'the guy we're looking for is A negative' — is a form of antibody testing. You can't test for blood type *per se*, just for the antibodies your body makes to attack foreign blood types."

"Interesting," I said. "But why are our techs still doing that, if it's dated?"

"Because this isn't just a blood-type test anymore, it's a test for the whole antibody signature," Hadley said. "Which my friend the tech thinks is fascinating, so she ran one on the semen we recovered from Perrin's body."

"And?" Santarella prompted.

"And, she found something really unusual: the antibody for lyssavirus rabies. Just to be sure, she went back and tested the blood from under Jessie Ryan's fingernails, too. No mistake; she got the same result."

"Our guy has *rabies?*" Vang said.

"Well, no, presumably not an active infection, since that leads pretty quickly to death," Hadley said. "What we're probably looking at is a guy who got the shots. Most likely it was after an animal bite, but it could have been as a precaution. People at risk get vaccinated, like wildlife-rehab workers or people who work in dairies."

"Dairies?" Santarella said, eyebrows rising.

"Cows get infected more than people realize. It's what's called a 'spillover' infection from the existing infected population, which is usually some kind of wildlife. In Minnesota, that'd be skunk."

Santarella leaned back thoughtfully. "Now, that's interesting," he said. "Not the skunk part, the workers-at-risk part. I think it'd be worth our while to cross-reference sex offenders with guys who've worked in animal husbandry or wildlife rehab. Sky, you opened up this new avenue, you want to take point on that?"

"Will do," Hadley said.

"The other thing is this," Santarella said. "Since the morning she went missing, we've been focusing all our attention on Cyd. Which is only natural; she's the newer victim and the fresher trail. But I don't want Jessie Ryan falling by the wayside. There still might be things to learn from her case." He tapped his pencil against the table. "Pribek, you did the initial victimology on her. Re-read the file and do follow-up interviews with her friends and family as you think necessary. Someone might remember something the second time around."

THIRTY-FIVE

When I caught up with Angie Eastman, Jessie's roommate, she was on the front porch of her house having a cigarette. As I shut off the engine of the Ford I'd checked out of the motor pool, she exhaled a long plume of smoke into the air.

When I'd called her last night, she'd said that her roommate Kori would be gone most of the morning, which suited me fine. Often it was helpful to talk to witnesses separately. Once again I was making a circle, but this time it went in the opposite direction, inward, tightening. I'd talk to Angie first, then to a few other casual friends. Then to Kori, who'd said she knew Jessie better than most, and from there I'd likely re-interview the mother and sister. Jessie herself was the center of the circle, but, of course, she was the one witness I could never reach.

"Hi, Detective Pribek," Angie said. "You want one?" She held out a pack of cigarettes with an Indian-head logo on it.

"No, thanks, I don't smoke anymore." I never really had, except a few times to be rebellious in high school, or to be sociable in college. But when you needed to bond with young people, *I don't smoke anymore* sounded less square than just *I don't smoke.*

Angie tossed the cigarette down into the snow. Then she held the screen door for me and we went in.

At the kitchen table, I asked her outright if there was anything new she'd thought of since the first time we'd talked. She said no. After that, I took her through the days leading up to Jessie's death: how much she'd seen her roommate, what they'd talked about, how Jessie had acted. I asked if anyone new had been by the house, if there were any repairmen or landscapers in the neighborhood, or if a car Angie didn't recognize had been parked near the house for long hours or on successive nights. She told me that Jessie had seemed normal, and that she hadn't seen a new car or any strange men around in the days leading up to Jessie's murder.

"You really should talk to Kori," Angie said. "She knew Jessie for longer than I did."

"I will," I said.

"I just got to know Jessie over the summer," she continued, "when they invited me to live here. They had the house together for all the previous school year, but with another girl who went home to Duluth for summer break."

"Jessie stayed here over the summer?" I asked. "That seems odd, given that her family is so close by."

"She wanted to stay," Angie said. "That's why she and Kori needed a third person, otherwise they'd end up splitting the whole rent. So Kori invited me to meet Jessie during finals. We all got along okay, and I moved in."

"Did you like her?"

"Sure," Angie said. "We weren't super close," she put up her hand and crossed her fingers, "which was why I wasn't one of her pallbearers at the funeral."

"That's right," I said, remembering the young women raising the heavy casket to their shoulders. "Whose idea was that?"

Angie thought for a second. "I couldn't tell you," she said. "Two nights before the service, Kori got together with some of Jessie's other friends, and when Kori came home, they'd come up with the pallbearer idea. That and the black ribbons, which I thought was really cool."

"Why?" I said. They'd seemed a generic statement to me: memorial ribbons in the traditional color of mourning.

"Because they chose black ribbons because of the black-skates thing."

"What black-skates thing?"

"Oh," she said, "Jessie told us that back when she was skating, she wanted a pair of black skates for competition. She just thought they looked more eye-catching than white ones. But her coach flipped out, told her she couldn't, because black skates would give the judges the impression of a 'bad girl.'" Angie shook her head. "She told us that so we'd understand how uptight the world of figure skating is. A little thing like that, wearing black skates instead of white, it would've made her a *bad seed.*"

"Jessie wanted to rebel?" I said.

"Not really. I think she wanted to change how people viewed her, but deep down, Jessie was never a 'bad girl.' She didn't smoke, she didn't really drink at all. She dressed hot, and she talked about sex like she was *dying* to get her freak on, but I got the feeling it was an act. She was always in her own bed on Friday and Saturday nights."

"You think she was a closet prude?"

"No, not a prude," Angie said. "I just think she was controlled. Like, really controlled. Her weight was always a perfect 115 pounds, her room was always clean. During really stressful times, like finals, she used to even leave a piece of foil-wrapped chocolate on her pillow for the end of the day."

"Really?"

"Yeah. Kori and I used to tease her about it, because it was something like a hotel maid would do." She paused. "When you found the pictures in her underwear drawer, it seemed out of character at first, then it started to make sense to me. There were hundreds of fairly hot guys around her, many of whom would've taken her to paradise for a night, but she had porn. Because porn's something you're in control of."

Control, I repeatedly, mentally. It was everyone's favorite illusion, that we were in control of our lives. Some of us chased that dream harder than others.

197

Not long after, I met Kori at a coffeehouse on the West Bank. She told me much the same things that Angie had. Jessie was controlled, studious, an exercise fanatic, but sweet and fun, too — and she'd seemed her usual self in the days leading up to her death.

Before this interview was even over, I'd more or less decided that Santarella had sent me on a wasted errand. We were almost certain that the attack on Jessie was a crime of opportunity, meaning our guy had seen her running and made an impulse decision to attack her. So why was I talking to her roommates about her demeanor in the days leading up to the attack?

I guess that's why I asked Kori about the female pallbearers. I had nowhere better to take the conversation.

"I...it was a group decision," Kori said. "We just wanted to do this for her."

"Why, though? She had male relatives."

"I know, but we'd lived with her, we were her friends. We wanted it to be girls taking care of girls until the...until the end."

She tipped her face down, keeping tears at bay. I put one hand on her shoulder until the moment passed.

Afterward, in the car again, I looked over the few notes I'd made. Nothing leapt out at me as significant, underscoring my sense that I'd wasted valuable time. I leaned my forehead against the glass of the driver's-side window, then almost immediately lifted it off again, embarrassed at the brief moment of self-dramatization. It was too easy, since Silverhus had fallen through as our chief suspect, to fall into gloom. All of us felt it; though they said nothing, I saw it on the faces of Vang and Hadley, of Santarella, even of the usually placid Syed Hasan.

Late-afternoon light, golden and cidery, limned the rooftops of the West Bank. The days were getting so short. It was hard not to feel that we were running out of time.

THIRTY-SIX

There are two schools of thought on facing brutal upper-Midwest winters: One is to go to ground, cranking up the thermostat, cracking open a good long book you've been meaning to get to, bundling yourself in goosedown when you have to venture outdoors. The second was to push back hard against winter, making no concessions. These were the people whose flaming Weber grills you saw in entry alcoves in mid-January, or who took out a garden hose and watered the icy front lawn to make a rink for the kids to skate on.

Then there were the exercise nuts: the cyclists who wore latex gloves under their fingerless ones so their hands wouldn't go completely nerveless with cold. And the runners who laced up their shoes and ran on the wet shining winter roads. That last was me, keeping up a practice I'd started as a teenager on the Iron Range.

After I got home from EMT class that night – a skills-lab night, one that I'd been profoundly relieved not to miss — the mercury in our front-porch thermometer was hovering at 23 degrees. But when I headed out for a run, the air felt cold and clean in my lungs, and I was hoping it'd clear my head, as well.

I ran as far as the bridge overlooking the Van Buren railway yards. A woman ran by in the opposite direction with a rotund Lab mix jogging beside her. He was having trouble keeping up with her, but his jaw was split in a panting smile, as if delighted to be out in the cold. He reminded me of the Lab that Silverhus had brought to the vet ER.

On the bridge, I stopped to pace, watching clouds of steam, tinted orange from sodium lights, roil upward to the nearly starless urban sky.

The truth was, Steven Silverhus and his miracle exoneration had never gotten very far from my mind. A stranger's dog had bled all over the trunk of Steven's car the very week he became a prime suspect in an abduction-murder. I didn't believe in coincidences like that. A dark sedan, like the one Silverhus drove, had been seen near each abduction site. I didn't believe in coincidences like that one, either.

I couldn't help it: I still liked him for it.

Nothing that grew out of that was good. First and simplest, it'd irritate Santarella. He'd already told me once not to "get married" to one suspect, and he had good reason. There are few worse characteristics in an investigator than mental inflexibility. To see that, we only had to look back at the sniper killings in Maryland and D.C. years ago, committed by two black men while everyone was fixated on the *lone white male* profile.

My heart rate had slowed to far below where I wanted it. Dismissing the case from my mind, I turned and headed back toward home.

When I came in through the back door, abandoning my dirty jogging shoes in the entryway, the kitchen was well-lighted, and Temple was making a grilled cheese sandwich for dinner. That was no surprise: the grilled cheese was a cornerstone of her diet.

"Someone called for you. Said his name was Jeremy," she told me, glancing away from her cooking.

"Jackson?" I said, thinking of Jessie Ryan's unrequited crush. It was rare enough for us to get calls on the house's landline, and I certainly hadn't given that number to Jeremy Jackson.

"Lambert," Temple corrected.

Lambert? That name was not familiar to me; I could feel my brows draw down in perplexity.

THIRTY-SEVEN

Driving across the Wisconsin countryside on Sunday morning, I found myself pursuing the forbidding clouds that had only just rolled out of the Cities. I pushed the Nova up to a higher speed than either the posted signs or the conditions called for, because this was a long trip, and I didn't have enough time off from work to stay overnight somewhere.

Jeremy Lambert, who had called yesterday, was a young guard at the prison where Shiloh was serving his time. He'd had an unusual offer: He'd asked if I'd like to visit my husband sometime outside normal visitors' hours — and, he added, in a more private location. Normally, with the investigation and night school demanding all my time, I wouldn't have been able to accept right away. But this was Sunday, and I hadn't taken a full day off from the investigation since the first day, when Jessie's body had been found.

"I'm here to see Jeremy Lambert," I said when I reached the entrance. Not technically true, but simplest.

The guard glanced down at a clipboard and nodded — I was expected — and made a phone call. A few minutes passed. The guard and I didn't make conversation, but neither did he go back to the techno-thriller he'd discreetly put aside when I'd approached.

A tall young man approached. He wore a stiff prison uniform but had an easy gait, and his face was broad and open. His blond hair looked as though it might curl if he let it grow any longer.

"Mrs. Shiloh?" The voice was familiar from our phone conversation.

"That's me."

"I'll take you up," Lambert said. "Your drive was okay?"

"Yes, it was fine," I said, following him.

"Sometimes the smaller roads around here get pretty bad. It helps to have four-wheel, do you have four-wheel?"

"No," I said, "but I'm used to what I drive."

"Mike says you're a detective. You must be pretty smart, like him."

Intelligent people will never know where words like those touch someone like me, someone who hasn't forgotten years of being an average student, semesters of pencil chewing over exams and succeeding only by working longer and harder.

"Not like him," I said.

We'd passed what I knew to be the visiting area. "Where are we going?" I asked.

"The medical wing," Lambert said.

Holy shit. Lambert had asked me to come, and now Shiloh was in the medical wing. Suddenly, I heard doctors' voices from my childhood: *We were out of surgery way ahead of schedule. It'll just be palliative care from here.* Disembodied auditory memories from my mother's last illness.

"Oh, no, it's nothing like that," Lambert said, reading my face. "Mike's fine. He's just waiting for you there."

The relief was like a shockwave, quick but intense. "Waiting for me?" I said. "I don't understand."

Lambert unlocked a door with a solid deadbolt above its handle and a cross-hatched window of safety glass. "Mike's a good guy," he said. "I owe him a favor. This was my idea."

We walked past an examining room, dark in disuse, then supply closets and rooms with shut doors and uses not known to me. Then Jeremy tapped on an unmarked door at the end of the hall, and, without waiting for an answer, opened it.

The room was very unlike a hospital room. There was a twin bed, low to the floor, covered in a counterpane; a simple nightstand and a freestanding wardrobe, both of cheap composite wood. One high bookshelf held a Bible and several books of prayers and devotions.

Shiloh turned from the window, where he'd been looking out at an empty field blanketed in unbroken snow. He was wearing the gray shirt and jeans of prison issue I'd seen him in before, and while his hair was short, it wasn't clipped as close as I would have expected.

"I'll be outside," Lambert said to him, "but not *right* outside, you know."

"Thanks, Jeremy," Shiloh said.

I understood now what Lambert had arranged for us. Shiloh had always spoken of conjugal visits with scorn. *Going out to some trailer for sixty minutes with guards knowing what you're doing in there. It's like some kind of government-run breeding project.* This wasn't like that. Clearly it was privately arranged between Shiloh and the guard he seemed to have a friendship with.

"Hey," I said. "What is this place?"

"A sickroom," he said. "Like everyone else, sometimes inmates get terminal illnesses. Usually they get a compassionate release when that happens and are sent home. But there are older ones, sometimes, who don't have any family. The ones who are used to prison, who've spent more time inside than outside. You know?"

I nodded.

"It'd be cruel to send those ones out to die alone on the streets, so that's why they have this room. It's like a hospice; they don't get treatment, just a comfortable place for the last weeks. It's done on the QT. Prison officials don't show this place off to the media, because then the state legislature would probably get involved. They'd want some kind of system for deciding who gets to use it, and whether the prison's budget should pay medical staff or if the money should come from somewhere else, and pretty soon the whole thing would be suspended indefinitely for 'further study.' You know how that goes." He looked more closely at me. "I've made you sad."

"No, I'm okay." But a silence followed that wasn't entirely comfortable. We were both suddenly reticent, unwilling to get close enough even to touch. So, after a moment, I filled the silence: "Listen, there's something I've really been wanting to ask you. It's about work."

"Work?"

"I hate to talk shop right now," I said, and I was sure my regret showed on my face. "But this might be our only opportunity. Most of the details of the case I'm working on are confidential, and your mail's monitored, so…" I lifted a shoulder.

"Go on."

"Can you think of a way that someone could cheat a DNA test, if he voluntarily gave a blood sample under textbook lab conditions?"

"Are you serious?" he said.

"You mean, am I serious about someone cheating a DNA test? Or am I seriously bringing it up at this moment?"

"The first thing."

"Yes, I am," I affirmed. "I know it's hard to wrap your mind around. DNA's like a religion for cops."

I'd been wanting to ask this question of Shiloh partly because he'd been a cold-case detective, and cold-case work, more than other subsets of homicide, demands a strong working knowledge of lab technology. But I also asked because Shiloh been considering medical school before being drawn almost unwillingly into police work. Medical science had always interested him.

"I never had to think about it before," Shiloh said. "You're sure it was a blood sample?"

"Yeah. I saw the guy give the blood, right in front of me."

"So this isn't a theoretical."

"Not at all."

"Offhand, I'd say…" he broke off, thinking. That moment stretched on before he finally said, "Nothing comes to mind."

"It didn't for me, either," I said, discouraged.

Shiloh came close to me, but not close enough to touch, as if saying he wouldn't encroach on my space without some sign of encouragement. Though we'd fallen into a comfortable rhythm in our letters, this was different. Things hadn't been easy between us since he'd gone to Blue Earth, since the days when he'd disappeared and I'd had to wonder if he were dead.

Not that I didn't have my own transgressions to own up to. Shiloh's, at least, were in the open between us.

"What's the favor you did for Jeremy?" I asked, finally. "He doesn't look like he needs any help breaking up fights."

"Oh, that," Shiloh said, equally relieved to be on more solid ground. "No, it wasn't a fight. Jeremy had a girlfriend; they'd been going out two years but were having troubles, and she packed up and moved to Milwaukee. Then he heard through the grapevine that her mother had died and she'd gone home to Louisiana for the funeral. He wanted to write a letter so it'd be waiting at her place in Milwaukee when she got back, but he doesn't write very well. He's not illiterate, just — "

"Couldn't find the words."

"Yeah. I helped him with what he wanted to say, about how he'd always thought her mother was special and he would miss her too, and how he hoped Charmaine, that's his girlfriend, was okay in Milwaukee, that he just wanted her to be happy, with or without him." Shiloh paused. "I didn't tell him what to say, just how to phrase it. She came to see him after she got the letter, and they decided to make another go of it. Jeremy told me about it, and then he thought of this. Bringing you here."

"That's great," I said. Then: "You look older. I mean … you've lost weight." I felt like Jeremy, needing someone to help me with the words.

"Prison food is about what you'd expect," he said, smiling. "You look the same. You look good." He moved closer, laid his hands gently on my ribcage. "Sarah, I didn't bring you here just to … I mean, if it doesn't feel right … "

"No, I want to," I said. "But there's something I have to tell you. I …"

When I broke off, Shiloh looked at me with his serious-minded curiosity. I sat down on the edge of the bed.

Since the summer, I'd known eventually I'd have to tell Shiloh about Cicero Ruiz. But I'd thought that moment wouldn't come until we were both on the outside. I hadn't expected to have this moment of both intimacy and privacy inside prison walls.

Shiloh sat down beside me and laid one hand over mine, prompting me without words. But I couldn't talk. My throat was stiffening as if I were going to cry.

Goddammit, I thought. Why did I feel I had to do this? Why couldn't I just give us this one brief good hour together?

"Last summer," I said finally, "there was someone else."

He didn't take his hand away, but I felt the words register.

"It was really short-lived. Just two times."

"Was it…" Shiloh spoke carefully, "was it someone I know?"

The question took me aback, but then I realized what he was really asking: He wanted to know if it had been Christian Kilander.

"No." I shook my head emphatically. "No, it wasn't."

Shiloh nodded, took a steadying breath. "Is it over?"

"Yes," I said. "It was just that… I admired him. He was a fine person, better than me. I know it doesn't excuse anything."

Shiloh pulled me against him and spoke quietly against my hair. "It's not always easy to be good," he said. "I should know."

"I'm sorry."

"I know. I know you are. It's all right."

I put my arms around him and my face in his neck, and the spasm of grief passed. "I miss you," I said.

"It won't be that much longer." Shiloh put me away from him just far enough to kiss me on the mouth.

"Shiloh, wait." I pulled back. "Don't do anything to screw up your release, all right?"

"Don't worry about that right now." He began pulling my shirt up.

"No, I mean it. I know how you are. At your parole hearing, just tell them what they want to — "

"Shhh." He kissed me under my chin, along my throat, a line of kisses. "Stop thinking about the future. Just be here."

He exerted a gentle pressure on my shoulders. The blanket on the sickbay bed felt deliciously coarse under the skin of my back as I lay down. "Shiloh," I said. "Oh, God."

"Easy. Slower than that."

"I can't. Don't tease."

"Wait, Sarah. I've waited."

But it was very quick after that.

THIRTY-EIGHT

Afterward, my skin felt sensitized all over, cool and warm at once. I was lying against Shiloh's chest; I'd almost forgotten what a comforting sensation that was. He'd never been muscular in the way of cops I knew who spent all their free time in the weight room; Shiloh had a long runner's build instead. But he was Shiloh, fierce and implacable in defense of people he loved, and that alone made lying in his arms like being in the protected waters behind a sea wall.

Then, Shiloh shifted his weight, suggesting that he wanted to get up and get dressed. There was a limit to the privacy even this secret room could confer. Outside these walls were hundreds of strangers. The pressure of modesty was closing in. I sat up, and he followed suit.

But when I saw Shiloh's face, he looked troubled in a way I couldn't explain. "Is something wrong?"

He shook his head.

I got off the narrow bed and began collecting my clothes. When I looked up again, he hadn't moved toward his own abandoned clothing at all. He was watching me.

"What?" I said.

"Was that — " he looked pointedly down at the mattress, " —was that kind of quick for you?"

"What? No, it was good."

"Are you sure?"

"Of course. Couldn't you tell?"

"I thought so, but I've been celibate a year, and unlike you, I haven't have recourse to other people."

Recourse to other people. It took a fraction of a second to register what that meant, that he was referring to my infidelity.

"You're angry with me," I said.

He shrugged.

"I thought you said — "

"That I understood about you being unfaithful?" he interrupted. "Yes, I said it. But I've been without sex a year, and you were sitting two inches away. On a *bed.* It made for a good distraction. In the harsh light of day, it might take a little longer than thirty seconds for me to get over this."

I swallowed involuntarily. This was where I was supposed to speak, to say something conciliatory, but everything I could think of — *I understand, take all the time you need* — felt patronizing. Finally I took refuge in the basic actions of getting dressed.

Maybe silence was the best tactic, because Shiloh sighed, arching his back and shoulders and then dropping his head to look down at the floor. Then he said, "Look, I'll get over it. I just need a little time."

"Okay," I said quietly, and out of the corner of my eye, I saw him start gathering his things, as well.

Before I left, he kissed me on the forehead. It wasn't a lover's kiss, but he was making an effort. Then he gave me back to Jeremy.

THIRTY-NINE

Santarella, at Monday's meeting, was in a dark mood. He had both of the Twin Cities' newspapers in front of him. The boldface headline on the *Pioneer Press*'s A1 read: **Few leads, little progress in slayings.** But it was the *Star Tribune* from which Santarella read aloud. Not a news story, but the Monday-morning contribution of a metro columnist.

"Former Captain Roy Nedegaard of the Minnesota State Patrol stands straight and tall," he read, "his posture befitting the paramilitary organization he served for almost three decades. But don't let his bearing deceive you: Roy Nedegaard is tired. Tired of waiting for information that doesn't come from the men and women investigating his beloved granddaughter's death."

Santarella went on as the columnist laid out Nedegaard's complaint: not just that Jessie's killer remained uncaught, but that the task force led by Joseph Santarella of the BCA was inaccessible, unwilling to share what leads and information they had obtained. Finally, when the writer backtracked to recap the basic points about Jessie and Cyd's murders, Santarella laid the newspaper down on the table.

"Cripes, I've been as responsive as I can with this guy," he said. "Nothing short of being invited to sit at this table with us is going to make him happy. Not that he told this guy — " indicating the column, "that."

Hasan leaned forward. "There's something interesting about the lead," he said. "The posture thing. A columnist isn't going to know

211

that from talking to someone on the phone. Nedegaard went to the newsroom in person."

"That sounds like him," Santarella said. "Look, bottom line, we catch someone and Nedegaard will shut up about our responsiveness." His impatient dark eyes ranged around the table, landing on me. "Pribek, you've been re-interviewing Ryan's peers. What'd you learn?"

"Nothing new, I'm sorry to say," I told him. "Her roommates said the same things the second time around: nobody strange around the house, no odd phone calls."

Santarella frowned. "Come on, that's not enough. You've got to have learned something new."

Down in my stomach, I felt the old tension from school days: caught unprepared by the teacher. I leafed quickly through my notebook, but already I knew there was nothing there to help. Yet —

"Jessie was different from how I'd been thinking of her," I said, slowly. "And different from how people around her viewed her."

"Go on," Santarella said.

"Angie told me this story about her wanting to wear black skates in competition, back in her figure-skating days. Her coach wouldn't let her, because black was for 'bad girls.' When she told me that, I remembered how I first came up with the theory that Jessie had gone running the night she died because her everyday workout shoes, the black ones, were missing. The ones in her closet were white. She didn't like her white Nikes as well." I could hear myself rambling. *Focus.*

"What I'm trying to say is, it seems like Jessie was always being pushed into the role of perfect daughter, perfect granddaughter, obedient white-skates girl. Part of her, maybe most of her, played along with it. But part of her wanted to break out of that mold and rebel."

Around the table were only uncomprehending faces. Hasan tried to help: "You think that Jessie had secrets from her family and roommates? Maybe she acted out in a way that put her in the path of her killer?"

I shook my head. "No, I still think our guy saw her running and made his decision on the fly. I just...she was so easy to sum up, an evening-news-friendly all-American girl. I bought into that too. I feel like I missed things about her, these hidden depths."

The guys were still looking at me with polite confusion and probably, underneath, a mild embarrassment. *You know women: Everything's personal for them. Send them out to solve someone's death, and they end up trying to solve their life.*

"Sorry," I said to Santarella. "I told you I didn't have anything. I've got a call in to Jessie's mother, to ask if I can talk to the younger sister again, but I haven't heard back yet."

"Well, stay on it," he said, his voice half a sigh.

He tipped back in his chair. "Here's something else. I know we didn't turn up any matches between sex offenders and guys who'd be eligible for rabies vaccination. But maybe we've been looking at this the wrong way. I think it's possible our guy is homeless."

That caught everyone's attention; Vang, in particular, looked up from his notes curiously.

"Look at the evidence." Santarella raised a hand and began counting off on his fingers. "One, Jessie was attacked near the riverbank, and Cyd lived along the river, too. It's where a lot of homeless people have their squats. Two, the killer used Cyd's car to transport her, which fits with him not having one of his own. Three, and this is most important, rabies exposure fits with someone who lives outdoors. Wild-land creatures carry rabies, with bats as a very frequent source of human infections. Homeless people are at risk because they're outdoors all the time."

Silence stretched out as we all considered his words. I saw the merit in what some of what Santarella had said, but not his second point. The killer had used Cyd's car, but only gone half a mile in it, which to me suggested a transfer to a second car he'd wanted to keep out of sight.

I was still weighing whether I should point this out when Vang spoke up. "Where'd he kill Jessie, then?" he asked. "She was drowned in a bathtub."

"She was drowned in municipal water, that's all we really know," Santarella corrected him. "He could have killed her by holding her head down in a sink, a bucket, anything."

He brought the chair down onto its front feet again, from the leaning-back position. "You know the main thing I don't like about this theory? It's labor-intensive. I want us to talk with the homeless population along the river and near the University, but we're going to need uniforms to help with that. That means overtime, which is a budget issue." He frowned, clicked his pen on and off. "I'll run it by Command, see how many hours they can give us. Bottom line is, you three — " he looked at Vang, Hadley and me, "are going to have to spend some shoe leather on this."

Hasan spoke up: "Let me help."

Santarella looked at him, mildly surprised.

"I know I'm here to do the psych side of things, but what good's a profiler with no suspects to profile?" Hasan asked. "My leg's not going to slow me down any. Let me get out in the field awhile."

"I can't think why not," Santarella said.

Hasan looked at the rest of us and said, "One thing I'd point out before we get started: Let's be careful. Some of these people aren't in close touch with reality. If they think they witnessed something, make sure they didn't also see JFK at the railing of a 19th-century riverboat a week before that."

FORTY

That evening, I once again had a glass of scotch over ice rather than my usual Heineken. It had been that kind of day.

No, that wasn't entirely true. Class had gone all right. The midterm was fast approaching, this Friday, and I felt in command of the material. The homeless-population interviews hadn't netted any promising leads yet, but they'd had to be done.

The truth was, I was still faintly itching with embarrassment over my botched summation of the Jessie Ryan interviews. At first, I blamed Santarella. He was grasping at straws and pushing his people to produce, that was understandable. But I didn't have to let him push me into a rambling off-the-cuff summary of, essentially, nothing.

Except, was it really nothing? What *had* I been trying to tell my boss?

Between my original interviews and the new ones today, a coherent picture of Jessie had emerged: a rigid, controlled young woman in the package of a sexily dressed, carefree college girl – the guise of a *coed*, as Rosamund Ross might irritably say. Jessie had exercised religiously and controlled her weight to the point that Kori had worried about an eating disorder. She had kept her room tidy as a hotel maid might, even leaving a piece of chocolate on her pillow during stressful times.

She'd had some sex issues, too, if Jeremy Jackson was any indication. She'd accused him of abandoning her for another girl because she hadn't had sex with him the very first night they'd kissed. More than that, according to Angie, Jessie had talked like she couldn't wait to get some action, but then she never really followed through. Jessie had downloaded pornography instead, a safe and private expression of sexuality.

I leaned back on the couch and propped my feet on the edge of the coffeetable — Temple and I had let it get piled up with mail and magazines and empty coffee cups, and the edge was the only place my boots could find. Tipping my head back, I closed my eyes.

Let it go, I told myself. *You didn't miss anything. You did what your boss asked, but there was nothing new to find.*

For a moment, my mind brought me only scent memories from the day's work: river water, decomposing leaves, and humus. The smells of the homeless squats where Hasan and I had talked to the unfortunate and the broken-minded at the river's edge of the Mississippi. Then one visual memory: a bird's nest that had fallen from a tree into the mud.

Are not two sparrows sold for one penny? Yet not one of them will fall to the ground apart from your Father.

The pallbearers were rising under Jessie Ryan's heavy black coffin. Not strong men. Not even really women, yet. Slight as sparrows; still only girls. *Girls taking care of girls until the end.*

My boot heel slipped off the edge of the coffee table, and its impact with the wooden floor rang up my body, jarring me out of reverie. All at once, I realized what I'd been missing about Jessie Ryan.

Emotional rigidity, strict control of diet and exercise, a push-pull mix of fear and fascination with sex: all of these were markers of childhood sexual abuse. But more than anything, it was the female pallbearers that clinched it for me. Jessie had had male relatives, her grandfather chief among them, who could have served in that typically male role. But her friends had insisted on doing it. They'd kept Jessie out of the hands of a male relative on the day of her burial. Somehow, without knowing, they'd known.

It wasn't anything to do with her murder, and it was just a theory. Yet suddenly I felt very sure of it, and certain that Roy Nedegaard was the abuser.

Part of my conviction on that was simply a numbers game: Who else was there? Jessie's father was dead, and she had no stepfather and no brothers. She'd had male relatives, but there was only one who'd been under the same roof with her for years, with that dangerous blend of intimacy and access. That was Roy Nedegaard, who'd been all bluster and rhetoric since his older granddaughter's death, calling Jessie the "gold in our sunshine," calling on old contacts in law enforcement and rattling his saber until the forces rallied to pursue Jessie's killer. Was that overcompensation for his guilt?

I retrieved my phone and sat down at the kitchen table. Santarella answered on the third ring.

"It's me," I said. "I've been thinking about Jessie Ryan. I have a new theory, but it's probably not going to be what you're expecting."

"Shoot," he said.

"I think Jessie Ryan might have been sexually abused at home."

Long pause. Then: "By the father, you mean, as a child?"

"By the grandfather," I said.

Concisely, I went over the red flags I'd seen in Jessie's behavior, as recounted by the people who knew her. When I was done, Santarella said, "It's kind of a leap. I mean, you're only getting this stuff from her friends."

"Well, I have to. The subject of the abuse — sorry, possible abuse — is dead."

"True," Santarella said. "But that's the other thing. Say you're right. When molestation is reported, it generally leads to a separation of child and abuser. Sometimes, later, there's a civil suit by the victim. It's too late for any of that for Jessie. Not to be cynical, but what difference does it make now?"

"Jen," I said, remembering her worming out from under Roy's arm at the funeral. "It's common for abusers to move on to a younger child. If he did it to one granddaughter, he could have done it to the other. Could still be doing it." I paused. "I was planning on talking to her anyway, somewhere away from her family. The mother and grandfather were both in the room during my first interview. For a teenager, that's not conducive to openness."

217

"I can see that."

"But I need your permission to take the interview in this new direction, the sex abuse."

He thought a moment about that. "Where do you want to interview her?"

"Downtown," I said. "And I want to pick her up from school myself. It'll take time out of my working day, but she doesn't drive yet, her mother works, and we can't let her grandfather do it. We'll never get anything out of her if she knows he's the first person she'll see when she walks out of the interview room."

"Agreed," he said. "But consider this from another angle. You're taking her into a sphere of police power and authority. In that environment, she might need to please you more than usual, which could lead to — "

"Fabrication? I doubt Jen's going to tell us that sex abuse happened if it didn't, no matter how intimidating her surroundings."

"She might not say she was abused," Santarella said, "but we're asking her about what might have happened with Jessie, who's dead now. That could lead her to speculate."

"I won't ask her to speculate. I'll cut her off, gently, if she starts," I said. "This interview is going to be about what she knows, and that's all."

He sighed, and I could almost see him rubbing his jawline. "Why don't you come in early tomorrow," he said, "and we'll strategize. Nedegaard's still got friends downtown. We need to be very careful here."

About ten minutes later, Temple's alarm went off. As usual, she ambled out in T-shirt and sweatpants. "What's up?" she said: a greeting, not a question.

"Can I talk to you for a minute, after you make your coffee?"

She glanced at me curiously. "What about?"

FORTY-ONE

At half past three the next afternoon, I was showing Jen Ryan into our "soft interview" room. That was our place for talking to witnesses who were under no suspicion of a crime, especially the young and the emotionally fragile. It was a room with a sofa and pillowy chairs, warm lighting, decorative prints on the walls.

Jen preceded me into the room, backpack in hand, her long reddish-blonde hair pulled back into a simple school-day ponytail. On the drive into the city, I'd tried to set her at ease by asking about her strong and weak subjects in school and about her extracurriculars. The small talk made me feel like somebody's aunt, but the difference in our ages didn't worry me. I'd planned around it.

Jen stood in the middle of the room with an air of composed awkwardness, studying the prints of delicate pastel irises on the wall. I silenced my cell phone and put it away in my bag. If there was any truly urgent task-force business, Santarella knew where to come get me.

"Please," I said, "have a seat." I set my shoulder bag down on the chair farthest from the coffee table, subtly claiming it. I wanted to be at the periphery of the action. I wasn't going to be the prime mover here.

There was a knock at the door, and then Temple stuck her head in. "Good," she said, "you're here."

"Jen, this is Officer Lockhart," I said.

Temple, carrying two paper cups of Caribou Coffee, came in and nudged the door shut with her foot. She was dressed in casual plainclothes today, blazer and T-shirt and jeans, with her badge visible at her hip.

Santarella had had reservations about this part. "She's a uniform and a rookie."

"I know," I'd said, "but Temple is only four years older than Jessie. There'll be a rapport."

"That's great, but she's had no training for this."

"I went over it with her last night in detail," I said. Which was true; the dark circles under my eyes this morning had attested to how late I'd stayed up. "The things she's going to be saying to Jen, those are mostly going to be my words. It's just better if they come from her."

Temple wouldn't just be drawing on my experience, either. I'd learned my interview techniques from Genevieve Brown, my former partner, who'd had a gift for coaxing information from witnesses, informants, and criminals alike.

"I want you in the room with them the whole time," Santarella had finally said, capitulating.

The thing I couldn't tell Santarella, the other reason I wanted Temple here, was that I knew she wouldn't push Jen too hard for personal reasons. I had my own childhood demons in this area; Temple, as far as I knew, didn't.

Jen had taken the center spot on the sofa. Her knees were together, hands on them with fingers laced, a discreetly defensive posture. I looked at coffee Temple had set on the table and said, "Is one of those for me?"

"Of course."

I winced apologetically. "I had coffee with lunch. I don't think I could stand any more."

"Really?" Temple said, sounding disappointed.

"Sorry."

Temple looked at Jen. "Would you like one of these? Caramel macchiato, they're really good." She set them both down on the table. Jen glanced at them and said, shyly, "Thanks."

Of course, the whole thing was arranged in advance. I'd once seen Genevieve, in an interview with a meth dealer's abused girlfriend, "accidentally" squirt too much hand lotion onto her hand, grimace, and ask, *Do you want some of this?* Genevieve had shared it directly, hand-to-hand. It was a gesture that close female friends made, and as the meth dealer's girlfriend rubbed the lotion into her skin, and the soft lily scent had diffused into the air, I'd seen her grow calmer by degrees.

At the time, I'd thought the gesture was one only Genevieve could pull off, but here I'd adapted it for Jen. The offer of a macchiato was more than hospitality. Jessie and her college-age friends would have drunk elaborate coffee confections from Starbucks and Caribou. Jen, when she visited her sister in the city, might have done so, too. Now, Temple and I were inviting Jen into the circle of adult women, and aligning Temple with Jessie's memory.

Temple took a seat next to Jen, though not too close. I leaned forward to resettle my shoulder bag nearer to them. The pen clipped to an outside pocket was a recording device, already on. Another of Santarella's conditions.

I said, "I didn't talk to you very long, the day I came to your house. So I wanted to check back, see if there's anything else that you remember that might be important."

Jen said, "I don't think so."

I shifted my weight backward, making eye contact with Temple. Taking my cue, she picked up the reins.

"This is the other thing," Temple said, and Jen's gaze shifted to her like a television-studio camera. "Your mother and your grandfather were both right there when Sarah was interviewing you. That can make it hard to talk freely, I know." She paused. "I'm sure you wouldn't deliberately keep anything from us that you thought might help, but if there's anything you didn't mention, you can tell us now."

"There was," Jen said, "but I don't think it means anything." She looked at me. "When you asked me what Jessie and I talked about, the last time I called her, I said it was just *Jane Eyre* and her costume for the masquerade."

"But it wasn't?"

Jen smiled nervously. "She wanted to get a tattoo, the Japanese character for *Courage,* on her ankle. We weren't telling Mom because she doesn't like tattoos."

Jessie the black-skates girl, always trying to bend the bars of her tasteful birdcage.

Temple said, "I want one, too. I haven't decided what yet. And I want Sarah to go get one with me."

"Really?" She looked to me.

"Yeah. Sarah's my roommate."

"She is?" Jen was surprised. Raised on TV dramas in which police detectives brooded by themselves in roomy urban lofts, Jen had probably never thought about cops economizing, taking in roommates, splitting the electric bill.

"Yeah. It's been great, because I never had a sister."

Temple continued in that vein a few minutes, talking about friendship, asking Jen questions about her relationship with her older sister. As she did, Jen's protective posture began to open up a little bit.

Then Temple said, "You know, one of the things we thought Jessie might have talked to you about is this guy she liked. The one who was coming to her party."

Jen looked puzzled. "She didn't mention a guy."

"Nobody's talked to you about why Jessie was out running that night, during her own party, have they?"

Jen shook her head.

"That was an odd detail, and Sarah and I believe it was because her feelings had been hurt by a guy. We can't prove that," Temple said, "and it's certainly not his fault she was killed, if it's true. But we've talked to friends about Jessie, and it seems like she had difficulty with men, trusting them. So we've been thinking that there's something we might not know about Jessie."

Temple drank a little bit of her coffee, giving Jen a moment to adjust to the turn the interview was taking. Then she said, "When a young woman is murdered by a stranger, it's so huge it gets everyone's attention. There's news coverage and white-candle memorials and everything else. But the truth is, it's much more common for girls and women to be hurt — abused or molested — in their own homes. And often that never comes to light, for all kinds of reasons. Because it isn't violent. Because he's family. Because he supports the family financially. But none of that makes it right."

Temple stopped there. I knew she didn't want to ask the key question outright. I'd told her she had to.

"Was that Jessie?" Temple said. "Was she abused?"

Jen stared down at her interlaced fingers and said nothing.

I was careful to stay still, but I was excited, because I knew silence was a confirmation. If Jen could have denied it outright, she would have done so immediately. There were two potential answers hanging in the air now: *Yes* and *I don't know for sure.*

"I don't enjoy having to ask that question," Temple said. "But Sarah and I think that Jessie was out running because she was upset. We think that if she had been more comfortable with her sexuality, one rejection wouldn't have hurt her that badly, and she'd have stayed at the party, and she'd be alive today."

Jen was very still, which wasn't entirely a good sign. Nothing was going to happen if she shut down completely.

"It's not like I want Jessie to have been abused by a man close to her," Temple went on. "But if she was, I think that man all but pushed her into the path of the man who killed her."

Jen was staring at her fingers. The nailbeds were pale, a sign of stress, blood retreating from the body's extremities. Quietly, she said, "Jessie didn't want anyone to know."

Temple waited.

"She only told me because she was leaving for college. She wanted me to call her if he ever started up with me."

"Did he?"

Jen nodded.

"And did you?"

"No," Jen said. "I didn't tell her. I wanted her to be happy away at school. I thought she was." A tear fell from her lower lashes. "Besides, when I'd asked her why she never told anyone, and she said, 'Because he's an ex-cop. Cops eat their guns.'"

An ex-cop. We were so close, but we needed her to say it.

Temple leaned forward. "When you say ex-cop, do you mean … "

Jen sniffled. "My granddad."

Temple's hands tightened and let go, and she released the breath she'd been holding. It was a very restrained expression of what I knew she was feeling: elation.

The details were bad, though not as bad as I'd feared. Nedegaard's molestation of his granddaughters hadn't gone as far as penetration; it had been exposure, groping and mutual touching. As Jen had told us, Jessie had never reported him because she feared he'd attempt suicide if unmasked as a criminal. I wondered, in addition, if Jessie had also realized that her mother couldn't support herself and her two daughters, should they have to move out of Nedegaard's home.

If that possibility hadn't occurred to Jen — she hadn't said anything about it in the interview room — it was surely going to hang over Katharine's head. I wondered how much she'd suspected about her father and her daughters.

I wouldn't want to be her in the weeks and months to come. Right now, she was with Jen in a social worker's office, dealing with the hole that had just been blown in her life.

"What's going to happen to Nedegaard?" Temple had asked me, as we climbed the stairs in City Hall, toward where Santarella waited for my report.

"Not much, I suspect," I said. "Social services will find Jen and her mom a place to stay until they can find somewhere permanent to live." Stopping on the landing, I switched my cell back on, checking for messages. "Nedegaard will rattle around that empty house and refine his excuses. He'll tell himself the girls didn't mind it, that they saw it as affection, and that the cops manipulated Jen into exaggerating the truth about him while she was still vulnerable from her sister's death. Eventually he'll convince himself.'"

Upstairs, Santarella listened first to my brief summary, then to the audio of our interview. He was satisfied with both. "Good work today," he told Temple, dry understatement making the praise authentic. Temple matched his nonchalance: "Thank you, sir."

He checked his watch. "Why don't you sit in on our late-afternoon meeting?"

I was about to tell him that Temple had a dogwatch shift that night and needed her sleep, but she was too quick. "I'd like that," she said.

When she'd preceded us into the conference room, Santarella pulled me aside. "We don't know how Nedegaard's going to take this," he said. "If he calls you, don't talk to him."

"Calls me to say what?"

"I'm not sure exactly," Santarella said, "but he might have accusations, try to impeach how you handled Jen's interview, threaten to have you investigated or demoted. Don't engage with him. You did the right thing. You're protected."

"Thank you," I said.

FORTY-TWO

B y the time I got home that evening, the thrill of having been right about Roy Nedegaard had faded. The fatigue was physical; I felt as if my larger muscles were laced with fibers of iron. I abandoned my plans to go for a run.

The day's biggest news, at the meeting Temple had attended, was that the homeless-person interview had seemed to result in a promising lead. A bag lady in her fifties had been confiding in Hadley about a young Iraq vet she knew, originally from Montana and now homeless, who had several pairs of girls' panties in his possession and knew a lot about the murders of Jessie and Cyd. Hadley had spent a long time trying to draw her out, but whenever he got close to an identifying detail — including a first or last name — the old girl's memory could never quite come into focus.

At length, Hasan was called in to talk with her one-on-one. After an hour, he came back with the news that the whole thing was a fabrication. The root cause: an instant infatuation with handsome, courteous Detective Hadley. She'd been telling him whatever would keep him talking to her.

It was a story that was good for a few chuckles around the table, except from Temple, who was too full of rookie sincerity at being in the war room to laugh.

She was sleeping now, apparently, door shut and room silent as they always were on her working nights. She'd only left City Hall a half-hour before me; she must have collapsed on her bed like a felled tree as soon as she'd closed her bedroom door.

For that reason, I left the radio and the television off, instead sorting through the day's mail, throwing circulars in the trash and setting bills aside until I came to the only piece of personal mail: a thick envelope, its return address central Wisconsin. Shiloh. For it to have arrived today, he must have written it very shortly after I left.

Carrying it to the living room, I sat down to read.

Sarah,

For reasons we'd probably both rather not revisit, I didn't give the question you asked — about a criminal beating a DNA test — enough thought. I've been thinking about it all night.

Because you said something about "textbook conditions," I'm assuming that the DNA sample was given voluntarily in a certified lab. Those are tough conditions to cast doubt on, but could a test under those conditions be wrong? Sure. DNA testing is a human activity, so it's imperfect. There are two possibilities: incompetence and corruption. Incompetence is pretty self-explanatory. Corruption usually means someone was bribed to fake test results. I don't have the science background I'd like, so I can't go into details about how exactly that faking would play out.

But if you want to argue that the DNA was manipulated on your subject's end — the guy who gave the sample — I can't figure out a way to make that happen. I've heard about doctors who passed drug tests by catheterizing themselves with someone else's urine. That works because drug tests look for the metabolites of drug breakdown in the urine, not for DNA. DNA comes from the nucleus of cells, and there's no cellular material in urine except for cells shed by the lining of the bladder, which is how sometimes resourceful technicians have gotten DNA from it. Hair and saliva are like that, too — there's no DNA in hair except in the follicle, if that's still attached.

And with saliva, there are usually some cells in it that have been shed from the cheek, tongue, et cetera.

My point is, if we accepted urine for a DNA sample and somebody catheterized himself with another guy's urine, it'd be a crapshoot whether that worked. The other guy's cells would be in the urine, sure, but so would some of the subject's own, having been shed from his own bladder wall. A cheek-cell swab — I'm assuming that's what your guy did, since it's become almost standard — would be even harder to beat. If your guy had kissed someone recently, some of her cells might have adhered to his cheek, but the vast majority that the swab would pick up would be his own.

I hope this helps, though re-reading it, I can see it probably doesn't. I wish I'd asked for more details when I had the chance. But generally I get the sense that you thought you had the right guy and then the DNA said no. Believe me, you're not the first cop to have that problem. I should tell you to move on to another suspect, but I won't. Not because it's a bad idea, but because it'd be hypocritical after all the time I spent pursuing Annelise Eliot with everyone around me thinking I was wrong. I don't want to feel hypocritical. I've got enough to feel guilty about these days.

I'm going to stop thinking about what you confessed to me during our visit. Many gangs have a "prison exemption" for infidelity. Maybe they've got it right.

Good hunting,

M.

My first feeling was relief not just at those last lines, but at my husband's equable tone throughout the letter. Maybe we'd inched back from the cliff's edge.

Then I made myself concentrate, going back and re-reading the letter's central four paragraphs again, just to be sure I'd absorbed everything. When I'd done that, I considered the possibilities Shiloh's answer had raised.

Corruption seemed unlikely: Steven Silverhus, a college student in his twenties, had no discretionary income with which to bribe a tech. He was even more unlikely to have a friend in the BCA lab: from what we'd observed, he didn't have friends, period.

Of course, his grandfather was a different story. Niels seemed to have had an active public life, and many of his friends would come from within the medical community. That was potentially huge.

One other thing about the letter leapt out at me: Shiloh assumed that we'd done a buccal-cell swab on Silverhus, taking material from the inner cheek. My fault; I hadn't told him we'd drawn blood.

But it was interesting because Santarella had mentioned cheek-cell testing recently, too. When we were thinking of the father of Cyd's baby as a suspect, Santarella had said we could acquire something close to the father's DNA by getting a buccal swab from Daniel, the son. It would be painless, Santarella had said, but he was nonetheless relieved not to have to do it.

A cheek swab was painless, so why had Silverhus given blood? A blood draw wasn't excruciating, but no one looked forward to it. Why hadn't he wanted a buccal swab? Or maybe he had, and Santarella had insisted on blood.

Whose idea had a blood draw been? There were only two people who could give me an answer to this question, and neither of them were going to be happy to hear me ask it: Joe Santarella and Steven Silverhus. Of the two, Santarella was the better choice. Silverhus would hang up on me or tell me lies. Santarella would be annoyed, but he'd give straight answers. I called him.

"Pribek," he said. "What's on your mind?"

"I have a question for you that you might not, um," — *just front up and say it, dammit* — "I have a question for you. Whose idea was it that Silverhus give us blood instead of a cheek swab?"

A silence followed that. A long one. Then he said, "Why are we talking about Steven Silverhus again?"

"Bear with me," I said. "Please."

230

He sighed. "I offered him a buccal swab instead, and he said that blood was the gold standard in testing. I thought he was confusing medical tests with DNA testing, but I didn't push the issue."

"You didn't find his choice strange?"

"It was his right. The test was voluntary; I couldn't demand a particular sample, not without a warrant. Besides, why would I? He's basically right. Blood is unimpeachable." He paused. "Am I hearing you right? Are you suggesting he cheated the test?"

"His grandfather is a doctor, and he still has practicing privileges at the hospital. He could have stolen blood from a lab, or even drawn it from a comatose patient. What if he did that, and then switched the samples?"

"That'd be a possibility if this were a rural jurisdiction in the 1950s, where the medical examiner was also the country doctor who births babies, and the morgue was also the county hospital, and his test samples got put in a fridge next to the secretary's brown-bag lunch. That's not how it works anymore. Niels has connections to the medical community, not the law-enforcement community. Those are two completely separate worlds. Maybe he could get his hands on someone else's blood, but he couldn't just stroll into our lab and swap out the samples. There's security, and then there's a half a dozen people who'd see him even if he slipped past security."

Then his voice dropped half an octave, calmer. "If it makes you feel better, I had my doubts too. After the results came back, I checked every step down the line. The procedure was completely according to Hoyle: a certified BCA phlebotomist did the draw, a Hennepin County sheriff's detective witnessed it, the chain of custody was unbroken, and the technician who did the test is a 17-year veteran. The sheriff's detective was you, remember? You *do* remember all this, right?"

"Yes."

"I'm saying this line of questioning is getting paranoid. It's time to let it go."

"I know," I said. "I'm sorry."

I did let it go, for all of an hour and a half. During that time I quietly fixed myself a grilled-cheese-and-tomato sandwich, scanned some news headlines online and checked my email, then sorted laundry to start later, after Temple was awake and the rumbling of the machines wouldn't bother her.

She and I threw casually our clothes into the same oversize basket with cracking plastic ribs, so I sorted out her things from mine. Hers ran to exercise clothes. I lifted a pale-gold U of M T-shirt out of the basket and stopped with it in my hands. There was a rust-brown stain on it I recognized from my rookie-cop days of breaking up fights and responding to accident scenes; it was dried blood. Temple had come out second best in a sparring match at her gym. I flicked a thumbnail over the stain, and scabby dark flecks came away at my touch.

Of course I thought of Silverhus, the day Vang and I had looked down into the trunk of his car and seen the same thing, dried blood matting the carpeting, so much that a faint ferrous scent had risen into the air.

It was the one thing I couldn't explain and I couldn't forget: Silverhus's trick with the black Lab, the blood that I still believed had covered up Jessie Ryan's.

Blood covered up blood.

Those words, however vague, shot adrenaline into my tired veins. Suddenly I was very glad Temple was sleeping; I had that feeling like a word on the tip of your tongue, when the slightest distraction will knock it back into a deep crevice in your brain.

That's why he didn't want a cheek swab. He needed blood to cover up blood. Blood that wasn't his.

I knew that was crazy, but it was the only answer that made sense: Someone else's blood was already inside his body. If Santarella had checked every step down the line and found nothing wrong, then the deception had to have been in place by the time I'd ushered Steven Silverhus into the little room where Mandy would draw his blood.

"Niels," I said aloud.

Santarella had shot down the idea that Steven's grandfather had used his connections to get a blood sample switched. But maybe that theory simply hadn't been ambitious enough; what if Niels had intervened at an earlier point? Didn't people have all kinds of medical equipment inside their bodies that wouldn't have been possible even 50, 60 years ago? Insulin pumps, ports and central lines for ease of injections, birth-control implants. How hard would it be for Niels to implant a tube of blood in his grandson's arm that wouldn't immediately show to the casual observer? Steven had worn a long-sleeved shirt that he couldn't slide up very far past his elbow. I remembered that because Mandy had suggested he wear short sleeves next time he had to have a draw.

What had he been hiding underneath that sleeve? Stitches? Bruising from a hasty DIY surgical implant?

I knew I had to talk to Niels.

FORTY-THREE

In addition to his limited practice, Niels Silverhus worked as a consultant for a line of medical textbooks, and several mornings a week he went in to their editorial offices on Dale Avenue in St. Paul. At 7:25 the next morning, I was outside those offices, yawning, a go-cup of coffee wedged between my shoulder bag and the passenger-seat backrest.

There were several good reasons to approach Niels when he was going in to work. Some of it was just practical; this was my first opportunity to see him. Beyond that, this was a location where Steven wouldn't appear, looming balefully in a doorway, instantly drying up what little willingness to talk I might coax from Niels. But most of all, I was hoping the surroundings would remind Niels of his values as a medical man. Those were what I was here to appeal to. First Do No Harm.

More strategy: I was only wearing a windbreaker, inadequate to the morning chill, and no gloves. I wanted to look cold and vulnerable, so Niels would invite me inside the building. I wasn't sure I could get as far as his office, not once I identified myself as a cop, but neither was Niels going to spend much time standing around outdoors. I had to get into the entryway if I wanted to talk to the man long enough to appeal to his conscience.

I sipped coffee and ran through some last-minute reminders. *Don't call him Mister. Always Doctor. Be respectful, and be nice as long as you can.*

Presently a red Cadillac sedan dipped low at the parking-lot entry and up again, Niels Silverhus recognizable behind the wheel. I open the Nova's door and poured the rest of my coffee out onto the snow. Niels climbed out of his sedan and locked it. I waited. This was a matter of timing: I needed to catch him right at the door, where it would seem only natural to allow me to step in.

I closed the distance between us just as he was reaching the door.

"Dr. Silverhus," I said as he raked his key card through the reader. The door buzzed and he opened it, but he turned, too.

"Dr. Silverhus, I'm Sarah Pribek." Wide smile. "I wanted to — I'm sorry, do you think we could go inside? This'll take a minute to explain."

"Certainly," he said with the affable tolerance old men save for sweet young things who can't sum up their thoughts, nor think to wear an adequate coat in 22-degree weather. He held the door, and I went ahead of him into a narrow entryway lined with locked mailboxes, ending in another doorway. It felt approximately 88 degrees in there. Entry alcoves are the warmest of all places in upper-Midwest buildings. A double-door system protects the interior rooms from drafts every time someone enters or exits, but in the process, entryways become delicious little cells of heat.

Niels was facing me, waiting. I noticed how sharp his eyes were, how tight and clean his skin, how excellent his posture. If he were sick from prostate cancer, either it wasn't very far along, or the growing physical weakness was disguised under a outer hull of sheer discipline.

"I guess my name wasn't familiar to you." I pulled back the light jacket and showed him my badge. "I'm Detective Sarah Pribek. I was at your house recently to take Steven to the lab."

His chin rose, like the prow of a boat facing rough seas. "I thought your business with Steven was done."

"Which is why I'm talking to you, not him."

"I don't have anything to say to —"

"You haven't even heard what I'm going to ask yet, Dr. Silverhus," I said. "Please."

He didn't look any happier, but his chin inched lower, as though he were psychologically standing down. He said, "What is it you want to know?"

There are plenty of times when it's best to circle around your central question, slowly tightening the thumbscrews. This wasn't one of them. With quiet, absolute civility, I said, "Please tell me how you helped Steven beat the DNA test."

There it was on Niels's face: *Doomsday*. His throat worked involuntarily. But he said, "I have no idea what you're talking about, young lady."

"I know this is hard," I said, "and I sympathize. But I have to put my cards on the table. There is a great deal of evidence against Steven, contradicted only by a DNA test."

"But DNA evidence is — "

"Don't." I put up my hand sharply. "There are many things you're qualified to lecture me on, but forensics is not one of them."

He blinked at the rebuke.

"I think the sample was manipulated. I think you know something about that," I continued. "You're a medical man. You've dedicated yourself to preserving life. If we don't put away the man who killed Jessie Ryan and Cyd Perrin, another young person could lose her life. Can you be part of that?" I paused, briefly. "This is the very essence of First Do No Harm."

"Don't use those words," he snapped. "You'll never take that oath. Don't be disrespectful."

"I'm not," I said. "But I watched a medical examiner cut up a 20-year-old's body last week. That was Cydney Perrin. The paramedic who had to help transport Jessie Ryan's body to the morgue is a personal friend of mine. He had to help remove her body from a dumpster. A container for *garbage.*"

Niels's face was growing darker.

"Steven is your grandson. It's human nature to protect family, maybe our first nature. But this isn't like bailing him out of jail after a night of drinking. This is too big. If you tell me how you helped him, I promise I'll do everything I can to make sure that you're shielded from any fallout."

"I did nothing," he said, stiffly. "My grandson is innocent. Please leave now."

But it was he who turned away, to the second doorway leading further inside. Too frustrated to let go, I reached out to catch his arm.

"Dr. Silverhus — "

He turned quickly, and his gaze shot down to my arm as if he couldn't believe I'd had the temerity to touch him. He pulled away, and his mouth pinched up into an odd kissing expression. Then, he spit neatly on my shoes.

"You're a very disrespectful young woman," he said, and disappeared through the doorway.

I stayed frozen where I was. He'd *spit* on me. Just my clothing, not my skin, but even so, the act was so out of line with his successful, urbane image that for a second or two, I couldn't move on.

Alone in the entry, I slowly bent to wipe the saliva off my boot before I decided I didn't want to touch it with my bare hand. There were sanitary wipes in the Nova's trunk, in the EMT kit I carried for our weekly skills lab.

My gait was stiff as I walked back to my car, as if I'd been in a literal fight and sustained an injury. It's uniquely embarrassing to be spit on. You try to tell yourself that it's the other person who should be embarrassed, not you, but that's not how it feels.

I was nearly to my car when I had the idea.

It was more to Shiloh's credit than mine: he'd written about how fluids that aren't made of cellular material, like urine, can still have DNA in them from shed skin cells. Saliva, too, fit in that category.

I unlocked the trunk and got out my EMT kit. Not only did it carry sanitary wipes, but also cotton swabs and sealed biohazard bags, much like the ones our forensic techs used. Carefully, I took out a swab, wiped it through the wetness on my boot, then dropped it into a bag.

FORTY-FOUR

The morning meeting had just broken up when I got to Minneapolis. I ran into Vang and Hadley as they were coming down the stairs.

"Where were you?" Hadley said, mildly. "Another thrilling day of questioning homeless people awaits. You're coming, right?"

"Can you give me a couple of minutes?" I said. "There's something I need to talk to the boss about."

When I reached the meeting room, Santarella didn't seem annoyed with me, just curious. "Traffic?" he said.

His question told me that Niels hadn't been on the phone five minutes after I'd left building, complaining to my supervisor. One small blessing.

"I have something for you." I laid the Ziploc bag with the swab on the table.

"What's that?"

The decision to take it directly to him hadn't been easy. I could've gone to Hadley first. He seemed to be on good relations with at least one of the forensic techs; he could have gotten his friend to run a DNA test.

Ultimately, though, an end run around Santarella would undermine my cause. I needed this DNA test to be done with his blessing.

"It's saliva," I said.

"Whose, exactly?"

"Niels Silverhus."

That got his attention. "What? You think *Niels* is our suspect?"

"No," I said. "I want to get DNA from that saliva and run a grandparentage index against our suspect DNA. I'm sure that the index will tell us Niels is the grandfather of our suspect, no matter what the official DNA profile on Steven Silverhus says."

Quickly, I explained the radical conclusion I'd come to last night, that somehow Niels had implanted foreign blood in Steven's arm. Then I explained how I'd followed up on that theory, and about Niels's extreme reaction to my questioning.

Santarella was shaking his head. "Look, whether or not I think there's any point in running a grandparentage index, the way you got this sample — "

"It's perfectly legal," I interrupted. "No one can say Niels didn't *give* me that saliva sample."

His expression had shifted from skeptical to annoyed. "I *told* you to let this go. Just last night I told you."

"I know. I couldn't," I said, lifting my hands appeasingly. "You're angry, I know, but there's no reason not to test — "

"It's not. About. The *test*." His olive skin was taking on a reddish color. "You went behind my back and made accusations against a relative of someone who isn't even a suspect anymore."

"I didn't accuse him. I made an appeal for his help."

"Help with what? Don't answer that," he said, before I could restate my case. "My point is, you harassed an old man."

"I didn't harass him. I was polite."

"Let me give you a small refresher in interpersonal relations: Anyone who spits on your shoes probably feels he's being harassed."

He went to the cork board, though I doubted he was really seeing the photos we'd pinned up there. He said, "You started out so strong, Pribek. Nobody on this team was getting me better stuff than you, figuring out we were wrong on Jessie's date of disappearance, realizing that she'd gone running. Getting us looking at the Stone Arch Bridge. Then your favorite suspect fell through, and you just went off the damn rails."

It was far from praise, but his voice was calmer, and that gave me hope. I stayed silent. Maybe Santarella was one of those people who talked himself out of a bad temper if you just got out of his way.

He went on: "Look, there's been some political stuff going on I haven't mentioned in the meetings. Even though Cyd and Jessie both lived in Minneapolis and were kidnapped from here, there was a bit of St. Paul involvement, in terms of where Jessie's body was found. Plus, there's always the prospect the next victim could be from Ramsey County." He paused. "In other words, it's ruffled some feathers that there's no St. Paul presence on the task force. They've offered a veteran from Ramsey County Sheriff's, and I think it's best I make room for her."

"Make room?" I said, the skin of my face beginning to heat.

Santarella took a push-pin out of a photo that was starting to come loose, a picture of Cyd and her son. Finding a spot of fresh cork, Santarella re-positioned the photo and firmly stuck the pin through. "Although this case is a 'redball,' it's not exactly the hunt for bin Laden. We don't have an unlimited budget," he said, turning to face me again. "If I bring somebody new in, yeah, I have to take someone off. I'm going to have to stand you down from this."

When I left, I went hurriedly down the rear staircase so as not to meet up with Hadley and Vang again. Santarella could explain it to them. I didn't think I could bear to.

When Prewitt first told me that I was his pick to serve on the Jessie Ryan task force, I'd expressed surprise and wondered if there wasn't someone better. It wasn't for show; I'd really believed that. Only when Santarella dismissed me did I realize how attached I was to the idea that I was the right person for the job.

And only when I was out on the sidewalk did I realize that I'd left the plastic bag with the swab upstairs, in our war room. The realization made me wince, but I couldn't go back for it now. If I did, Santarella's thoughts would go instantly to the prospect of me taking it to the lab myself, and persuading one of the forensic scientists there to test it. Which, I had to admit, would be a temptation. Maybe it was for the best I'd forgotten it.

At least, that was what I kept telling myself.

FORTY-FIVE

A civilian who'd seen too many cop shows would expect me to have left work Wednesday and gone to the nearest day-drinking bar, drowning my sorrows in several shots of whiskey with a beer back. The truth was much less sexy: I went across the street to the government center and went back to work. Prewitt was out of the office on budget meetings, so I didn't have to explain my reappearance to him. I just slipped quietly into the role of house detective, waiting to catch whatever came in via phone or by reports from uniforms in the field. My open cases had long since been reassigned.

Occasionally, I thought about the Silverhus case, as I'd come to call it, and about the nasty incident with Niels. Santarella had blamed me for getting spit on, saying that I'd provoked it. But few people, even when pushed, resort to that kind of primitive behavior. I couldn't help but wonder if Niels — no matter how cosmopolitan he was on the outside — had a buried streak of anger at women, and if so, if he'd subtly infected his grandson with it. Niels and Steven were very different on the outside, and I'd blamed Steven's assaults on women, the crudeness of them, on the very ways he was different from Niels — less confident, far less successful.

But deep down, was there a similarity between them, a shared fear and hatred of the female that expressed itself in different ways? Maybe Niels had merely coped with it much better, had covered for it. He'd married and had a son, after all. Perhaps Steven's shyness and insecurity had only brought his grandfather's buried misogynist tendencies to the fore. Maybe what was like a dormant viral infection in Niels had spiked like a fever in his grandson?

The ringing of my cell interrupted those thoughts. The number on the screen wasn't familiar to me, and the prefix wasn't the Cities' familiar 612. Frowning slightly, I connected the call.

"Detective Pribek." The voice was soft and dry as autumn leaves. "This is Katharine Ryan. Is this a bad time?"

"No," I said, "it's all right." Santarella had warned me against talking to Roy Nedegaard, but he'd said nothing about Katharine. She could be feeling anything from rage to gratitude. I proceeded cautiously: "How can I help you?"

"I wanted to thank you," she said. "For helping Jennifer to tell us about — well, you know."

"It wasn't me who drew her out," I said. "That was Officer Lockhart."

"But it was your idea to have Jen talk to anyone at all, wasn't it?" she said. "Officer Lockhart didn't come to our house, and she wasn't working on Jessie's case. It was you who recognized the signs of abuse. You came to my house and saw something I didn't, even after living with the situation for so many years."

I said, "Maybe it took an outsider's eye to see it."

"Maybe," she said. "I just had no idea my father had that in him."

"So he never hurt you," I said, "when you were young?"

"No," she said, her response quick, emphatic. "If he had, I never would have let my daughters be in the same house with him."

I'd known mothers who had, because they were in denial, because they needed a place to live and financial support too badly to do anything else. Even so, I wanted to believe Katharine when she said she would have been different.

Just then there was a chirp on the line, the one that meant an incoming phone call. I didn't even look at the screen; this wasn't a time when I could say, *Can you hold while I take another call?*

Katharine said, "The worst part is that it was Jessie, not just Jen. I mean, Jen is still here, so there are things I can do to help her get over it. With Jessie, it's too late."

"I know," I said. It was blunt, but to suggest anything else would have been glib. She didn't need to hear that symbolic gestures, like a donation in Jessie's name to a sex-abuse-awareness organization would make any sort of difference, now.

There was a click on the line, telling me the other call had gone into voicemail. Katharine didn't hear it. She said, her voice strengthening, "Well, I just wanted to call and thank you for what you did." She'd gone back to the formal script.

"I'm glad I could help," I said.

After I'd hung up, I thought about Roy Nedegaard.

I'd heard nothing from him; as far as I knew, Santarella hadn't either. No angry accusations of wrongdoing, that I'd manipulated his vulnerable younger granddaughter. Perhaps Nedegaard was doing what I'd told Temple he would: walking the empty confines of his house, drinking too much, mentally rehearsing his excuses and evasions. Good. Better he internalize his anger than externalize it onto me and my superiors.

Remembering the call I'd let go to voicemail, I checked my call log. This time, I recognized the number on the screen immediately: It was Hadley. I let out the breath I'd been holding, and my shoulders dropped. This would be condolences, I thought, over my dismissal from the task force. But I listened to the message immediately anyway, in case it was a lingering question about Jessie or Cyd only I could answer.

I'd been right the first time: It was condolences.

"Listen, John and I both think Joe's overreacting," Hadley's recorded voice said. *"He might get over it, you never know. Give me a call when you can, we'll get a beer or something."*

Mentally, I filed that away to do later. By mid-afternoon, though, I still hadn't called. I'd slipped into a fatalistic mood, suddenly convinced that Santarella was right about me, that I'd been chasing the wrong guy all along. The last nail in the coffin, I thought, would be a breakthrough in the case, and I kept checking for the headline on my phone: *Suspect arrested in Ryan, Perrin murders; charges imminent.* That didn't happen.

Late in the day, Prewitt dropped by my desk. I set aside my work and looked up, steeling myself to explain why I was here at my desk when the rest of the Ryan-Perrin task force was doing something else.

But my boss opened with, "I heard from Joe already. I know what's going on."

"Oh." Mildly relieved, I rubbed the back of my neck. "Well, okay."

"I've been at this job a long time," he continued. "It's not the first time I've seen differences of opinion split up a team. It happens. Don't get too bent out of shape."

"Thank you," I said. He'd surprised me.

"Look, why don't you take tomorrow and Friday off," Prewitt said. "Not as a punishment, just as an opportunity for you to regroup a little."

I nearly said no, out of pride, but then I thought about my approaching midterm in EMT class, and I accepted.

FORTY-SIX

Friday midafternoon found me shoveling snow on our front walk, breaking up underlying ripples of ice with the hard corners of the shovel. It was good hard work, much needed. Between yesterday and this morning, I'd studied for my midterm until I realized I was at risk of overpreparing. I didn't want my mind to be numb when Shigawa passed out the test.

Earlier, the skies had been mostly occluded with cloud, but now they were breaking up. Tonight was predicted to be clear. The air was warm enough that I had to take off Shiloh's old thigh-length parka; a fine sweat was rising on my skin as I cracked ice under my shovel blade.

A muted noise distracted me. It was my phone, still in the parka I'd hung over the fence. I had to scramble to catch it in time.

"Detective Pribek," a warmly confident, masculine voice said.

"Yes?"

"This is Rob Donovan. Remember me?"

"Professor Donovan," I said, and tried briefly to remember the name of the anti-violence group that he led, that Silverhus was part of, but it wouldn't come. "What can I do for you?"

"Nothing specific," he said. "I've just been following the Perrin and Ryan investigations since you and I first talked. It doesn't seem like there's been any progress."

"Not a lot, no." I braced my shovel in the snow, so I could support it with just one hand.

"If I were to ask you whatever became of your interest in Steven Silverhus, would you tell me that you're not allowed to comment on that?"

If I wasn't before, I'm certainly not now. "That is what I'm supposed to say, yes," I told him. There didn't seem to be a point in mentioning I'd been bounced from the task force. "Has Steven talked to you at all about it?"

"He never even told me he was under suspicion," Donovan said, "and I didn't tell him that I knew, either. Listen, Detective Pribek, I haven't drawn any conclusions about Steven, but there's something you might find interesting." He paused . "He's dropped out of my group."

The name came to me then: "Men Against Interpersonal Violence?"

"Right."

"Did he say why?"

"He claimed he was too busy with schoolwork, but I'm not sure that's it. He seemed uncomfortable. On edge, or possibly sick."

"Sick?" I let go of the shovel, letting the handle fall against the moon-gray shingles of the house.

"His eyelids were reddish, and he looked like he'd lost weight. I don't know, perhaps his grandfather really isn't doing well."

"I just saw his grandfather yesterday. He looked good and was on his way to work."

"So Steven *is* still a suspect."

He understood that I wouldn't have been talking to Niels otherwise. He was quick, Donovan.

"Technically, no," I admitted. "It's complicated. I shouldn't be talking to you about this, either, as you pointed out."

"I wouldn't have asked you to, but I get the feeling something's going on with him, and not a good something. Knowing that you'd identified him as a suspect, I wouldn't have felt right not letting you know."

After that, I went back to shoveling, but somewhat more mechanically than before.

Donovan had wanted me to know that Steven had quit his group. It wasn't hard to grasp the meaning behind that. Hasan had said that if our guy was involved in a group like MAIV, he might be trying to resist tendencies he feared in himself. Donovan had indirectly agreed with that idea when he'd said that some men came to his group trying to escape — what was it he'd said? An "unhealthy interest in pornography."

If Silverhus had come to MAIV to escape urges more serious than a taste for pornography, and now he was quitting, one potential conclusion was obvious: He'd stopped trying to resist those urges. Maybe he was even embracing them. If he was our killer, why *wouldn't* he embrace his needs? With the DNA test results, he'd forged himself a free pass to act out on them.

By now, I'd nearly cleared the front walk. I moved down to the final stretch, the one nearest the gate. Using the shovel blade as a rake, I dislodged light powdery snow, revealing the translucent ridges and bumps of ice below. Then I raised the shovel and brought it down hard. Chips flew, the ice turning opaque white as it broke up into slivers.

The Victoria house, the one Niels owned, had an unshoveled walk. I'd noticed it when I'd gone to check out the place.

We'd never identified the place where Jessie and Cyd had been taken to be killed. Profilers sometimes called that the "secondary crime scene," and it was the case's biggest question mark.

My phone call with Marty Washington, the tenant, had seemed to resolve that; she'd assured me that she and her family were in residence. Now, though, I was remembering how the Victoria house had looked: wan and listless, to put it anthropomorphically. More that that, the grounds had looked empty. No kennels, coops or cages for animals, and no ruins of a summertime garden.

This was significant because a home halfway out to the countryside was a significant amount of work, even when it was a a rental. There was upkeep a landlord wouldn't do, like shoveling the walk and keeping the driveway clear, or laying in emergency supplies for a storm that left roads impassable. Why would you take all that on if you didn't want to grow vegetables or keep a 4-H animal for the kids?

Within 20 minutes, I was behind the wheel of my car. I wanted a second look at that house.

I didn't think about Santarella, who was already deeply frustrated with me, nor about Prewitt, who'd taken my dismissal from the task force with more equanimity than I'd deserved. Instead, I cranked the key in the ignition. A second after the engine turned over, the radio came alive: " — *November 20, 2005, and these are the stories we're following.*"

Sharply, I spun the dial away from Minnesota Public Radio, found a station playing Metallica, and turned the music up just loud enough to override thought.

FORTY-SEVEN

Even a new dusting of clean white snow didn't make the Victoria house look any more inviting than it had on my first visit. It seemed to crouch down in the cold, all the window blinds closed, no steam escaping the vents. I eased the Nova onto the shoulder of the road and turned off the engine.

My business card was gone from the front door; I could see that from across the road. But as I crossed the road and stood closer to the house, it became clear that the front walk still hadn't been shoveled. The open space alongside the house, leading up to the free-standing, two-story garage, was likewise unmarked by tire tracks. We hadn't had enough snow recently to completely cover the deep ridges that would have been made by a car's weight. I should have been able to see evidence of the Washington family's comings and goings.

I didn't because there wasn't any. They lived elsewhere. I didn't know her motives, but Marty Washington had lied to me.

I pulled on a pair of thin black leather gloves and walked along the side of the house. A back door often had a lock that was easier to circumvent.

The credit-card-in-the-doorframe trick isn't as easy as people think; on a quality lock it wouldn't have worked at all. As it was, I spent long minutes teasing a card back and forth along the tongue of the lock, with my face sideways nearly against the wall like a milkmaid's against a cow's flank, before the lock yielded to my pressure.

Inside, brown-checked linoleum flattened and bubbled back up under my footsteps. My breath still clouded faintly on the air. This place hadn't been heated in a while.

I walked through like a prospective tenant. Every room was unfurnished, but in the living room stood a cluster of medium-to-large cardboard moving boxes, all sealed with packing tape. I counted eleven. The Washingtons' things? Or Silverhus's trophies and souvenirs? I took out my penknife and chose a box at random. I'd gone too far already to kid myself I was respecting anyone's privacy.

The knife blade slid through brown packing tape. In the box were paperback novels, cookbooks, and calendars from the late '90s and the past few years. I picked out the 2004 calendar and leafed through it. Appointments and birthdays were noted in feminine handwriting. These were Marty Washington's things. She was using the living room as a storage unit for things that wouldn't fit into her family's home, wherever that really was.

The last room I inspected was the bathroom. When I flicked on the light, my shoulders sank with disappointment at what I didn't see: there was no bathtub, just a stall shower.

Of course it was still possible that Silverhus had simply held Jessie's head down in a kitchen sink or a bucket. Santarella had pointed that out, in support of his homeless killer theory. I turned the cold-water tap on the sink, but nothing happened; the pipes were clearly frozen.

The lack of running water wasn't the only problem. There was no other evidence that this was where Jessie or Cyd had died: no faint stains on the floor, no trophies, no tools of a killer's work.

I turned off the bathroom light, went back outside and looked at the garage. If I'd been smart, I would have started there. For Silverhus, it was a marginally safer choice than the house, in terms of being walked in on. Possibly, it was even off-limits to the Washingtons. That happened in rental contracts all the time: *That building's not included, I keep some of my stuff out there.*

The door wasn't on an automated opener, and its hinges and springs were stiff, but with some effort I got it to rise. Inside, the floor was concrete, the ceiling high with bare wooden rafters. I'd missed a simple opportunity to see inside: several rear windows were shattered. Not a small hole, but an open area about the size of a microwave oven, ringed with jagged glass teeth.

The cement of the floor was spattered with what looked at first like gray-white drops of paint. Except it wasn't paint; the splashes were too regular in size and shape, like rounded starbursts. They were bird droppings. I raised my eyes. In the rafters were several lumpen dull-black shapes: bats, hanging upside down in sleep. The droppings on the floor were guano.

Rabies. Bats are a very frequent source of human infection.

I should have felt elation, but mostly I wanted to back carefully out of the garage and stay out. *Get a grip. They're nocturnal. They'll probably just sleep through your visit.*

Forcing myself to look away, I scanned the perimeter. An old bicycle frame without wheels, several electrical boxes, a small collection of hand tools hanging on the wall, and — was that a bathtub? My gaze had stopped on a long, two-foot-high rectangle of dirty white ceramic, standing just under the broken window.

I couldn't identify it for a second because this wasn't a graceful clawfoot like you saw in old western movies, but something left over from a bathroom redesign, torn out from a wall and put in storage here. The side facing me had rough patches of off-white plaster stuck to it, and at the top was a flat horizontal lip where the tub had once met a bathroom wall. Nearby, a sea-green garden hose had been threaded through a hole in the wall and was coiled on the floor. When I drew nearer I saw alluvial drifts of fine dirt, like river silt, on the bottom.

I'd never felt such a strange mix of sadness and relief as I did then, feeling certain I'd found the place where Jessie Ryan had died. In a sense, I was standing over a grave.

Cyd Perrin had not died here, and I suspected that was because the pipes feeding the spigot had frozen recently, as the pipes inside the house had. Possibly that was why Steven had thrown Cyd into the river. When he'd killed Jessie, the weather had been warmer, and water had still flowed through the garden hose to his bathtub. With Cyd, he'd had to change his methodology.

One thing remained to be checked out. Along the far wall was a door, and behind that almost certainly were the stairs to the storage area. There was no other visible access to the second story.

The door didn't have a locking knob but a hinged latch held shut by a combination lock. Someone had taken an extra precaution to make sure the loft area wasn't intruded on. When I saw that, I felt a trickle like ice water along my spine. *If anywhere out here is the place, this is it.*

Smashing a combination lock wasn't like jimmying a door with a credit card; it was violent and obvious, and I was going to do it anyway. I walked over to the collection of tools on the wall.

Hammer in hand, I turned the lock sideways to rest against the wall and held the very bottom of it in my gloved fingertips. Then I lined up the head of the hammer with the spot where the shackle met the body and made one gentle practice stroke that didn't actually connect. Then I swung for real.

The impact shuddered through my gloved fingers and into my hand. It wasn't a comfortable sensation. Even so, I swung a second time, then a third. The lock held on.

I took a deep breath. Carefully, I lined up on the weak spot where the shackle met the round body, taking extra care because this time, I was going to close my eyes. Which I did, and brought the hammer down yet harder. This time, I felt the shackle give way. The lock didn't spring open, but it yielded when, opening my eyes again, I gave the body a hard yank.

Hooking the injured lock around the eyebolt in the wall, I felt a touch of queasiness down in my stomach. There was no covering up the damage; Silverhus would know someone had been here. I'd crossed a bright line. Pulling the door wide, I went in and climbed the narrow interior staircase.

Upstairs was Steven Silverhus's nest.

A simple bed was against the wall — mattress, pillow, and a covering of brown velveteen fabric. Nearby, several items were perched on the open two-by-four beams along the wall: a camp lantern and a Polaroid camera, several candles partly burned down, their wicks black with use. There was a pile of notebooks and sketch pads near the head of the bed. Along the walls on both sides of the bed, Steven had hung Polaroids. Jessie Ryan, unconscious, lying on her back with her hair spread out on the pillow. Cyd Perrin, similarly posed.

Oh, Jesus. My heart kicked my chest wall, and I dropped my hand to touch my gun. The movement was reflexive and comforting. Even though Silverhus wasn't here now, and I didn't expect him to turn up, his malignant energy clung to this place, a place where unconscious women were used like sexual furniture. Touching my service weapon was my way of reassuring myself, *Not me.*

I took a deep breath, then another and a third, and finally I was able to shift my hand from gun to cell phone.

Santarella picked up on the second ring.

"It's me," I said. "Silverhus is our guy. I'm at the rental house near Victoria. There's — "

"Sarah — "

" — trophies and a bathtub that I'm sure has DNA in it our techs can find. I know there's — "

"Sarah — "

" — going to be evidentiary problems with how I found this but we've got to get him off the streets before he does it again *because it's him."*

"Sarah, will you *listen?* I know it's him."

"You do?" This was such an abrupt turnaround that my knees felt wobbly, like I'd been running full-out on an airport's moving sidewalk and suddenly hit the end.

"I was just about to call you. After I cooled down a little bit, I realized that it couldn't hurt to ask the lab if they could find cheek cells in that saliva sample you gave me, and if so, to run a DNA test on them. They did, and I got the results about 20 minutes ago. You were right. Niels Silverhus is the grandparent of the suspect in all three cases, Ryan, Roback, and Perrin. Hasan thinks Niels used some kind of

255

soft surgical tubing to plant the blood in Steven's arm, something that wouldn't provide much resistance to a needle."

I knew it, I thought. Niels's rage, the bizarre act of spitting at me ... it had grown out of shame at the way he'd betrayed his profession.

"I'm getting an arrest warrant on Steven. Niels, too, for obstruction. The ink will be dry on both warrants by the time you get back downtown," Santarella continued. "I'm sending Vang to carry them out, but I think you should be in on the collar."

"I'd like that."

"Good. Get out of there; leave everything untouched and come on in."

"Thank you, sir."

"Joe."

"Joe," I said.

FORTY-EIGHT

About an hour later, Vang and I were pulling up in front of Niels Silverhus's home on Portland Avenue. We were hoping to find Niels at home alone, with Steven still at school. The general plan was to arrest Niels, have him transported back to Minneapolis by uniforms, and then wait for Steven to return home and arrest him as well.

Hasan had shaped this plan, predicating it on the idea that Steven was a risk to take hostages in an arrest situation, and that his elderly grandfather would have been ideal, in that he was a low risk to fight back. In other words, Niels's arrest was partly a way to get him safely into custody.

I'd seen reason in everything Hasan had said. I just wasn't at all certain that Steven was still attending classes at the University. Donovan had said that Steven had dropped out of MAIV. Had he lost interest in his psychology studies altogether? Was his whole life, now, about the things I'd seen in his nest out in Victoria?

I looked out the window at the tall, high-shouldered house. The garage door was closed, and the windows revealed nothing about who might be inside. Uncertainty roiled in my stomach.

There was a second reason I was feeling reluctant: The sun was sinking into the horizon, and in about three hours, my EMT-class midterm started. I stepped down hard on that feeling of anxiety. There was plenty of time. I'd make it.

"How do you want to do this?" I asked Vang.

"Let's walk over to the garage first, see whose car is in there," he said, opening the driver's side door.

We walked the perimeter of the house, me glancing at the windows for signs of life. The garage crouched behind the house like an afterthought. There I went up on tiptoe to look through a high line of windows. Inside, I saw Niels's cinnamon-red Cadillac, not the dark-blue Taurus that Steven drove. Good. Maybe this really was going to go as planned.

But nothing ever does. When Vang and I knocked on the door, no one answered. Vang knocked more assertively, using the side of his fist instead of his knuckles. Still nothing.

I scowled. "I really hope Steven didn't drive Niels somewhere in his Taurus."

"Yeah, that'd throw a wrench in things." Vang's brows were lowered in thought. "This isn't likely, but maybe he's just somewhere he can't hear us knocking. Let's try a hail-Mary and give him a call on his cell."

I didn't have high hopes either, but I got out my phone, drew Niels's number up from the call log, and handed it over. Vang connected the call and raised the phone to his ear.

In a moment we both heard it: the faint sound of a cell phone ringing behind the walls of the house. It was undoubtedly a window which conveyed the sound through its glass; in a house of this quality, the walls were solid and well-insulated.

Vang disconnected the call. "Well, he's in there."

"Or he went out and left his phone behind."

"Maybe." He shrugged. "Let's call on the house's line."

"That might tip off Steven that we're here."

Vang frowned, then walked over to the house and stood right alongside the wall. I followed his lead. He was positioning us so that Steven wouldn't see us if he looked out an upstairs window.

When Vang dialed, we heard the jangling ring of a traditional telephone. It sounded six times before Vang gave up.

"Looks like Steven did drive his grandfather somewhere," I said, glumly.

"No." Vang shook his head, certain, dissatisfied. "Something's not right here."

He dialed a third time, and again we heard the faint ringing of the cell phone inside. Without disconnecting the call, Vang walked along the side of the house in the general direction of the sound, stopping in front of a window. He raised himself on the balls of his feet and looked inside, then drew back and gestured me forward.

"Come here," he said, stepping back so we could exchange places, "and tell me what you think you see."

I pressed my face against the glass like he had done. Beyond the leaves of a jade plant, I saw the familiar contours of a kitchen: pine cabinetry, a refrigerator, a tiled floor. Sticking out from the kitchen doorway was what looked like brown-and-white dress shoes, toes upward, and the cuffs of pants.

"Damn," I said, stumbling quickly back. Vang had been awfully calm; I hadn't been expecting that. The feet most likely belonged to Niels; the dress shoes didn't look like anything Steven would wear.

"We should call for some uniforms and an ambulance, do you agree?" Vang said.

"We should go in," I said firmly. "One, this clearly falls under the 'emergency' exclusion to the need for a search warrant. Two, one of us is a medic in training, and we don't know for sure the person in there is dead."

Vang put his hand on my arm. "We also don't know that the person who *made* the person in there dead, or almost dead, is gone. Do we care about that?"

My EMT textbook warned readers about "unusual silence." It said that emergency scenes are generally noisy, chaotic places, and that a still, silent scene is, paradoxically, the most dangerous for EMTs to enter unawares. Shigawa, too, had always been clear on this point: EMTs and paramedics waited until a scene was safe before entering. Job One was not creating secondary victims.

Sorry, Nate, but for now I'm still a cop. "I'm going in," I told Vang. "I back you up, you back me up. Right?"

It had occurred to me that maybe this wasn't murder; maybe it was suicide. I couldn't help but think of the way I'd pressed Niels for the truth at his office, the way he'd rounded on me and spat at my feet. That was the action of a man who knew the walls were closing in.

If he's dead by his own hand, it's not your fault, I told myself as we headed to the front door. *He chose to do what he did, falsifying evidence, protecting a murderer.*

I pounded on the back door while Vang called in what we knew, asking for both medical and police assistance. When no one answered, I broke a diamond-shaped pane of glass with a rock and reached inside for the knob.

Niels Silverhus lay in the hallway leading to the kitchen. He'd been knocked backward by a gunshot to the chest, but there was no gun near the body. Not suicide.

I sat on my heels to do the vitals. He wasn't breathing, had no pulse, and his flesh was beginning to cool. I looked up at Vang and shook my head *No.*

Vang was on high alert, his back nearly at the wall, weapon at chest level, dark eyes steadily scanning all around us. We hadn't checked out the rest of the house.

"Let's clear the rooms," he said.

We did, covering each other in doorways until we'd done every room and closet and were sure Silverhus wasn't still hiding in the house.

"Killed granddad and took off with his gun," he said, standing with me in Niels's bedroom upstairs, the last room of our search. "What do you think set Steven off?"

"Betrayal, maybe," I told him. "Niels might have been ready to come to us and confess. I tried to get him to do that Wednesday, and he wouldn't, but maybe it just took a little time for remorse to set in. Maybe today Niels tells Steven he's going to come clean to the police, and Steven goes for the rifle."

We both remembered Niels's Olympic triumph: He'd been a competitive shooter. It looked like it'd been a bad decision to keep a rifle in the house, loaded and in working condition.

Vang said, "You think Niels'd be that stupid, to tell his grandson he was thinking about turning him in?"

"From what I've heard about Steven, he's been a yes-grandpa, no-grandpa type all his life." I stood up before my calves started to ache from the sitting-on-my-heels position. "I don't think Niels imagined a Steven who could talk back to him, much less shoot him."

Vang said, "Do we know if Niels owned any other guns? A handgun, something concealable?"

"Santarella's probably got that information in the paperwork. I don't know off the top of my head."

Dull thudding noises came from outside: car doors slamming. Our backup from the St. Paul police had evidently beaten the ambulance here. Vang moved toward the stairs. "Wait," I said. "There's something else I want to run by you. When I went to the Victoria property, there were bats nesting in the building where Silverhus had his den."

"Bats?" he repeated. Then he got it: "Rabies? You think the infection's active? Untreated, I mean?"

"If Silverhus ever slept out there, yes. People have been known to get bitten in their sleep and not even realize it. The incubation period can take months."

"So we could be looking at brain involvement," Vang said. "There'd be irrational thinking and paranoia as the virus starts to work on the brain."

Like shooting the man who raised him from childhood.

He went on: "At worst, we could have a paranoid man who's already killed three people loose in the Cities with a rifle in his hands. Goddamn, we've to call Santarella."

Heavy boots pounded on the front steps and masculine voices called out to us, announcing their arrival. And finally, the siren of the ambulance began to wail in the distance.

FORTY-NINE

Ten minutes later, the whole 911 circus was camped out on Silverhus's snow-crusted front lawn. Darkness was falling, making the emergency lights brighter in contrast. Neighbors gathered, wide-eyed but at a respectful distance. It was in the middle of all this that Vang tried, with difficulty, to have a conference call about the unfolding situation. He was standing on the front porch, where the wide glass windows protected him from being overheard, if not seen, by the milling neighbors. The EMTs and uniformed officers were inside; for the moment Vang and I had this glassy cocoon to ourselves.

On the phone with Vang were Santarella, the assistant SAC from the Minneapolis field office of the FBI, and the chiefs of police of Minneapolis and St. Paul. I stood nearby, available in case Vang fielded a question only I could answer.

That wasn't a great idea from a legal standpoint: Some of the things I knew, I couldn't admit to knowing, not until Santarella got his search warrant and Vang and Hadley officially "told" me what was in the room over the garage in Victoria. But at this point, with lives at stake, our concerns about evidentiary rules were falling away, down into the darkening vortex that this case was becoming.

It was also in the back of my mind that I clearly wasn't going to be at my desk when Shigawa's midterm started, not with a seven-county manhunt under way. I couldn't let myself feel anything about that. Just another thing that was free-falling into the vortex.

I paced, hands in my coat. The house's door was open behind me, letting heated air drift out and with the yellow light that spilled onto the floor in a long trapezoid. Vang was explaining to the bosses what we'd found at the Silverhus house and told them about the prospect that we had an unstable gunman on the loose. He advised that we get Steven Silverhus's photo on the news and every officer in both counties looking out for him and his blue Ford Taurus.

After that, the chiefs and the FBI's assistant SAC apparently hung up, leaving just Santarella and Vang on the phone. Vang motioned me closer. "Joe, Sarah's right here," he said. Looking at me: "Do you have anything you want to add?"

"I do," I said. "I think we should find Jen Ryan. We know that Steven — "

"Wait," Vang said. He handed me the phone. "Tell him directly. I can listen from here."

I took the phone and repeated what I'd just said, continuing with, "We know that Steven's seen Jen Ryan at the public memorial, because she was up at the microphone, and he was right there watching her. We also know — "

"That she's his type, just like Jessie was," Santarella finished.

"Right," I affirmed.

Normally, I wouldn't have believed that Silverhus would target the younger sister of his prior victim. He'd proved to have a crafty self-preservation streak, and going after Jen was risky. She and her mother would be on heightened alert still, the way people always are after crime touches them personally. They'd be locking doors and looking twice at every shadow. But if Silverhus were decompensating psychologically...

"If he's falling apart and ready to go out in a blaze of glory, he might take a risk in going after her," I went on. "He might snatch her right off the street or kick down the front door to her house."

Santarella thought about that. "I'm not too worried about Jen," he said. "School's out for the day, meaning Steven can't find her there, and she and her mother have moved into a new apartment."

264

Vang had moved away, nearer to the glass wall that fronted the porch. To a casual observer, he'd have looked bored. He wasn't; he was paying attention to every word, and also to everything going on in the street.

"Still," Santarella continued, "just to be sure, I'll get an officer to babysit Jen and Katharine until all this is over."

"Can I make a suggestion?" I said. "It's going to be pretty traumatic for Jen to hear that her sister's murderer might be fixated on her now. It might soften things to have a cop she knows around. I think Officer Lockhart would be a good choice."

"Your roommate."

"I'm not suggesting this *because* she's my roommate."

"I know you're not. It's a good idea," Santarella said. "We'll also put a car outside Nedegaard's house. Just because Jen isn't there doesn't mean Steven won't show up looking for her."

We signed off, and at almost that moment, an EMT began backing out of the house. He was shepherding a wheeled stretcher between himself and his partner, which bore a human-sized burden in a black zippered bag: Niels Silverhus, physician and surgeon, going to the hospital for the last time.

The pair reached the door between the porch and the outside world, folded the stretcher's wheels, and carefully inched onto the steps. As they descended, their burden became visible to the crowd, who *ohhh'd* softly at the sight of the body bag.

Inside that black bag was the young man who'd once stood astride his skis on a California mountaintop like Apollo on Olympus. He'd trained his body and sharpened his mind, established a home and family, amassed a small fortune. Maybe he'd been arrogant, maybe he'd had a touch of old-school medical man's hubris, but all in all, he'd lived well.

Then one day he made a big misstep. His grandson came to him and said, *I'm in trouble*, and Niels protected him. We'd never know exactly why. Probably family loyalty had played into his decision to fake the DNA results, but I felt there was more at play. The surface of Niels's personality might have resembled a sunlit lake, but there had been darker, colder waters underneath; my close-up encounter with him had attested to that.

Or, possibly, he just feared being alone. He'd already lost his wife, his son and his daughter-in-law. Perhaps, no matter how great a disappointment Steven had been to him, he hadn't wanted to lose the last of his family. Faced with that prospect, Niels Silverhus did a terrible thing.

And how long did that benefit him? Ten days, at the end of which the same grandson he'd protected took his own rifle and blew a hole in his chest. The end.

If a man like Niels Silverhus couldn't bring his life to a graceful close, what hope was there for the rest of us?

FIFTY

Sometimes, when things really change, you feel it in the air. It's like the ripple that runs through a public place when the news breaks that a president has been shot, or a space shuttle has exploded on re-entry. Before you know exactly what's happened, you just know *something* has.

That charge was in the air when Vang and I got back to City Hall. Even though there'd been nothing on news radio about Steven Silverhus, it clearly wouldn't be long. Reporters were beginning to mill on the ground floor of City Hall. Vang saw them and said, "Let's go around the side."

Up in the war room, our usual number had more than doubled. The St. Paul detective whom Santarella had taken on to replace me was present, and a slender blonde woman whom I recognized as the MPD's public-information officer, whose first name I knew as Nina. Also in attendance were the PIO for the St. Paul police, the special agent in charge of the Minneapolis field office of the FBI, Santarella's immediate superior at the BCA, a young female BCA intern, and liaisons from both the Minneapolis and St. Paul mayor's offices. Hadley quietly identified everyone after Vang and I had edged over to where he stood.

"But where's Joe?" I said.

"Not sure," Hadley said. "He might be talking to a judge about the search warrant for the Victoria place. He's eager to get one of us out there to look around, see if there's any evidence there we can use." His face was smooth, his words innocent, avoiding any reference to the fact that he knew very well how much evidence was waiting in that garage.

I nodded and looked around. Someone had rolled a television on a cart into a corner of the room, and a handheld radio crackled on the table. We also had two thermal carafes of coffee and mugs, plus a pitcher of water and glasses. All niceties we hadn't had on a daily basis. Say what you will about catastrophes: the amenities do improve.

There was an air of waiting in the room, with several small conversations going on. I had time to notice how everyone affiliated themselves along professional lines: The PIOs were standing together, as were the mayor's-office staffers, and the FBI's special agent in charge had come over to talk to Hasan. Vang and I had done the same, I realized, immediately going to Hadley.

Santarella arrived, phone to his ear, responding in fragments to someone on the other end. "Yeah, in fifteen minutes, more or less. Thanks. Good. Goodbye."

After he disconnected, he spoke briefly to the BCA intern, who nodded and left the room. When she was gone, Santarella went over to shut the door. That caused all the little satellite conversations in the room to stop. It meant Santarella had something to say he didn't want to be overheard.

"There is some good news," he said. "Jennifer Ryan is safe. Officer Temple Lockhart of the MPD is staying with her and her mother until this situation is resolved."

I smiled. He'd found a way to drop Temple's name into some important ears.

"I'm guessing there's also bad news?" one of the mayor's liaisons asked.

"There is," Santarella said. "Roy Nedegaard is dead."

A ripple of reaction went through the room.

"The officers I sent out to his place found him," Santarella continued. "They went up to the house to tell him that they'd be parked near the end of his driveway and to explain why, but when they got to the door, it was open. They went in and found Captain Nedegaard lying in his entryway, shot in the back." He paused. "He was almost to the doorway of his den. It seems likely that Silverhus thought the gun would buy him instant submission from Nedegaard, but it didn't. We think that he tried to get to his own gun, and Silverhus shot him twice from behind."

Vang interrupted: "Have they cleared the house? Are they sure Steven's gone?"

"They're sure," Santarella told us. "Apparently he took Nedegaard's car, because the Taurus was in the garage."

Tricky, I thought. I also wondered how far gone from the rabies infection Silverhus was. Was he putting analytical thought into tactics like switching up the cars, or was that just animal cunning, a residual survival instinct even as his brain broke down?

"What kind of car?" Nina, the Minneapolis public-information officer, asked.

"Nedegaard's? It's a Ford Five Hundred. I know the change of cars is a pain in the...uh, the neck for you guys. You'd only just gotten out the information about Steven's Taurus. But I've got the information about the Five Hundred out to our officers in the field already. That was what I sent Michelle — " the intern, " — out to take care of."

He tugged at his tie again. "The other bad news is this: Captain Nedegaard's gun doesn't appear to be at the scene, which probably means Silverhus took that, too. In addition, gun-registration records show that Niels Silverhus didn't just own the rifle, he had a handgun. A Sig Sauer."

Nobody looked happy about that news. Our guy was getting ever more well-armed.

Santarella looked at Hadley. "Sky, I told the officers at Nedegaard's place I'd get a detective out there. Can you take that? I need Vang here in case of a standoff with Silverhus. John's had the best rapport with him; he'd be the best guy to negotiate."

"On it," Hadley said, taking his holster off the back of a chair and sliding it over his shoulders.

Both the Minneapolis and St. Paul PIOs put their heads together, conferring. When Hadley was gone, Nina spoke again. "Agent Santarella, we've promised the reporters downstairs a statement shortly. It'd be best if you did it personally. Steven Silverhus is the biggest public-safety issue in Minnesota tonight, and you're the point man on this."

"I can do that," he said. "What do I need to tell them?"

I spoke without thinking: "What about — ?"

Every face in the room turned toward me, and I stopped short. I'd been thinking about Silverhus's potential rabies infection and what Vang had said about paranoia. I glanced at him now, but he wasn't up to mind reading; he didn't guess what I wanted to say and take over for me.

"Detective Pribek?" Santarella prompted.

Clearing my throat, I summarized: the antibody profile, the bats, the possibility that Silverhus had a active rabies infection that had gone to his brain.

"God Almighty," said Santarella's boss, a gray-haired man with a deeply-lined face.

Santarella sighed heavily. "It's a valid theory, but it shouldn't be on the news just yet. We already have to tell people he's armed and dangerous. If we say, 'armed, dangerous, and *rabid*' there's going to be panic. We're going to fill up the ERs with people shot by trigger-happy neighbors and roommates."

"I tend to agree," the St. Paul PIO said.

"Can I bring something up?" Syed Hasan said, quietly. "Has anyone contacted Robert Donovan?"

"Who?" Santarella's boss said. It was a question reflected on several other faces.

"One of Silverhus's psychology professors, with whom he had a closer relationship than most," Santarella explained. To Hasan: "You think he's going to have good insights on where Steven is?"

"No, I'm worried about him," Hasan said, leaning forward. "Silverhus has already killed two male authority figures tonight. Donovan might be a failed father figure, someone Silverhus thinks could have helped him, but didn't."

Santarella lifted his eyebrows. "I can see that," he said. "Pribek, would you take care of that? Tell Donovan to stay somewhere private and safe until we've got Silverhus in custody. And if you can't raise Donovan personally, contact the University police, have them make sure he's not in his office ignoring his phone."

"I will," I said.

As the two PIOs and Santarella began drafting his statement, I pushed back from my place at the table, ready to excuse myself and make the phone call in private. But almost as I touched the phone, it buzzed once in my hands, indicating an incoming text message. I stood by the window and took out the phone.

Did you forget about tonight? Exam starting NOW. NS.

Nate Shigawa. Regret pricked me, and I sighed without meaning to. The message didn't require a response. He didn't really mean *Did you forget?* He meant, *Get over here right now.* But I couldn't, even if it meant an automatic incomplete in the course. Which it probably did.

Behind me, there was a rustle at the head of the table. Santarella and his helpers had finished with their statement. Santarella stood and began adjusting his necktie, restoring the knot to a professional-looking height.

"Be back in fifteen," he said, looking specifically at Vang, Hasan, and me. "We'll think about the next steps."

There weren't going to be a whole lot of "next steps," I knew. We were playing a reactive game now, everything dependent on what Silverhus did.

Hasan said mildly, to Santarella, "Let me go down with you." He got to his feet. "I could use a cigarette anyway."

They went out, trailed by the public-relations people and the head of the BCA. Those who were left began to shift their attention to the television set, where Santarella's statement would soon be broadcast, live.

I didn't join them, turning back to the window instead. It was full dark by now, though I couldn't see any stars in the narrow slice of sky visible between the roofline and the surrounding tall buildings. But if I put my face hard by the glass, I could see the congregating reporters down below, gathering on the steps.

Rob Donovan didn't answer his cell. Instead I heard his voice-mailbox message.

"Professor Donovan, this is Sarah Pribek," I said. "If you're watching the news, you'll understand what I'm about to say: We think you should stay away from campus until this current situation is, uh, resolved. I can explain the rationale behind that a little better when you call me. Please *do* call me. I need to be sure you got this message."

I was just about to dial 411 for the number of the University Police when a someone behind me said, "It's starting."

I glanced backward. On the TV screen, the scene had changed to the steps of City Hall. Santarella appeared, his complexion two shades lighter in the television lights. I felt the strangeness of seeing someone you know on the other side of the screen.

For reasons I'll never be able to reconstruct, I didn't leave the window and join my colleagues around the TV. Instead, I looked out the window again, steeply down to the crowd. It must have numbered more than 60 people now: reporters and cameramen and sound guys, uniform cops, some curious passers-by. The angle was too steep for me to see Santarella at his microphone, but I could make out the coppery curls of Rosamund Ross's head.

"Good evening," Santarella's disembodied voice said behind me. *"I'm here tonight to ask for help and vigilance on the part of the people of the Twin Cities. The joint task force on the murders of Jessica Ryan and Cydney Perrin has identified a suspect in those deaths."*

Down below, everyone was looking straight ahead, at Santarella. Nobody was looking behind them. But from my vantage, I saw it: a tall figure was moving toward the steps.

"Hey," I said, quietly.

The approaching man had a bearlike gait I'd seen before. The bald spot at the crown of his head was clearly visible.

"Hey," I said, louder.

The gun in the approaching man's hand was either his grandfather's Sig Sauer or Roy Nedegaard's Glock.

"His whereabouts are currently unknown —"

I raised both hands and banged hard on the glass, a futile gesture I'd think back on many times in the days to come. How close I was, yet much too far away.

"What are you doing?" That, behind me, was Vang's irritated voice.

I turned around, and whatever Vang saw in my face was enough to make his hand jump and coffee splash over the rim of his cup.

"His name is Steven Mark Silverhus."

The shooting started.

FIFTY-ONE

Fresh snow turned to cherry-colored slush. Carnival-like emergency lights flickering off snowdrifts and stone surfaces. The spike heels of the Minneapolis public-information officer's ultrafeminine shoes scrabbling against wet stone as EMTs tried to treat her. My own blood-wet hands trying to hold down the blood that was trying to leap from a chest wound.

Whenever I closed my eyes, I saw those images from the front steps, and I was afraid they were only a tame prelude to the dreams I'd have if I fell asleep. So I sat up in the ICU, next to the bed of one of Silverhus's victims, staying when Natalie had to go back to the apartment to rest.

Hasan had been right about Silverhus going after another male authority figure. He'd been wrong about which one. It was Joe Santarella he'd been aiming for when he fired his first shots. But his grandfather's gift for shooting didn't run in the family. Santarella wasn't hit at all. It was Hasan, standing next to him, who took the first two slugs. Even so, he'd stayed on his feet long enough to draw his Glock and fire at Silverhus, hitting his upper arm, very good shooting for a profiler whose job didn't involve a lot of gun-range practice.

Hasan's was the chest wound I'd tried to hold together with just my bare hands and my upper-body weight. He flatlined just outside the ER, but the doctors got him back.

Rosamund Ross, the *Star Tribune*'s 27-year-old crime reporter, they could not save.

The final toll: three dead, nine injured. One of the dead was Steven Mark Silverhus, hit ten times by shots from two police officers on the scene. The final fatality was Nina Svenhard, the public-information officer for Minneapolis P.D., who succumbed to multiple organ failure minutes before midnight. Though on his last night of life Silverhus had turned his rage toward men, his final two kills were women.

Hasan made it through the night, which made the doctors optimistic about his chances for recovery. Around dawn, I realized I couldn't keep up my vigil until he was awake; it was time to pack it in. At the same time, I realized I was too exhausted to safely drive, I called Temple and asked her if she'd come pick me up.

Down in the hospital lobby, a familiar figure caught my eye: Nate Shigawa, heading for the elevators I'd just emerged from. He saw me, lifted his chin in greeting, and changed course.

"I figured you'd be here," he said. "Are you all right?"

"Tired. Otherwise, fine."

He scanned my face, as if not sure he believed that. "You told me once you have a kind of phobia about doctor's offices," he said. "You want me to do a quick assessment, maybe outside at my car? I've got my bag in the trunk."

"Really, it's not necessary," I said, "I wasn't hurt. I was several stories above the action. The shooting was over by the time I got down there."

"Mm." He looked thoughtful. "Tell me you're not disappointed about that."

"Not disappointed. Guilty, I guess."

"Survivor guilt. It happens," he said. Then: "You know you've missed two classes and the midterm. According to the academic code, I'd be within my rights to AI you."

Automatic Incomplete. I'd have to start over next quarter, take the class from day one.

"Nate," I said, the single word a remonstration.

"I know: Tonight was a public-safety emergency. Probably I should give you a pass this one time, let you make up the exam sometime this weekend."

Shigawa looked away, at a group of passing nurses in cranberry-colored scrubs. Then he looked back at me. "Here's the thing: There's a reason why you were where you were tonight. Since you first came to class, I've wondered how ready you are to leave police work behind you. I think tonight was my answer."

"What? That's not true."

"Hmm," Shigawa said. "I guess we'll find out. I'm giving you the AI."

The physical shock I felt, rising from my core to the surface of my skin, made me realize I hadn't really expected him to go through with it.

"I'm teaching the class again next quarter," he said evenly. "If you come back, if you make all the skills labs and the exams, then we'll both know." He paused. "This is my life's work, Sarah. I don't want people out there next to me who aren't truly committed to it. Take some time and think about it. Be sure."

FIFTY-TWO

S ome things we learned in the following days:
    A search of the Silverhus home turned up a four-inch surgical
drain, a soft rubber tube with clotted blood still inside it, stuffed behind
a broken electric razor in a bathroom cupboard. Steven had known
enough to not throw it in the trash, which, once taken out to the curb,
can be seized without a warrant. He should have dropped it off a bridge
into the Mississippi, but maybe he hadn't wanted to think about it. Out
of sight, out of mind.

We would probably never know whose blood it contained. There
were too many comatose or just heavily-sedated patients at the hospital
whom Niels could have taken a sample from, not to mention the
prospect that he'd stolen a vial from a phlebotomy lab. There was no
reason to investigate that issue further; the case was over.

Because we couldn't prove what Niels had done, that detail never
went public. For that reason, the obituary packages that ran in sports
pages nationwide were kind and respectful. Many used the photo of the
dark-haired, abundantly healthy Niels in Squaw Valley, and spoke of his
later medical accomplishments in glowing terms.

Those images and feats were hard to reconcile with the blood-
clotted surgical drain. But only a few of us had to try.

In addition to the things I'd seen in the Victoria garage — the
Polaroids of Jessie and Cyd, for example — Silverhus's loft yielded up
Jessie's and Cyd's clothing from the nights they were abducted, a bolt

of the same material Jessie's body had been wrapped in, several diaries, and two sketchpads full of fantasy drawings. The drawings depicted women in poses of extreme submission, ones with generously-built bodies and full rosebud mouths, but no eyes. Sometimes there was a man as well, one with exaggerated male sexual attributes.

Since Hasan was in no shape to do it, Hadley took on the task of looking through the diaries and the sketchpads. It wasn't just professional curiosity. He needed to make sure that nothing suggested that Silverhus had committed other crimes, ones no one had connected him to.

Hadley called the drawings "disturbing, but pretty generic." The diaries, meanwhile, had a lot to do with Silverhus's childhood, his grievances against the world in general, his sense of loneliness and isolation, but nothing about his crimes. Clearly, he'd channeled all that ideation into his art.

With no next of kin to claim them, I suspected that all the materials would sit untouched in a sub-basement until a reporter filed a Freedom of Information request for them, as research for a book-length project on the Ryan and Perrin murders. The tamer of Silverhus's fantasy drawings would end up as photographic inserts in the center of a true-crime paperback.

One interesting sidenote about the Victoria house: Martha "Marty" Washington was an editor for a Minneapolis small-press newspaper with a strong voice on working-class issues. As such, she felt pressure to live inside Minneapolis city limits, near the heart of the community she served, and so the Washington family did. However, the public schools out near Victoria were much higher-rated in nearly all areas: higher test scores, smaller class sizes, et cetera. Marty's income and her husband's was just adequate to renting the place in Victoria, which in turn allowed them to send their son to school there. Rattled by a call from a police detective — me — she'd been too nervous to come clean about not really living out there. So she'd lied.

It would have been an innocent-enough deception, except that if I'd known two weeks earlier that the Victoria place was unoccupied, I might have been able to get a warrant. We might have searched, and might have found evidence of Jessie Ryan being taken there.

That was a lot of "mights," but it came down to this: We might have saved Cyd Perrin. If we'd found Polaroids of Jessie in the apartment over the garage, we would have arrested Silverhus immediately and held him without bail. He would have been taken directly to the BCA laboratory under a court order. There would have been no chance to go home and allow his grandfather to implant a tube full of blood in his arm. Cydney would still be alive, as would Niels and Roy Nedegaard.

I never spoke about this detail publicly, and neither did Vang or Hadley. But with interest in the Silverhus case running high, eventually a reporter was going to make the connection. I had a feeling Marty Washington's days as a respected editor in the alternative press were numbered.

In the waning days of November, Syed Hasan had recovered enough to travel, and this time it was me, not Hadley, who drove him and Natalie to the airport for their flight back to D.C. Outside the domestic terminal, in the pale, chilly morning light of late autumn, Natalie shook my hand, but Syed surprised me by giving me a hug. Recovering from that minor shock, I whispered "Stay safe," into his ear, and he promised me that he would.

EPILOGUE

January 8, 2006

A few minutes before midnight, in one of the earlier days of the new year, I was sitting at the kitchen table, in a pool of light from the overhead fixture. All the other lights in the house were off. Temple was out, but I wasn't alone. Shiloh sat across the table from me.

Except that there was no rain, our reunion at the prison had been a great deal like my dream: Shiloh had come out through an unmarked metal door, carrying his possessions in a brown paper bag. But instead of casual street clothes, Shiloh was wearing his best suit. Which made sense: It was the suit he'd worn to his sentencing, after which he'd been taken directly to prison.

The formal clothing looked out of place here, in our kitchen. Shiloh himself looked out of place, really. Which was odd, given that this house had been his home before it had been ours together, and long before Temple had shared it.

"The roommate's at work?" Shiloh asked.

I shook my head. "She's on a date," I explained, breaking the seal on the bottle of Scotch I'd purchased the day before. "She's seeing the instructor of my EMT class."

Briefly, I'd been angry at Nate Shigawa, but his decision hadn't been personal. With time, I'd seen that it had probably taken some backbone to make the choice he had, and also to come to the hospital and tell me to my face. So I'd called him, being likewise direct in telling him that I was staying on my chosen path, and I'd be in his next EMT class.

It was a friendly conversation, and when we'd finished talking business, Nate asked after Temple. I'd remembered how taken he'd seemed with her, the night he'd dropped by the house. It seemed time hadn't diminished the attraction any.

So I'd put in a casual good word with Temple, and they'd gone out on their first date the night after Christmas. Tonight's date was their third, and the fact that she wasn't home by nearly midnight seemed like a good sign. I knew what it meant when third dates went late into the night.

It also provided Shiloh and me some very welcome privacy in his first hours home.

I poured two fingers of whisky into his glass, and then mine. We didn't toast; that would have been glib. This moment was no celebration. We were simply recovering our footing after more than a year of very difficult times, of hardships largely of our own making.

Shiloh drank, head tipped back, then half-closed his eyes in pleasure: "God, that's good," he said. Despite the gentle golden light from overhead, he appeared older than he had even back in November, when I'd been with him in the hospice room. But also more real, more vulnerable.

I'd changed too, I knew. There was a lot of water under the bridge between us, turbulent and muddied water. But I could hope that from here on, we could both be better navigators.

"What?" Shiloh asked. He hadn't missed the serious way I was surveying him over the table.

Not ready to share such sober thoughts, I shook my head, saying, "Nothing." Then: "This might sound petty, but do you think you might let your hair grow out a bit, now that you can?"

"That does sound petty," he said, and we both laughed a little. "But maybe. If you'll consider something in exchange."

"I'm not going blonde."

"No," he reassured me. He swirled the remaining whisky in the glass, the liquid coating the sides before slowly ebbing back down. "Would you consider living somewhere other than Minneapolis?"

That wasn't what I'd been expecting. I said, "I never thought much about it."

That wasn't entirely true. Had Shiloh not made his rash trip to Blue Earth, by this time he would have been a newly fledged agent of the FBI, and we'd have moved to wherever he'd gotten his first posting. But I'd put that prospect out of my mind long ago.

"It's not that I couldn't deal with life after prison here, in the Cities," he continued. "I can live with the fact that I'll run into cops and prosecutors I know on the street and have to tell them that I'm working construction. I could do that." He paused there, drank a bit more of his Scotch. "But I never thought Minnesota was our endgame, yours and mine. Except for a year of college in Nevada, you've been in Minnesota since you were, what, thirteen? There's a big world out there beyond it." Then: "You're very quiet. Is that a bad sign?"

"No," I said. "I'm just surprised. You've only been out of prison a few hours."

"That's part of the reason, though," he said. "We're both at a crossroads. I haven't started looking for a job. You haven't re-taken your EMT class yet, much less signed on with an ambulance service. Neither of those things would be huge commitments, but..."

But they were tendrils. Given time, tendrils became vines, vines became a thicket, and soon you needed a machete to slash through the commitments you'd made.

"Did you have somewhere in mind?" I asked.

"I was thinking about one of the coasts," Shiloh said. "Seattle, maybe. Baltimore. Or the Gulf Coast. Biloxi or Pass Christian would be fairly inexpensive to live in."

In my mind's eye, I saw a new kitchen window. One in a cheap apartment, to be sure — but maybe with a view of a distant slice of water. Opened, the window would let in the scent of the ocean beyond, or of a thunderstorm brewing over the Gulf.

My heart had picked up its pace just a little. Not with nerves, but with anticipation.

"Let's do it," I said.

"Really?"

"Yes." I was sure. "Let me find my legal pad, and we can make a list of all the places we might want to live. We can narrow them down to our top two choices, and just flip a coin."

Would he think I was being too frivolous? But no, the idea pleased him. I could tell just by the way he splashed a little more whisky into my glass.

I was just starting up from my seat, to retrieve my yellow notepad, when Shiloh caught my hand.

"Thank you," he said, quietly. "For waiting for me."

"There's no one else."

Shiloh said, "For me, either."